Never in a Hurry

Essays
on
People
and
Places

Never in a Hurry

Essays
on
People
and
Places

NAOMI SHIHAB NYE

UNIVERSITY OF SOUTH CAROLINA PRESS

Thanks to Samuel Hazo for his ever-good advice.

Copyright © 1996 University of South Carolina

Published in Columbia, South Carolina, by the
University of South Carolina Press

Manufactured in the United States of America

06 05   9 8

Library of Congress Cataloging-in-Publication Data

Nye, Naomi Shihab.
    Never in a hurry : essays on people and places / Naomi Shihab Nye
        p.   cm.
    ISBN 1–57003–082–0 (pbk)
    I. Title
PS3564.Y44N48   1996
814'.54—dc20   95–41778

With gratitude to Judith Kitchen
and Elizabeth Mills

"It's really fun if you can stand it."
—Dorothy Stafford

When I was a child in Chatta-nooga, seven or eight years old, I re-member sometimes in April when that spring gold light would come in at the end of the day and just be there for about ten minutes . . . that gold time, well, I could hardly stand it as a child. I would lie down and hug myself and my mother and father would be play-ing bridge with the Penningtons. Ly-ing on the floor hugging myself, I'd look at her and say, "Mama, I've got that full feeling again," and she'd say, "I know you do, honey." So I grew up in an ecstatic world in which it was okay to lie on the floor and hug your-self or maybe just sit out on the bluff and watch the river.

—Coleman Barks

Contents

Acknowledgments

The author is grateful to the journals, anthologies, and newspapers that first published some of the selections:

Cradle and All, edited by Laura Chester (Faber and Faber)—"The Rattle of Wheels Toward the Rooms of the New Mothers"; *Food for Our Grandmothers,* edited by Joanna Kadi (South End Press)—"Banned Poem"; *Going Where I'm Coming From,* edited by Anne Mazer (Persea Books)—"Thank You in Arabic"; *The Iowa Review*—"My Life with Medicine"; *Journal of Palestine Studies*—"One Village"; *Manoa*—"Camel Like Only Camel"; *Michigan Quarterly Review,* edited by Anton Shammas—"Speaking Arabic," "Broken Clock," "White Coals"; *Mid-American Review*—"Marie," "One Moment on Top of the Earth"; *New Growth,* edited by Lyman Grant (Corona Press)— "Tomorrow We Smile"; *Northern Lights*—"Women of the West"; *Ploughshares,* edited by Rosellen Brown—"The World and All Its Teeth"; *Southwest Review*—"David Crockett's Other Life," "Three Pokes of a Thistle"; *Stories*—"Local Hospitality" (in a slightly different form); *Sycamore Review*—"Bread"; *The Georgia Review*—"The

Cookies," "Maintenance"; *The Austin Chronicle*—"Nineties," "Talk, Talk, Talk," "Neighborhood Quartet in a Minor Key"; *The Houston Chronicle*—"Home Address," "Favorite Cleaners, San Antonio," "Field Trip"; *The San Antonio Express News*—"Roses for Lubbock"; *The Virginia Quarterly Review*—"Pablo Tamayo"; *Third Woman*— "Tulips"; *Willow Springs*—"Commerce."

"Pablo Tamayo" also appeared in *New Stories by Southern Women,* edited by Mary Ellis Gibson (University of South Carolina Press), and *South by Southwest,* edited by Don Graham (University of Texas Press); "Maintenance" also appeared in *Best American Essays 1991,* edited by Joyce Carol Oates and Robert Atwan (Ticknor & Fields), and *The Pushcart Prize* (1991 edition, Pushcart Press), edited by Bill Henderson; "The Cookies" also appeared in *Necessary Fictions: Selected Stories from "The Georgia Review,"* edited by Stanley W. Lindberg and Stephen Corey (University of Georgia Press); "Newcomers in a Troubled Land" also appeared in *The Contemporary Essay,* edited by Donald Hall (St. Martin's Press); "Tomorrow We Smile" also appeared as a limited edition chapbook made by James Escalante, Iguana Press, Madison, Wisconsin.

Never in a Hurry

Essays
on
People
and
Places

Growing

I pressed my face to the car window, sobbing heavily. Ten years old and my mother had just said that my little bit of childhood was nearly gone. If I pinched my brother, if we tussled in the back seat, the last few morsels would disappear. I cried and cried, wanting to eat the sweet kernels of days flagging out behind us.

Ten years later I banged my head against a wall because I loved my parents too much and didn't want to move out. How could you tell someone you loved them too much? It sounded ridiculous, like you just didn't want to get a job. My father called, "What's going on in there?"

I wouldn't move out, so my parents did. They left me in the house with their old Danish sofas and the chipped enamel pan my mother heated milk in when I was a baby. A few nights later I was certain I heard a UFO land in the backyard.

After you separate, stories have their own lives within your lives.

For a while I wanted to dial the phone every time something happened.

Now we have a boy with jumbled curly hair who began asking for coffee when he heard that children who drink coffee might not grow. He asked about the word "stunting." Someone else's phrases living in my mouth. Isn't there a tale where you open your mouth and rocks fall out?

The whole world divides itself between four and five. *Will this happen when I'm four?*—means close, soon. *I won't do that till I'm five*—far away, a mountain.

Our grandfathers are standing on the mountain.

My great-grandmother whose letters live in a battered box in my closet.

My great-great-uncle John who wrote in 1889, "I feel so alone, not even a story can afford me pleasure." And the little boys with curly hair dot each slope, deep green pine trees. We breathe each other's air.

This morning a woman in the post office wasn't sure what day it was. "Ever since I got old I think Friday is Saturday and Saturday is Friday." She asked my boy, "Are you a girl or a boy?" then said, "Once I had a little boy with curly hair and his daddy cut off his hair and I cried and cried." She said to me, "Soon you'll have to share him with the world, with school—it sounds so easy, but it's not."

I was buying stamps to stick on big brown envelopes tossed onto the new computerized scale. He was reading signs out loud, "Please Form Line Here"—"Exit Only"—and every word had weight.

Newcomers in a Troubled Land

Our four-year-old is printing his name on a piece of yellow construction paper. I bend to see which name it is today. For awhile he wanted to be *called* Paper. Today he's gone back to the real one. Each blocky letter a house, a mountain, a caboose . . . then he prints my name underneath his. He draws squiggly lines from the letters in my name to the same letters in his own. "Naomi, look, we're inside one another, did you know that? Your name is here, inside mine!"

Every letter of *Naomi* is contained in his name *Madison*—we pause together, mouths open. I did not know that. Although we have been mouthing one another's names for years, and already as mother and son we contain one another in so many ways it would be hard to name them all.

For a long time he sits staring, smiling at the paper, turning it around on the table. "Do I have any friends," he asks, "who have *their* mother's names inside their names?" We try a few—none does. And the soft afternoon light falling into the kitchen where we sit says, *this is a gift.*

When I was small, the name *Naomi,* which means *pleasant,* seemed hard to live up to. And *Shihab, shooting star* or *meteor* in Arabic, harder yet. I never met another of either in those days. My mother, Miriam, whose name meant *bitter,* said I didn't know how lucky I was.

Hiking the tree-lined streets of our St. Louis borough en route to school, I felt common names spring up inside my mouth, waving their leafy syllables. I'd tongue them for blocks, trying them on. Susie. Karen. Debbie. Who would I be if I'd had a different name? I turned right on a street called Louise. Did all Karens have some region of being in which they were related? I called my brother *Alan* for a week without letting my parents hear. He was really Adlai, for Adlai Stevenson, a name that also means *justice* in Arabic, if pronounced with enough flourish.

Neither of us had middle names.

I admired our parents for that. They hadn't tried to pad us or glue us together with any little wad of name stuck in the middle.

Not until I was sixteen, slouching sleepily in the back seat of my best friend's sister's car, did I fall in love with my own name. It had something to do with neon on a shopping center sign, that steady color holding firm as the nervous December traffic swarmed past. Holding my eyes to the radiant green bars of light as the engine idled at a corner, I felt the soft glow of my own name stretch warmly awake inside me. It balanced on my tongue. It seemed pleasurable, at long last, to feel recognizable to oneself. Was this a secret everyone knew?

Names of old countries and towns had always seemed exquisitely arbitrary, odd. The tags in the backs of garments, the plump bodies of words. We had moved from the city of one saint to the city of another, San Antonio, whose oldest inner-city streets had names like *Eager* and *Riddle*. We had left the river of many syllables, with a name long enough to be used as a timing device, Mississippi, for a river so small you could call it Creek or Stream and not be too far off. We ate *kousa, tabooleh, baba ghannouj*—Arabic food—on a street called Arroya Vista.

Earlier, I'd stood with my St. Louis schoolmates as the last gleaming silver segment of the Gateway Arch was swung into place by a giant crane. We held our breaths, imagining a crash as the parts clanged together, or a disaster if the piece were to slip loose. Worse yet, what if the section didn't fit? Each of us had been keeping close watch on the massive legs as they grew and grew in what used to be a weedy skid-row riverfront lot, a few blocks from the licorice factory. Each of us had our own ideas about whether we'd really trust the elevator inside that thing. But I doubt if anybody questioned the slogan accompanying its name— Gateway to the West. In those days we probably accepted "winning the West" as something that had really happened.

Studying history in grade school, we learned that everything our country had ever done was good, good, good. Nothing smoldered with dubious implications. Occasionally my father offered different views on foreign policies, but no one ever suggested a pilgrim or pioneer might have been less than honorable. I recall preferring Indian headdresses to Pilgrim hats. The Indians had a more powerful mystique. I recall feeling profound indignation over missionaries. Somehow they seemed so insulting—like coming into someone else's neighborhood and telling them how to do things. My father, sent to Kansas as an immigrant student because he wanted to go "to the middle" of the country, left his first university town because local evangelists wouldn't leave him alone.

Long later, I'd read the Chilean poet Pablo Neruda, who

wrote, "Why wasn't Christopher Columbus able to discover Spain?"

Long later, after our country was able to "celebrate victory" in a war that massacred scores of people no more criminal than you or I, our son sat quietly reading a book called *Stanley,* in which cavemen come out of their caves and build houses for the first time. The animals speak in human tongues. They say, "Don't eat my grass and I'll let you live by me." The cavemen plant flowers around their doorways. They learn how to be nice to one another. They put down their clubs. "Isn't it strange," my son said, "that a caveman would be called Stanley?" He had an older man friend named Stanley. It just didn't seem like a caveman kind of name.

I passed under the Gateway to the West into the land of many questions. On a Christmas Eve as far west as we could go in "our own country," we sat in downtown Honolulu in the back pew of the historic Kawaiho Church, the "Westminster Abbey of the Pacific." We each held a candle with a crimped white collar as short-sleeved men and women filed into the pews, wearing leis over Christmas-patterned Aloha shirts. I grew quietly aware that a group of people had entered and were now sitting in the carved wooden box behind us, the space once reserved for royalty, still set aside by a velvet rope. The matriarch of the group wore black, and a distinguished hat, unusual for Honolulu. She stared straight ahead with handsome, queenly elegance. The rest of her family, while attractive, could have blended easily into the crowd.

I don't know why I grew so obsessed with her presence behind us, as we rose for "Joy to the World!" or took seats again for the handbell choir. Maybe it was the row of royal portraits on the second-floor balcony visible over the rail, or my growing curiosity over the ways our fiftieth state had been acquired. I just kept wondering what she thought about it all. Once her family had ruled this little land most remote from all other lands on the globe—a favorite Hawaiian statistic. And now? She was served her wafer and tiny cup of grape juice first, before the rest of the packed congregation. And she walked out into the warm streets, this daughter of Hawaii's last king, on her own two feet when it was over.

My husband first appeared to me in a now-vanished downtown San Antonio eatery with a pleasantly understated name, Quinney's Just Good Food. Businessmen in white shirts and ties swarmed around us, woven together by steaming plates of fried fish and mashed potatoes. I knew, from the first moment of our chance encounter, that he was "the one"—it felt like a concussion to know this.

Walking up South Presa Street later with my friend Sue, who'd introduced us, I asked dizzily, "What *was* his last name?" She said, "Nye, like eye," and the rhymes began popping into my head. They matched our steps. Like *hi,* like *why,* like *bye*—suddenly like every word that seemed to matter. She waved at her corner and I stood there a long time, staring as the crossing signal changed back and forth from a red raised hand to a little man walking. And I knew that every street I crossed from that moment on would be a different street.

Because I am merely a tenant of this name Nye—it is not the house I always occupied—it inspires a traveler's warm affection in me. I appreciate its brevity. Reading about the thirteenth-century Swedes who fled internal uprisings in their own country to resettle in Denmark in settlements prefixed by *Nye*—meaning new, or newcomer—deserves a border-crosser's nod.

Hundreds of families listed in the *Nye Family of America*

Association volumes gather regularly at Sandwich, Massachusetts, to shake hands and share each other's lives. I would like to join them, which surprises me. They started their tradition of gathering in 1903. R. Glen Nye writes, "How can we reach you to tell you how important it is for you to know your origins.... Those who read this are the oldsters of tomorrow ... a hundred years hence, we will be the very ones someone will yearn to know about. Who will they turn to then, if we do not help them now?"

Because my own father came to New York on the boat from his old country of Palestine in 1950, I am curious about these Nyes who came on the boat just following the *Mayflower,* who stayed and stayed and stayed, who built the Nye Homestead on Cape Cod, now a museum pictured on postcards and stationery notes. They have kept such good track of one another. Thick volumes list them, family by family, birthdates, children, occupations.

On a driving trip east, my husband and I paused one blustery day to walk around the cemetery at Sandwich. It felt eerie to sidestep so many imposing granite markers engraved with our own name. Oh Benjamin, oh Katherine and Reuben, you who had no burglar alarms, what did you see that we will never see? And the rest of you Nyes, wandering out across America even as far as Alaska where cars and trucks and jeeps all have their license plates set into little metal frames proclaiming NYE in honor of some enterprising car dealer who claimed the Land of the Midnight Sun as his territory, where did you get your energy? What told you to go?

Once my husband and I invited every Nye in the San Antonio telephone book to dinner. Such reckless festivity would have been more difficult had our name been Sanchez or Smith; as it stood, the eleven entries for Nye seemed too provocative to pass up. Eleven groups of people sharing a name within one city—and we didn't know any of them.

Handwritten invitation—"If you're named Nye, you're invited." Would they *get it?* I was brazen enough to style it a "potluck"—a gathering where the parties themselves would be a potluck—and asked all to RSVP. A week later each family had responded positively, with glinting curiosity, except one humorless fireman, whom I telephoned at the last minute. He was too busy for such frivolous pursuit.

Later I would remember how the picnic table in our backyard spilled a rich offering of pies and green beans and potato salads, how the talk seemed infinite in its variety, how the laughter—"What a wacky idea, Babe!"—some Nye slapping me on the back with sudden gusto—rolled and rolled.

The experience I'd had at a Women's Writing Weekend in Austin where a visiting poet singled me out with displeasure—"What are these three names of yours? So, you've compromised yourself to marriage? I supposed you'd let a *man* publish your work?"—seemed nullified, erased. I'd walked out of that place, throat burning. It probably wouldn't have made any difference had I told her that I happened to *like* the name, or that sometimes it's a pleasure to become someone else midstream in your life. Had the name in question been Smithers or Lumpkin, I might have passed. But this little syllable, this glittering eye, held mine. I could almost have made it up.

No one encouraged us much when we set out one July to drive across the wide western expanse of the United States with a two-year-old. I had a job lined up through rural libraries of the state of Oregon, to be a visiting writer town-to-town for three months. It sounded delicious. It bore the aroma of blackberry jam and grilled salmon. For years I'd said I hoped to live in Oregon someday, if I were lucky enough to get old.

"You'll get old all right, before your time," advised our dubious friends. "A two-year-old? Strapped in a car seat for hours on end? You'll be pulling your hair out. *He'll* be pulling your hair out. How will he stand it? How will he be able to sleep in so many strange places?"

One friend asked if we were going to haul his crib on the roof of the car.

I lay awake nights and worried. I rolled his socks into tight balls. Our son, on the other hand, seemed anxious to depart. He'd been throwing things into his tiny blue suitcase for weeks. I'd find the salt box in there. Or a wad of dried clay. "I'm ready for Oregon," he kept repeating. "When do we go? I won't stand up in my car seat!"

The moment we rolled onto the highway, exhausted by the tedium of departure, a familiar flood of relief washed over us. We found ourselves driving slowly, casually, absorbing the countryside. Home again! Hadn't Americans become too destination-oriented, hurtling forth toward places when we barely had time enough to get there, driving fast all the way? We didn't want to do that. We wanted to fall back into waltz rhythm. To pull into the long driveway that said FRESH CORN MEAL GROUND TODAY even though we didn't know when we'd have an oven again.

It worked out. We stopped at every playground between San Antonio and Portland. (The best one, for anyone following our circuitous route, is at Baker, Oregon—an old-fashioned paradise of high slides and well-oiled merry-go-rounds.) We ate Japanese food in Santa Fe. We unrolled our moldy-smelling tent on a spot of ground in Utah and by morning were encircled by clamoring chipmunks, who had found a wealthy source of cracker crumbs. They were calling for more.

We camped high up in Idaho's Sawtooth Forest near the Sublette junction, where pioneers of the Oregon Trail split off south toward California or continued west toward the Columbia River. Some legends say the signs toward Oregon were written in fancy handwriting (Oregon favored literate settlers) while the signs toward California bore only a painted gold chunk. We had been reading aloud in a series of *National Geographics* about these early vagabonds, how the trail was littered with furniture they pitched from their wagons. How many people died, how many got all the way there, paused awhile, and turned back? What was it they didn't find? Some places in Wyoming, Idaho, Oregon, the deep ruts of their wheels are still engraved in the earth.

Inside our zippered tent I finished reading the essays about the Oregon Trail by flashlight, one of those fancy flashlights that do three different things. I felt scared to walk to the car for something I had forgotten. It was so *big* out there. Where had everyone gone? That night I would dream a bear grabbed my toe through the tent's opening and shook it, hard. Long wild voices pulled at us out of the air.

To consider our evolution into good-gas-mileage sedans, with well-fingered atlases tucked between the seats, seemed critical. Long trip? You call this a long trip?

On one of those Idaho back roads, I contemplated deeply the sweet emblem of a stranger's hand raised in passing, a car or truck traveling the other way whose driver wanted somehow to say, "Good journey, I've been where you're going, travel well." I wanted to tell my friends back home who were teaching their children not to talk to strangers that they had it all wrong. *Do* talk to strangers. Raise your hand to them in strange places, on back roads where leaning fields of tasseled grass have more identity than you do.

Ask strangers anything you want. Maybe they'll have an answer. Don't go home with them, don't take off your pants with them, but talk, talk, talk. Anyway, in this mobile twentieth century, who among us is *not* strange?

I remember thinking, that night, that talking to strangers has been the most important thing I do in my life. It seemed doubtful two wagons on the Oregon Trail would have overtaken one another without a word or message being exchanged.

How much have we lost in this cornucopia land?

When my eye picked out a town named Nye on the map near Pendleton, the place famous for woolens in eastern Oregon, it became suddenly imperative to visit it. Only twenty-eight miles off the interstate—I didn't care how far it was. At our stop for lunch I wrote quick, wild messages to every Nye I could think of, planning to mail them from there. Like Thoreau, New Mexico, or Valentine, Texas—a luminous postmark. This would be better than the tucked-away alley called Nye in El Paso, which no house even faces. Better than the old schoolhouse called Nye in Laredo, named for a beloved teacher.

The road south from Pendleton loomed rolling and golden as the road to Oz. It held its breath— no signs, structures, other cars. The men slept in the back seat.

I couldn't stop imagining it. Maybe there would be a Nye Café. We could swivel on stools at the gleaming counter, ordering cocoa in thick white cups, or vanilla milkshakes. When people looked at us curiously—you here to visit someone?—we'd say the best thing possible to a little lost place in America: "No, we just came here to see the town." Maybe they'd take us around.

The first thing my husband and I ever did together, after that initial meeting at Quinney's, was stare at a map of Texas and pick out a little village called Sweet Home. We drove there in the first excited flush of our togetherness, simply to see what could *be* at a place called that. All day we sat in a pool hall with the regulars, at a metal-topped table inscribed with the name of some beer. An older woman with a gravelly voice showed us her gold wedding band. "Lemme tell ya, I waited," she proclaimed. Waited?

"Met Randolph back high school days, but wasn't no way he was going to stick around this little old place after we was through. He took off, *off,* and I stayed here in Sweet Home, with my mama and daddy, all my relatives was here, did farming, my daddy fixed those old kinda tractors nobody uses anymore. I was just a small-town girl, ya know? But I don't marry no one else, no matter who comes along, I keep thinkin' a Randolph and I say to myself, Randolph's the one fer me. Well he marry somebody else, up some bigger town by Houston, and they stay married all her life but God bless her she died. And one day last year Randolph come through here just to see how we all turned into nothin'."

She grinned.

"Nothin'?"

"Sure, like small-town people do. They happy just to stay home and turn into nothin' else than what they started out to be. Yeah? It's not a bad nothin'. So he come through and here I am, not married yet, age sixty-nine and still waitin'! He sweep me off my feet." Her face grew rosy. "I'm here to say some things can happen good. Ain't it pretty?" She turned the shiny band over and over in the soft afternoon light.

Where was Randolph today? "Up to Shiner buying seed." Had Sweet Home changed much in fifty years? "Oh yeah. Went downhill completely. But we still love it."

After dark we drove back to San Antonio on one of those old two-lanes without much shoulder on either side. I grew sleepy and curled up on the front seat with my head in my husband-to-be's lap. And dreamed, and dreamed. Some things can happen good.

At the junction where Nye, Oregon, was supposed to be, a single ragged spoke spun on a crooked windmill over a leaning, empty shack of a barn. Purely desolate. No human, no house, nothing to indicate this was the place.

We drove one leg of the junction, looking. Fields of lush range grass. The long, lonely land. We tried the other leg—emptier yet. Back at the battered windmill, I turned off the engine. Our boy chanted for juice. While he sucked at the tiny straw and the wind blew through our open doors, a deer bolted, bright-eyed, from a ditch.

It approached our car instead of heading the other way. The deer stared and stared and did not run, examining us with no evident sense of danger. More petite than Texas deer, it sidestepped gracefully around our car, then tiptoed into the brush.

"I think we're here," my husband said, looking down at the map and up again at the small black number that indicated the junction. There was no other sign.

I felt suddenly panicky, my voice shrill in the giant silence. "But where is it? We must be turned around! Wouldn't there be some indication?"

We compared the size of Nye on the map with a few Oregon towns we'd already been through. "Look, this Nye is bigger than the name of that town we passed through that had a thousand people. This is the size of a three-thousand-person town. Weird! It's got to be here!"

My husband gazed. "I've seen ghost towns better looking than this."

Heaving my stiff legs out the door, I walked around. A tumbled chimney whistled *Home.* Wishing for some scrap of women, or love—lace, a wad of pinned hair—I caught instead the wisp of a woman's gaze staring far off, the sweet hinges of cloud that held it. That long look that said *something else.*

If this were indeed it, where had the toughened settlers gone? Perhaps they wished neighbors to lay down wheels, saying, "I'll build here too"—the slim-sided seed of a town, awakening. Perhaps they wished, and everybody passed them by. Among thistles and broken trough, I poked for a sign. And the ache in the throat of that long wind kept hurting.

Finally a red pickup truck appeared on the highway, and we flagged it. A blonde woman squinted at us, scratched her head. "Yep, that's Nye. Not much to look at, is there? When I was little, someone still lived in that beat-up house, but we never knew him. I have a memory of an old guy bending down in the weeds. It didn't look much better then, that's for sure. Actually, none of us around here ever thought of Nye as anything more than a turnoff, you know? I mean, it seems strange that the map makes it look like a town."

Before she drove off, she apologized. We stood around a while longer, as you would at a grave, before driving off toward Portland quietly. I don't think anyone spoke for a hundred miles.

Later the *Oregon Directory of Geographical Names* would say this point on the highway once boasted a post office named Nye, service discontinued 1917. It had probably been named for A. W. Nye, a well-known early resident, though why he was well known, or anything else about him, had filtered into the wind above Umatilla County and disappeared, perhaps toward the town of Echo, relatively nearby on the road back toward life.

"Go to Newport," people in Portland told us later. "There's a street called Nye in Newport. There's a beach called Nye, and an art center." We saved it for another time.

Sometimes the calls come late at night. "I'm looking for a Nye who was a well-known country and western singer in the 1950s. He wore these pants printed with rainbow-colored spurs. That wouldn't happen to be your husband, would it?"

Or, "I'm looking for my great-aunt's friends named Nye—she had a real bad dream, few nights ago, that they drove off a cliff, and she keeps begging us to call them. She can't remember the man's first name. Do you happen to know Celia Withers of Weatherford?"

One evening a rich, musical voice phones from small-town east Texas. She's seen my husband's name in the Corsicana newspaper, and says she's been looking for him for seventeen years. Her name is Peachy Gardner. "Honey! I took care of babies all my life and no baby ever got into my heart like that little Nye did. He'd tweak my ear and kiss me. *Honey!* I loved him so much. I just want to see what he grew into. When his parents moved away I nearly died. They sent me Christmas cards for a while but then— you know what happens. People just get lost."

Then she says they lived in Dallas. My husband never did. And when was the loving baby born? Four years after my husband. I hate to tell her this.

"Are you positive? Are you sure his daddy's name isn't James?"

We talk a while longer. She wrote to the place they had moved and her letter came back. America, she says, eats people up. They get too busy. I promise to start looking for the man with my husband's name, taking her number, in case he appears. We talk about the trees in her part of Texas;

she lives in a thicket so dense the light barely shines through. She says, "I guess it's strange to want to see someone so bad this long after. I mean, he wouldn't look twice at me now. I know that. But I can't forget how he said—Peachy. I can't forget—his little hand."

The Cookies

On Union Boulevard, St. Louis, in the 1950s, there were women in their eighties who lived with the shades down, who hid like bats in the caves they claimed for home. Neighbors of my grandmother, they could be faintly heard through a ceiling or wall. A drawer opening. The slow thump of a shoe. Who they were and whom they were mourning (someone had always just died) intrigued me. Me, the child who knew where the cookies waited in Grandma's kitchen closet. Who lined five varieties up on the table and bit from each one in succession, knowing my mother would never let me do this at home. Who sold Girl Scout cookies door-to-door in annual tradition, who sold fifty boxes, who won The Prize. My grandmother told me which doors to knock on. Whispered secretly, "She'll take three boxes—wait and see."

Hand-in-hand we climbed the dark stairs, knocked on the doors. I shivered, held Grandma tighter, remember still the smell which was curiously fragrant, a sweet soup of talcum powder, folded curtains, roses pressed in a book. Was that what years smelled like? The door would miraculously open and a withered face framed there would peer oddly out at me as if I had come from another world. Maybe I had. "Come in," it would say, or "Yes?" and I would mumble something about cookies, feeling foolish, feeling like the one who places a can of beans next to an altar marked *For the Poor* and then has to stare at it—the beans next to the cross-—all through the worship. Feeling I should have brought more, as if I shouldn't be selling something to these women, but giving them a gift, some new breath, assurance that there was still a child's world out there, green grass, scabby knees, a playground where you could stretch your legs higher than your head. There were still Easter eggs lodged in the mouths of drainpipes and sleds on frozen hills, that joyous scream of flying toward yourself in the snow. Squirrels storing nuts, kittens being born with eyes closed; there was still everything tiny, unformed, flung wide open into the air!

But how did you carry such an assurance? In those hallways, standing before those thin gray wisps of women, with Grandma slinking back and pushing me forward to go in alone, I didn't know. There was something here which also smelled like life. But it was a life I hadn't learned yet. I had never outlived anything I knew of, except one yellow cat. I had never saved a photograph. For me life was a bounce, an unending burst of pleasures. Vaguely I imagined what a life of recollection could be, as already I was haunted by a sense of my own lost baby years, golden rings I slipped on and off my heart. Would I be one of those women?

Their rooms were shrines of upholstery and lace. Silent radios standing under stacks of magazines. Did they work? Could I turn the knobs? Questions I wouldn't ask here. Windows with shades pulled low, so the light peeping through took on a changed quality, as if it were brighter or dimmer than I remembered. And portraits, photographs, on walls, on tables, faces strangely familiar, as if I were destined to know them. I asked no questions and the women never questioned me. Never asked where the money went, had the price gone up since last year, were there any additional flavors. They bought what they remembered—if it was peanut-butter last year, peanut-butter this year would be fine. They brought the coins from jars, from pocketbooks without handles, counted them carefully before me, while I stared at their thin crops of knotted hair. A Sunday brooch pinned loosely to the shoulder of an everyday dress. What were these women thinking of?

And the door would close softly behind me, transaction complete, the closing click like a drawer sliding back, a world slid quietly out of sight, and I was free to return to my own universe, to Grandma standing with arms folded in the courtyard, staring peacefully up at a bluejay or sprouting leaf. Suddenly I'd see Grandma in her dress of tiny flowers, curly gray permanent, tightly laced shoes as one of *them*— but then she'd turn, laugh, "Did she buy?" and again belong to me.

Gray women in rooms with the shades drawn. . . . Weeks later the cookies would come. I would stack the boxes, make my delivery rounds to the sleeping doors. This time I would be businesslike, I would rap firmly. "Hello Ma'am, here are the cookies you ordered." And the face would peer up, uncertain . . . cookies? . . . as if for a moment we were floating in the space between us. What I did (carefully balancing boxes in both my arms, wondering who would eat the cookies—I was the only child ever seen in that building) or what she did (reaching out with floating hands to touch what she had bought) had little to do with who we were, had been, or ever would be.

Commerce

My parents did not scrimp on a name for their enterprise; the boxy white cottage, small as a bachelor uncle's daily resignation, became WORLD GIFTS. My mother painted a sign. The small building didn't even sit on a thoroughfare—it sat back behind someone else's house. And the people of that town who so rarely seemed to travel, though they had come from Italy or Quebec or Grand Rapids to begin with, filtered through the screen door one by one wearing their dubious faces.

From behind the counter, we guessed if they would buy or only browse, curling with our library books, on Moroccan hassocks, camel saddles. I loved the stack of white paper bags as they lay together, anticipatory on their shelf, and the ream of new tissue. I'd crease the folds as my smooth father in dark suit and daily drench of cologne counted change. Or we'd help unpack crates: nested Russian dolls, glossy mother-of-pearl earrings from Bethlehem, a family of sandalwood fans. Something wonderful was always on its way. It would sell big; it would be what people craved. Better than boring brass candle-snuffers and napkin rings, better even than Mexican piñatas sharpening the air with their crisp exotic allure. I wanted to live where people cracked pink and green turtles open with a stick.

Occasionally whole days passed and no one came in. We could read my mother's face when we swirled through the door after school. A tablet of blank tickets lay open on the counter. It never made sense to me when people talked about luck; more, it seemed a question of hope, how much you had, how long it lasted when only the slow drone of the clock held it up.

Above the shop a gnarly apple tree twisted its branches. We climbed in it, but our interest in climbing felt short-lived. Scarred apples thudded onto the roof, softening into winey fists. One day when no one had come in for a long time, my brother smashed a hard apple through the glass of the life insurance company next door. A secretary cupped her bleeding knuckles in front of our mother, who made my brother apologize, and promised to pay. Nobody cried. But a man from Texas who declared he'd return to buy all the dolls in the shop, and never showed up again, became unmentionable; we waited for him, that's all. When the door opened on a fluttering woman looking for her lost hair salon, or a postman with a stack of invoices, we thought of the Texan and shook our heads. Promises. It was like someone telling my father he'd call him back. I felt my father always waiting. Another day my brother and I walked two doors down to Mannino's Grocery and smashed a watermelon on the ground.

I was reading a book about the Happy Hollisters, who had banisters in their home, whose daughters gave slumber parties and made lists of things to do on happy Saturdays. Christmas jingled inside those pages, coin purses, bangle bracelets, sugar cookies—I'd fallen in. Sometimes people would address me and I'd be a Happy Hollister when I answered.

Waiting for someone to give you money for what you had—it seemed so strange. But that's what they did everywhere, at every store. I'd seen the CLOSEOUT signs plastered across storefronts on Florissant Avenue, Union Boulevard. A Chinese couple offered dozens of salt and pepper sets at their going-out-of-business sale. Streaked napkin dispensers, flattened lanterns . . . while our parents considered the lanterns, the Chinese couple stood back against the bushes, murmuring. In a few months The Emperor's Palace would fall from local consciousness, as if it had never steamed and souped us onward.

Our parents did well enough, briefly, for our father to branch out to the Sheraton Hotel downtown, even enlarging the name of the business to WORLD GIFTS LTD. British, he said. Our mother ran the little shop. Why Limited? I thought it should be Unlimited. Items kept arriving, nestled in shredded packaging. Sometimes we'd go downtown with him and ride the elevators all day. The hotel restaurant let me sign the check, and I'd order a roast beef sandwich because it seemed so American. We'd write letters to mail in the old-fashioned chutes connecting floors; I'd stand on the eighth and my brother on the seventh to see the letter whiz by. Lyndon Johnson passed through the lobby once, and Monique Van Vooren entertained at the Can-Can Room, breezing past us with her puff of frozen hair. Danny Thomas invited us up to his suite, after purchasing something Lebanese. I wrote Danny Kaye a letter, completely forgetting about it until a creamy handwritten envelope arrived for me; "Sylvia and I loved hearing from you—we both thank you for your sweet thoughts. . . ." I pressed the rich paper to my cheek, feeling giddy. So then I knew his wife's name. Beyond the world of commerce, all the possible transactions one could make through the mail!

That's what I held close when things didn't work out;

Danny Kaye wrote me back. On the night my friends called me "Liar!," on the long days of No Sales, I held the quiet voice of Danny's letter in my throat. Might our saving graces all be so unexpected? I never dreamed Danny would die years later within weeks of my other masculine heroes, Robert Preston and Desi Arnaz. We never guessed, pushing DOOR CLOSE in the elevator's velveteen cage, how the sensations of dropping and soaring would stay with us, the click of the key in the large lock, the flood of light over onyx animals, chessboards, silken scarves.

My father opened two more shops before a roar of flames in the subterranean Sheraton stockroom consumed the entire pre-Christmas inventory. We'd gone on a late vacation, driving up into the Wisconsin Dells, riding steamers, eating hotcakes. It felt like a place the Happy Hollisters might go. But the insurance on the business lapsed during our absence, right before the blaze. I kept tonguing the word, *lapsed, lapsed.* My father, who often proposed his belief in fate as ruling the universe, received a call at our motel; the stunned slant of his jaw, his hands gripping the wheel for the long drive back. And our mother's infinite gaze, she who had waited and waited, rearranging shelves, who had penned the perfect tags with calligrapher's ink.

After that our homes held little traces: a string of olivewood camels linked by chain, a Mexican box whose lid slid back as a snake with slithery tongue flipped out to greet you. A single doll from India stayed to sleep with me, the red dot imprinted on her forehead, a delicate sari edged in gold. She told me I would travel in India someday, and see how much there was to buy, how many people to buy it. Not explaining why I would wander those markets wanting nothing, even the ancient quilts of Rajasthan with their dark scrolls of satiny stitching, feeling I'd already owned it all, and given it back. Or that sense of something coming that would dog me, someone unknown and unknowable about to step through the door and gaze at our gathered splendors . . . Did we have . . . ? My desire to please, between the full shelves, the earth's sad abundance.

Three Pokes of a Thistle

HIDING INSIDE THE GOOD GIRL

"She has the devil inside her," said my first report card from first grade. I walked home slowly, holding it out from my body, a thistle, a thorn, to my mother, who read the inside, then the note on the back. She cried mightily, heaves of underground rivers, we stood looking deep into the earth as water rushed by.

I didn't know who he was.

One day I'd smashed John's nose on the pencil sharpener and broken it. Stood in the cloakroom smelling the rust of coats. I said No. No thank you. I already read that and it's not a very good story. Jane doesn't do much. I want the spider who talks. The family of little women and their thousand days. No. What I had for breakfast is a secret. I didn't want to tell them I ate dried apricots. I listened to their lineage of eggs. I listened to the bacon crackle in everyone else's pan. Thank you.

What shall we do, what shall we do? Please, I beg you. Our pajamas were flying from the line, waists pinned, their legs fat with fabulous air. My mother peeled beets, her fingers stained deep red. She was bleeding dinner for us. She was getting up and lying down.

Once I came home from school in the middle of the day in a taxi. School gave me a stomachache. I rode in the front passenger seat. It would be expensive. My mother stood at the screen door peering out, my baby brother perched on her hip. She wore an apron. The taxi pulled up in front of the blue mailbox I viewed as an animal across from our house—his opening mouth. Right before I climbed out, another car hit the taxi hard from behind so my mother saw me fly from the front seat to the back. Her mouth wide open, the baby dangling from her like fringe. She came toward us running. I climbed up onto the ledge inside the back window to examine the wreckage. The taxi driver's visored cap had blown out the window. He was shaking his head side to side as if he had water in his ears.

You, you, look what a stomachache gets you. Whiplash.

The doctor felt my neck.

Later I sat on the front steps staring at the spot where it had happened. What about that other driver? He cried when the policeman arrived. He was an old man coming to mail a letter. I was incidental to the scene, but it couldn't have happened without me. *If you had just stayed where you belonged . . .* My classmates sealed into their desks laboring over pages of subtraction, while out in the world, cars were banging together. Yellow roses opened slowly on a bush beside my step. I was thinking how everything looked from far away.

Then I was old. A hundred years before I found it, Mark Twain inscribed the front of his first-edition leatherbound book, "BE GOOD—AND YOU WILL BE LONESOME." In black ink, with a flourish. He signed his name. My friend had the book in a box in her attic and did not know. It was from her mother's collection. I carried it down the stairs, trembling. My friend said, "Do you think it is valuable?"

LANGUAGE BARRIER

Basically our father spoke English perfectly, though he still got his *b*s and *p*s mixed up. He had a gentle, deliberate way of choosing words. I could feel him reaching up into the air to find them. At night, he told us whimsical, curling "Joha" stories which hypnotized us to sleep. I especially liked the big cooking pan that gave birth to the little pan. My friend Marcia's father who grew up in the United States hardly talked. He built airplanes. I didn't think I would want to fly in anything he made. When Marcia asked him a question, he grunted a kind of pig sound. He sank his face into the paper. My father spilled out musical lines, a horizon of graceful buildings standing beside one another in a distant city. You could imagine people living inside one of my father's words.

He said a few things to us in Arabic—fragrant syllables after we ate, blessings when he hugged us. He hugged us all the time. He said, "I love you" all the time. But I didn't learn how to say "Thank you" in Arabic till I was fourteen, which struck me, even then, as a preposterous omission.

Marcia's father seemed tired. He had seven children because he was a Catholic, Marcia said. I didn't get it. Marcia's mother threw away the leftovers from their table after dinner. My mother carefully wrapped the last little mound of mashed potato inside waxed paper. We'd eat it later.

I felt comfortable in the world of so many different people. Their voices floated around the neighborhood like pollen. On the next block, French-Canadians made blueberry pie. I wanted a slice. It is true that a girl knocked on our door one day and asked to "see the Arab," but I was not insulted. I was mystified. Who?

Sometimes Marcia and I slept together on our screened-in back porch, or in a big green tent in her yard. She was easy to scare. I said the giant harvest moon was coming to eat her and she hid under her pillow. She told me spider stories. We had fun trading little terrors.

When I was almost ready to move away, Marcia and I stood in Dade Park together one last time. I said good-bye to the swings and benches and wooden seesaws with chipped red paint. Two bigger boys rode up on bicycles and circled us. We'd never seen them before. One of them asked if we knew how to do the F-word. I had no idea what they were talking about. Marcia said she knew, but wouldn't tell me. The boys circled the basketball courts, eyeing us strangely. Walking home with Marcia, I felt almost glad to be moving away from her. She stuck her chest out. She said, "Did you ever wish someone would touch you in a private place?"

I looked in the big dictionary at home. Hundreds of F-words I didn't know reached their hands out so it took a long time. And I asked my mother, whose face was so smooth and beautiful and filled with sadness because nothing was quite as good as it could be.

She didn't know either.

BRA STRAP

It felt like a taunt, the elastic strap of Karen's bra visible beneath her white blouse in front of me in fifth grade. I saw it even before Douglas snapped it. Who did she think she was, growing older without me?

I spent the night with her one Saturday. In the bathtub together, we splashed and soaped, jingling our talk of teachers, boys, and holidays. But my eyes were on her chest, the great pale fruits growing there. Already they mounded toward stems.

She caught me looking and said, "So?" Sighing, as if she were already tired. Said, "In my family they grow early." Downstairs her bosomy mother stacked cups in a high old cabinet that smelled of grandmother's hair. I could hear her clinking. In my family they barely grew at all. I had been proud of my mother's boyishness, her lithe trunk and straight legs.

Now I couldn't stop thinking about it: what was there, what wasn't there. The mounds on the fronts of certain dolls with candy-coated names. One by one, watching the backs of my friends' blouses, I saw them all fall under the spell. I begged my mother, who said, "For what? Just to be like everybody else?"

Pausing near the underwear displays at Famous and Barr, I asked to be measured, sizing up boxes. "Training Bra"— what were we in training for?

When Louise fell off her front porch and a stake went all the way through her, I heard teachers whispering, "Hope this doesn't ruin her for the future." We discussed the word "impaled." What future? The mysteries of ovaries had not yet been explained. Little factories for eggs. Little secret nests. On the day we saw the film, I didn't like it. If that was what the future meant, I didn't want it anymore. As I was staring out the window afterwards, my mouth tasted like pennies, my throat closed up. The leaves on the trees blurred together so they could carry me.

I sat on a swivel chair practicing handwritings. The back-wards slant, the loopy up-and-down. Who would I ever be? My mother was inside the lawyer's office signing papers about the business. That waiting room, with its dull wooden side tables and gloomy magazines, had absolutely nothing to do with me. Never for a second was I drawn toward the world of the dreary professional. I would be a violinist with the Zurich symphony. I would play percussion in a traveling band. I would bake zucchini muffins in Yarmouth, Nova Scotia.

In the car traveling slowly home under a thick gray sky, I worked up courage. Rain, rain, the intimacy of cars. At a stoplight, staring hard at my mother, I asked, "What really happens between men and women to make babies?"

She jumped as if I'd thrown ice at her.

"Not *that!* Not *now!*" From red to green, the light, the light. "There is *oh so much you do not know.*"

It was all she ever told me. The weight of my ignorance pressed upon us both.

Later she slipped me a book, *Little Me, Big Me.* One of the more incomprehensible documents of any childhood: "When a man and a woman love one another enough, he puts his arms around her and part of him goes into part of her and the greatness of their love for one another causes this to feel pleasurable."

On my twelfth birthday, my father came home with our first tape recorder. My mother produced a bouquet of shiny boxes, including a long, slim one. My Lutheran grandparents sat neatly on the couch as the heavy reels wound up our words.

"Do you like it? Is it just what you've been waiting for?"

They wanted me to hold it up to my body, the way I would when I put it on. My mother shushing, "Oh, I guess it's private!"

Later the tape would play someone's giggles in the background. My brother? Or the gangs of little girl angels that congregate around our heads, chanting, "Don't grow up, don't grow up!"

I never liked wearing it as much as I did thinking about it.

Thank You in Arabic

Shortly after my mother discovered my brother had been pitching his Vitamin C tablets behind the stove for years, we left the country. Her sharp alert, "Now the truth be known!" startled us at the breakfast table as she poked into the dim crevice with the nozzle of her vacuum. We could hear the pills go click, click, up the long tube.

My brother, an obedient child, a bright-eyed, dark-skinned charmer who scored high on all his tests and trilled a boy's sweet soprano, stared down at his oatmeal. Four years younger than I, he was also the youngest and smallest in his class. Somehow he maintained an intelligence and dignity more notable than that of his older, larger companions, and the pills episode, really, was a pleasant surprise to me.

Companions in mischief are not to be underestimated, especially when everything else in your life is about to change.

We sold everything we had and left the country. The move had been brewing for months. We took a few suitcases each. My mother cried when the piano went. I wished we could have saved it. My brother and I had sung so many classics over its keyboard—"Look for the Silver Lining" and "Angels We Have Heard on High"—that it would have been nice to return to a year later, when we came straggling back. I sold my life-size doll and my toy sewing machine. I begged my mother to save her red stove for me, so I could have it when I grew up—no one else we knew had a red stove. So my mother asked some friends to save it for me in their barn.

Our parents had closed their imported-gifts stores, and our father had dropped out of ministerial school. He had attended the Unity School of Christianity for a few years, but decided not to become a minister after all. We were relieved, having felt like impostors the whole time he was enrolled. He wasn't even a Christian, to begin with, but a gently non-practicing Muslim. He didn't do anything like fasting or getting down on his knees five times a day. Our mother had given up the stern glare of her Lutheran ancestors, raising my brother and me in the Vedanta Society of St. Louis. When anyone asked what we were, I said, "Hindu." We had a Swami, and sandalwood incense. It was over our heads, but we liked it and didn't feel very attracted to the idea of churches and collection baskets and chatty parish good-will.

Now and then, just to keep things balanced, we attended the Unity Sunday School. My teacher said I was lucky my father came from the same place Jesus came from. It was a passport to notoriety. She invited me to bring artifacts for Show and Tell. I wrapped a red and white *keffiyah* around my friend Jimmy's curly blond head while the girls in lacy socks giggled behind their hands. I told about my father coming to America from Palestine on the boat and throwing his old country clothes overboard before docking at Ellis Island. I felt relieved he'd kept a few things, like the *keffiyah* and its black braided band. Secretly it made me mad to have lost the blue pants from Jericho with the wide cuffs he told us about.

I enjoyed standing in front of the group talking about my father's homeland. Stories felt like elastic bands that could stretch and stretch. Big fans purred inside their metal shells. I held up a string of olive wood camels. I didn't tell our teacher about the Vedanta Society. We were growing up ecumenical, though I wouldn't know that word till a long time later in college. One night I heard my father say to my mother in the next room, "Do you think they'll be confused when they grow up?" and knew he was talking about us. My mother, bless her, knew we wouldn't be. She said, "At least we're giving them a choice." I didn't know then that more clearly than all the stories of Jesus, I'd remember the way our Hindu swami said a single word three times, "Shanti, shanti, shanti"—peace, peace, peace.

Our father was an excellent speaker—he stood behind pulpits and podiums easily, delivering gracious lectures on "The Holy Land" and "The Palestinian Question." He was much in demand during the Christmas season. I think that's how he had fallen into the ministerial swoon. While he spoke, my brother and I hovered toward the backs of the auditoriums, eyeing the tables of canapés and tiny tarts, slipping a few into our mouths or pockets.

What next? Our lives were entering a new chapter, but I didn't know its title yet.

We had never met our Palestinian grandmother, Sitti Khadra, or seen Jerusalem, where our father had grown up, or followed the rocky, narrow alleyways of the Via Dolorosa, or eaten an olive in its own neighborhood. Our mother hadn't either. The Arabic customs we knew had been filtered through the fine net of folktales. We did not speak Arabic, though the lilt of the language was familiar to us—

our father's endearments, his musical blessings before meals—but that language had never lived in our mouths.

And that's where we were going, to Jerusalem. We shipped our car, a wide golden Impala the exact color of a cigarette filter, over on a boat. We would meet up with it later.

The first plane flight of my whole life was the night flight out of New York City across the ocean. I was fourteen years old. Every glittering light in every skyscraper looked like a period at the end of the sentence. Good-bye, our lives.

We stopped in Portugal for a few weeks. We were making a gradual transition. We stopped in Spain and Italy and Egypt, where the pyramids shocked me by sitting right on the edge of the giant city of Cairo, not way out in the desert as I had imagined them. While we waited for our baggage to clear customs, I stared at six tall African men in brilliantly patterned dashikis negotiating with an Egyptian customs agent and realized I did not even know how to say "Thank you" in Arabic. How was this possible? The most elemental and important of human phrases in my father's own tongue had evaded me till now. I tugged on his sleeve, but he was busy with visas and passports. "Daddy," I said. "Daddy, I have to know. Daddy, tell me. Daddy, why didn't we ever *learn*?" An African man adjusted his turban. Always thereafter, the word *shookrun*, so simple, with a little roll in the middle, would conjure up the vast African baggage, the brown boxes looped and looped in African twine.

We stayed one or two nights at the old Shepherd's Hotel downtown, but couldn't sleep because of the heat and honking traffic beneath our windows. So our father moved us to the famous Mena House Hotel next to the pyramids. We rode camels for the first time, and our mother received a dozen blood-red roses at her hotel room from a rug vendor who apparently liked her pale brown ponytail. The belly dancer at the hotel restaurant twined a gauzy pink scarf around my brother's astonished ten-year-old head as he tapped his knee in time to her music. She bobbled her giant cleavage under his nose, huge bosoms prickled by sequins and sweat.

Back in our rooms, we laughed until we fell asleep. Later that night, my brother and I both awakened burning with fever and deeply nauseated, though nobody ever threw up. We were so sick that a doctor hung a Quarantine sign in Arabic and English on our hotel room door the next day. Did he know something we didn't know? I kept waiting to hear that we had malaria or typhoid, but no dramatic disease was ever mentioned. We lay in bed for a week. The aged doctor tripped over my suitcase every time he entered to take our temperatures. We smothered our laughter. "Shookrun," I would say. But as soon as he left, to my brother, "I feel bad. How do you feel?"

"I feel really, really bad."

"I think I'm dying."

"I think I'm already dead."

At night we heard the sound and lights show from the pyramids drifting across the desert air to our windows. We felt our lives stretching out across thousands of miles. The Pharaohs stomped noisily through my head and churning belly. We had eaten spaghetti in the restaurant. I would not be able to eat spaghetti again for years.

Finally, finally, we appeared in the restaurant again, thin and weakly smiling, and ordered the famous Mena House *shorraba,* lentil soup, as my brother nervously scanned the room for the belly dancer. Maybe she wouldn't recognize him now.

In those days Jerusalem, which was then a divided city, had an operating airport on the Jordanian side. My brother and I remember flying in upside down, or in a plane dramatically tipped, but it may have been the effect of our medicine. The land reminded us of a dropped canvas, graceful brown hillocks and green patches. Small and provincial, the airport had just two runways, and the first thing I observed as we climbed down slowly from the stuffy plane was all my underwear strewn across one of them. There were my flowered cotton briefs and my pink panties and my slightly embarrassing raggedy ones and my extra training bra, alive and visible in the breeze. Somehow my suitcase had popped open in the hold and dropped its contents the minute the men pried open the cargo door. So the first thing I did on the home soil of my father was recollect my underwear, down on my knees, the posture of prayer over that ancient holy land.

Our relatives came to see us at a hotel. Our grandmother was very short. She wore a long, thickly embroidered Palestinian dress, had a musical, high-pitched voice and a low, guttural laugh. She kept touching our heads and faces as if she couldn't believe we were there. I had not yet fallen in love with her. Sometimes you don't fall in love with people immediately, even if they're your own grandmother. Everyone seemed to think we were all too thin.

We moved into a second-story flat in a stone house eight miles north of the city, among fields and white stones and wandering sheep. My brother was enrolled in the Friends Girls School and I was enrolled in the Friends Boys School in the town of Ramallah a few miles farther north—it seemed a little confused. But the Girls School offered grades one through eight in English and high school continued at the Boys School. Most local girls went to Arabic-speaking schools after eighth grade.

I was a freshman, one of seven girl students among two

hundred boys, which would cause me problems later. I was called in from the schoolyard at lunchtime, to the office of our counselor who wore shoes so pointed and tight her feet bulged out pinkly on top.

"You will not be talking to them anymore," she said. She rapped on the desk with a pencil for emphasis.

"To whom?"

"All the boy students at this institution. It is inappropriate behavior. From now on, you will only speak with the girls."

"But there are only six other girls! And I only like one of them!" My friend was Anna, from Italy, whose father ran a small factory that made matches. I'd visited it once with her. It felt risky to walk the aisles among a million filled matchboxes. Later we visited the factory that made olive oil soaps and stacked them in giant pyramids to dry.

"No, thank you," I said. "It's ridiculous to say that girls should only talk to girls. Did I say anything bad to a boy? Did anyone say anything bad to me? They're my friends. They're like my brothers. I won't do it, that's all."

The counselor conferred with the headmaster and they called a taxi. I was sent home with a note requesting that I transfer to a different school. The charge: insolence. My mother, startled to see me home early and on my own, stared out the window when I told her.

My brother came home from his school as usual, full of whistling and notebooks. "Did anyone tell you not to talk to girls?" I asked him. He looked at me as if I'd gone goofy. He was too young to know the troubles of the world. He couldn't even imagine them.

"You know what I've been thinking about?" he said. "A piece of cake. That puffy white layered cake with icing like they have at birthday parties in the United States. Wouldn't that taste good right now?" Our mother said she was thinking about mayonnaise. You couldn't get it in Jerusalem. She'd tried to make it and it didn't work. I felt too gloomy to talk about food.

My brother said, "Let's go let Abu Miriam's chickens out." That's what we always did when we felt sad. We let our fussy landlord's red and white chickens loose to flap around the yard happily, puffing their wings. Even when Abu Miriam shouted and waggled his cane and his wife waved a dishtowel, we knew the chickens were thanking us.

My father went with me to the St. Tarkmanchatz Armenian School, a solemnly ancient stone school tucked deep into the Armenian Quarter of the Old City of Jerusalem. It was another world in there. He had already called them on the telephone and tried to enroll me, though they didn't want to. Their school was for Armenian students only, kindergarten through twelfth grade. Classes were taught in three languages, Armenian, Arabic and English, which was why I needed to go there. Although most Arab students at other schools were learning English, I needed a school where classes were actually taught in English—otherwise I would have been staring out the windows triple the usual amount.

The head priest wore a long robe and a tall cone-shaped hat. He said, "Excuse me, please, but your daughter, she is not an Armenian, even a small amount?"

"Not at all," said my father. "But in case you didn't know, there is a stipulation in the educational code books of this city that says no student may be rejected solely on the basis of ethnic background, and if you don't accept her, we will alert the proper authorities."

They took me. But the principal wasn't happy about it. The students, however, seemed glad to have a new face to look at. Everyone's name ended in *-ian*, the beautiful, musical Armenian ending—Boghossian, Minassian, Kevorkian,

Rostomian. My new classmates started calling me Shihabian. We wore uniforms, navy blue pleated skirts for the girls, white shirts, and navy sweaters. I waited during the lessons for the English to come around, as if it were a channel on television. While my friends were on the other channels, I scribbled poems in the margins of my pages, read library books, and wrote a lot of letters filled with exclamation points. All the other students knew three languages with three entirely different alphabets. How could they carry so much in their heads? I felt humbled by my ignorance. Again and again and again. One day I felt so frustrated in our physics class—still another language—that I pitched my book out the open window. The professor made me go collect it. All the pages had let loose at the seams and were flapping into the gutters along with the white wrappers of sandwiches.

Every week the girls had a hands-and-fingernails check. We had to keep our nails clean and trim, and couldn't wear any rings. Some of my new friends would invite me home for lunch with them, since we had an hour-and-a-half break and I lived too far to go to my own house.

Their houses were a thousand years old, clustered beehive fashion behind ancient walls, stacked and curled and tilting and dark, filled with pictures of unsmiling relatives and small white cloths dangling crocheted edges. We ate spinach pies and white cheese. We dipped our bread in olive oil, as the Arabs did. We ate small sesame cakes, our mouths full of crumbles. They taught me to say, "I love you" in Armenian, which sounded like *yes-kay-see-goo-see-rem*. I felt I had left my old life entirely.

Every afternoon I went down to the basement of the school where the kindergarten class was having an Arabic lesson. Their desks were pint-sized, their full white smocks tied around their necks. I stuffed my fourteen-year-old self in beside them. They had rosy cheeks and shy smiles. They must have thought I was a very slow learner.

More than any of the lessons, I remember the way the teacher rapped the backs of their hands with his ruler when they made a mistake. Their little faces puffed up with quiet tears. This pained me so terribly I forgot all my words. When it was my turn to go to the blackboard and write in Arabic, my hand shook. The kindergarten students whispered hints to me from the front row, but I couldn't understand them. We learned horribly useless phrases: "Please hand me the bellows for my fire." I wanted words simple as tools, simple as *food* and *yesterday* and *dreams*. The teacher never rapped my hand, especially after I wrote a letter to the city newspaper, which my father edited, protesting such harsh treatment of young learners. I wished I had known how to talk to those little ones, but they were just beginning their English studies and didn't speak much yet. They were at the same place in their English that I was in my Arabic.

From the high windows of St. Tarkmanchatz, we could look out over the Old City, the roofs and flapping laundry and television antennas, the pilgrims and churches and mosques, the olive-wood prayer beads and fragrant *falafel* lunch stands, the intricate interweaving of cultures and prayers and songs and holidays. We saw the barbed wire separating Jordan from Israel then, the bleak, uninhabited strip of no-man's land reminding me how little education saved us after all. People who had differing ideas still came to blows, imagining fighting could solve things. Staring out over the quiet roofs of afternoon, it seemed so foolish to me. I asked my friends what they thought about it and they shrugged.

"It doesn't matter what we think about it. It just keeps happening. It happened in Armenia too, you know. Really, really bad in Armenia. And who talks about it in the world news now? It happens everywhere. It happens in *your* country one by one, yes? Murders and guns. What can we do?"

Sometimes after school, my brother and I walked up the road that led past the crowded refugee camp of Palestinians who owned even less than our modest relatives did in the village. The kids were stacking stones in empty tin cans and shaking them. We waved our hands and they covered their mouths and laughed. We wore our beat-up American tennis shoes and our old sweatshirts and talked about everything we wanted to do and everywhere else we wished we could go.

"I want to go back to Egypt," my brother said. "I sort of feel like I missed it. Spending all that time in bed instead of exploring—what a waste."

"I want to go to Greece," I said. "I want to play a violin in a symphony orchestra in Austria." We made up things. I wanted to go back to the United States most of all. Suddenly I felt like a patriotic citizen. One of my friends, Sylvie Markarian, had just been shipped off to Damascus, Syria, to marry a man who was fifty years old, a widower. Sylvie was exactly my age—we had turned fifteen two days apart. She had never met her future husband before. "Tell your parents no thank you," I urged her. I thought this was the most revolting thing I had ever heard of. "Tell them you *refuse*."

Sylvie's eyes were liquid, swirling brown. I could not see clear to the bottom of them.

"You don't understand," she told me. "In United States you say no. We don't say no. We have to follow someone's wishes. This is the wish of my father. Me, I am scared. I never slept away from my mother before. But I have no choice. I am going because they tell me to go." She was sobbing, sobbing on my shoulder. And I was stroking her long, soft hair. After that, I carried two fists inside, one for Sylvie and one for me.

Most weekends my family went to the village to sit with the relatives. We sat and sat and sat. We sat in big rooms and little rooms, in circles, on chairs or on woven mats or brightly-covered mattresses piled on the floor. People came in and out to greet my family. Sometimes even donkeys and chickens came in and out. We were like movie stars or dignitaries. They never seemed to get tired of us.

My father translated the more interesting tidbits of conversation, the funny stories my grandmother told. She talked about angels and food and money and people and politics and gossip and old memories from my father's childhood, before he emigrated away from her. She wanted to make sure we were going to stick around forever, which made me feel very nervous. We ate from mountains of rice and eggplant on large silver trays—they gave us plates of our own since it was not our custom to eat from the same plate as other people. We ripped the giant wheels of bread into triangles. Shepherds passed through town with their flocks of sheep and goats, their long canes and cloaks, straight out of the Bible. My brother and I trailed them to the edge of the village, past the lentil fields to the green meadows studded with stones, while the shepherds pretended we weren't there. I think they liked to be alone, unnoticed. The sheep had differently colored dyed bottoms, so shepherds could tell their flocks apart.

During these long, slow, smoke-stained weekends—the men still smoked cigarettes a lot in those days, and the old *taboon,* my family's mounded bread-oven, puffed billowy clouds outside the door—my crying jags began. I cried without any warning, even in the middle of a meal. My crying was usually noiseless but dramatically wet—streams of tears pouring down my cheeks, onto my collar or the back of my hand.

Everything grew quiet.

Someone always asked in Arabic, "What is wrong? Are

you sick? Do you wish to lie down?"

My father made valiant excuses in the beginning. "She's overtired," he said. "She has a headache. She is missing her friend who moved to Syria. She is feeling homesick."

My brother stared at me as if I had just landed from Planet X.

Worst was our drive to school every morning, when our car came over the rise in the highway and all Jerusalem lay sprawled before us in its golden, stony splendor pockmarked with olive trees and automobiles. Even the air above the city had a thick, religious texture, as if it were a shining brocade filled with broody incense. I cried hardest then. All those hours tied up in school lay just ahead. My father pulled over and talked to me. He sighed. He kept his hands on the steering wheel even when the car was stopped and said, "Someday, I promise you, you will look back on this period in your life and have no idea what made you so unhappy here."

"I want to go home." It became my anthem. "This place depresses me. It weighs too much. I hate all these old stones that everybody keeps kissing. I'm sick of pilgrims. They act so pious and pure. And I hate the way people stare at me here." Already I'd been involved in two street skirmishes with boys who stared too hard and long, clucking with their tongues. I'd socked one in the jaw and he socked me back. I hit the other one straight in the face with my purse.

"You could be happy here if you tried harder," my father said. "Don't compare it to the United States all the time. Don't pretend the United States is perfect. And look at your brother—he's not having any problems!"

"My brother is eleven years old."

I had crossed the boundary from uncomplicated childhood where happiness was a good ball and a horde of candy-coated Jordan almonds.

One problem was that I had fallen in love with four different boys who all played in the same band. Two of them were even twins. I never quite described it to my parents, but I wrote reams and reams of notes about it on loose-leaf paper that I kept under my sweaters in my closet.

Such new energy made me feel reckless. I gave things away. I gave away my necklace and a whole box of shortbread cookies that my mother had been saving. I gave my extra shoes away to the gypsies. One night when the gypsies camped in a field down the road from our house, I thought about their mounds of white goat cheese lined up on skins in front of their tents, and the wild *oud* music they played deep into the black belly of the night, and I wanted to go sit around their fire. Maybe they could use some shoes.

I packed a sack of old loafers that I rarely wore and walked with my family down the road. The gypsy mothers stared into my shoes curiously. They took them into their tents. Maybe they would use them as vases or drawers. We sat with small glasses of hot, sweet tea until a girl bellowed from deep in her throat, threw back her head, and began dancing. A long bow thrummed across the strings. The girl circled the fire, tapping and clicking, trilling a long musical wail from deep in her throat. My brother looked nervous. He was remembering the belly dancer in Egypt, and her scarf. I felt invisible. I was pretending to be a gypsy. My father stared at me. Didn't I recognize the exquisite oddity of my own life when I sat right in the middle of it? Didn't I feel lucky to be here? Well, yes I did. But sometimes it was hard to be lucky.

When we left Jerusalem, we left quickly. Left our beds in our rooms and our car in the driveway. Left in a plane, not sure where we were going. The rumbles of fighting with Israel had been growing louder and louder. In the barbed-wire no-man's land visible from the windows of our house, guns cracked loudly in the middle of the night. We lived right near the edge. My father heard disturbing rumors at the newspaper that would soon grow into the infamous Six-Day War of 1967. We were in England by then, drinking tea from thin china cups and scanning the newspapers. Bombs were blowing up in Jerusalem. We worried about the village. We worried about my grandmother's dreams, which had been getting worse and worse, she'd told us. We worried about the house we'd left, and the chickens, and the children at the refugee camp. But there was nothing we could do except keep talking about it all.

My parents didn't want to go back to Missouri because they'd already said good-bye to everyone there. They thought we might try a different part of the country. They weighed the virtues of various states. Texas was big and warm. After a chilly year crowded around the small gas heaters we used in Jerusalem, a warm place sounded appealing. In roomy Texas, my parents bought the first house they looked at. My father walked into the city newspaper and said, "Any jobs open around here?"

I burst out crying when I entered a grocery store—so many different kinds of bread.

A letter on thin blue airmail paper reached me months later, written by my classmate, the bass player in my favorite Jerusalem band. "Since you left," he said, "your empty desk reminds me of a snake ready to strike. I am afraid to look at it. I hope you are having a better time than we are."

Of course I was, and I wasn't. *Home* had grown different forever. *Home* had doubled. Back *home* again in my own country, it seemed impossible to forget the place we had just left: the piercing call of the *muezzin* from the mosque at prayer time, the dusky green tint of the olive groves, the sharp, cold air that smelled as deep and old as my grandmother's white sheets flapping from the line on her roof. What story hadn't she finished?

Our father used to tell us that when he was little, the sky over Jerusalem crackled with meteors and shooting stars almost every night. They streaked and flashed, igniting the dark. Some had long golden tails. For a few seconds, you could see their whole swooping trails lit up. Our father and his brothers slept on the roof to watch the sky. "There were so many of them, we didn't even call out every time we saw one."

During our year in Jerusalem, my brother and I kept our eyes cast upwards whenever we were outside at night, but the stars were different since our father was a boy. Now the sky seemed too orderly, stuck in place. The stars had learned where they belonged. Only people on the ground kept changing.

WORLD GIFTS

One Village

It is fifteen years since I have seen my grandmother. I feel some guilt about this, but her face, when we meet in the village, betrays no slant of blame. She is glad to see me. She blesses me with whispered phrases, Mohammed this, Mohammed that, encircling my head with her silver ring. Later she will ask, "Why didn't you ever write a letter?" and the guilt will return, unabsolved by fact: *She can't read. Who would have thought she'd want a letter?* I had forgotten she is so small, barely reaching my shoulder as I hug her tightly, kissing both cheeks. I am stunned with luckiness; so much can happen in fifteen years.

The village smells familiar—a potent soup of smoke, sheep wool, water on stone. Again it is the nose retrieving memory as much as eyes or ears—I poke into courtyards, filled suddenly with lentil broth, orange blossom, olive oil soap. Whole scenes unfold like recent landscapes; a donkey who once entered the room where we were eating, a dusty boy weeping after a wayward kickball knocked him on the head. I was a teenager when last here, blind in the way of many teenagers: I wanted the world to be like me. Now there is nothing I would like less. I enter the world hoping for a journey out of self as much as in. I come back to this village remembering, but it is more like I have never been here before. This time I am awake.

"What do you do every day?" I ask my grandmother. She replies in Arabic, *cod*. Every day I sit. What else would you want me to do?

But I will find this is not quite true. Each morning she prays, rising at 4:30 to the first muezzin's call. It seems strange that the sun also rises this early. The days stretch out like gauze—we are pulled up from sleep by too much brightness.

Each morning my grandmother walks across the road to *the cow*, singular, to carry home a teakettle of fresh warm milk. Take me with you, I say. And she will take me, laughing because I like this black and white cow enough to touch it on the head and thank it, *Shookrun, haleeb*. She speaks to cows, my grandmother will say later, pointing at me. This is a girl who speaks to cows.

Every day she lights the oven, fat stone mound heated by the dung of sheep and goats, *taboon* for bread cooked on the black rocks. She enters barefooted, her headdress drifting about her. "Could be dangerous," says my father, "I don't think she should light it anymore," but it is one of the ways she remains a vital part of her corner of the village, one of the things she does better than anyone else.

Her face is deeply mapped, her back slightly bent. Three years ago she made a pilgrimage to Mecca, became a *Hajji*. For a year afterward, she wore only white. Today she alters this slightly, wearing a long white dress embroidered with green over black-and-white pajamas. It is cool here in the West Bank in late May; people think of the whole Middle East as a great hot desert, but here in this high, perched village the days feel light and breezy, the land a music of terraced hills.

Feelings crowd in on me; maybe this is what it means to be in your genetic home. That you will feel on fifty levels at once, the immediate as well as the level of blood, the level of uncles, of weeping in the pillow at night, weddings and graves, the babies who didn't make it, level of the secret and unseen. Maybe this is heritage, that deep well that gives us more than we deserve. Each time I write or walk or think, I drop a bucket in. Staring at my grandmother, *my Sitti,* as she sits on the low bed, rocking back and forth in time with conversation, tapping her fingertips on her knees, I think, this is the nectar off which I will feed.

"Does he beat you?" she asks of my husband, back home in Texas. "No? Ah, good. Then he is a good man." It is simple to define things here. If God wills it, it happens. A bird poops on my head in the courtyard. "That means you will soon have a boy." Looking up, Sitti says, "It's an impolite mother who didn't put underpants on her baby." Conversation stops. My uncle slaps his head and laughs. "She's always saying things like that."

It's amazing what facts we have about each other. She knows I "write." What does that mean to someone who never did? I know her husband had three simultaneous wives, but my Sitti was in some way "favored." Her husband, my grandfather, died when I was five. We were living in St. Louis; my father lay in silence across his bed for a whole day. "Be kind to him," my mother whispered. My grandmother had a daughter, Naomi, *Naimeh* in Arabic, then five or more babies who died, followed by two sons, of which my father was the last. Naimeh had two children, then died suddenly. My grandmother was having my father at the same time Naimeh birthed her second boy. My grandmother suckled her son and grandson together, one at each breast. I know these things, I grew up on them. But this trip I want to find out more: the large bird-like tattoo on her right hand, for example, from where?

"Many years ago, a gypsy passed through. She was hungry and offered to tattoo someone in exchange for food. She poked pins in me and the blood poured out like water from a spring. Later the skin came off five times and I was left with this. Beautiful, no?" She turns her hand over and over, staring at it. It is beautiful. It is a hand preparing to fly away. I want to hold on to it.

Across the valley, a new Jewish settlement sits, white building blocks shearing off the graceful green hill. At night the lights make a bright outline. No people are visible from here—just buildings, and lights. "What do you feel when you look at that?" I ask my grandmother. "Do you feel like those are your enemies?" In 1948 she lost her home in the Old City of Jerusalem to Israeli occupiers. She moved with her family back to this village. I've always heard that my father's best friend was killed in his presence. My grandmother is a refugee who never went to a camp. My father was a refugee who moved to the United States and married an American. What does Sitti think about all this now, in a region the Arabs will only refer to as the West Bank *via* Israel? Does she feel furious or scared?

She waves at the ugly cats lurking in every corner of the courtyard. Most have terrible fur and bitten-off ears. She pitches a loquat pit at a cat with one eye, and it runs. "See those cats? One night last year an Israeli jeep drove into this village and let them all out. Everyone saw it. What could we do? I think about that. And I think about the good ghosts we used to have in the big room, who floated in the corners up by the ceiling and sang songs late at night after we were asleep. I used to wake up and hear them. Happy friendly ghosts, with warm honey voices, the ghosts of the ones under the ground who used to live here, you know? I tell you, they had parties every night. They were a soft yellow light that glowed. Then the Jews built that settlement across the valley and the ghosts were scared. They all went away. Now you wake up, you hear no singing. And I miss them."

My uncle, a stately Arab in a white headdress, functions as *mukhtar,* or mayor, of the village. He is proud of his new yellow-tiled bathroom. It has a toilet, sink, bathtub, and shower, as well as the traditional hole in the floor—for my grandmother. He is planning a new kitchen under the stairs.

His wife, a good-humored woman with square, manly eyeglasses, bore twenty children; eleven survived. Her dresses are a rich swirl of Palestinian embroidery—blue birds and twining leaves, up one side and down the other. Her two daughters remaining at home, Janan and Hanan, are the ones who can sew. Of herself, she says, "I never learned how."

Sitti lives with this family, our family, in one of the oldest homes in the village. My father estimates it at more than two hundred years. Stone walls and high arched ceilings grace the main room, where most of the visiting and eating take place. Sitti sleeps in her own smaller room off the courtyard. The rest of the family sleeps communally, parents on mattresses on the floor, guests on the beds. Everyone gets covered with weighty calico comforters stuffed with sheep's wool. I swear I have come back to something essential here, the immediate life, the life without refrigerated food.

"How did this rice pudding get so cool?" I ask dumbly one morning, and Hanan leads me to the stone cupboard where food is kept. It is sleek and dark, like the inside of a cave. She places my hand against the face of stone and smiles. Goat cheese floats in olive oil in a huge glass jar. A honeydew melon tastes almost icy.

One afternoon a breathless red-faced woman appears in the doorway with a stack of freshly-picked grape leaves. She trades them with my aunt for a sack of *marimea* leaves, good for stomach ailments, brewed in tea. I can see by their easy joking this is something they do often. The woman motions to me that I am to walk home with her, but I'm not sure why. Her Arabic is too jazzy for my slow ear.

Down alleyways, between houses where children spin tops on the flattest stones—as children our father taught us to pare the tops off acorns to make quick spinners—up ancient stairs, past a mosque with its prayer rugs and mats spread out, waiting. Where is this woman taking me?

I stand in the courtyard of her home. Pigeons are nesting in rusted olive oil tins nailed to the wall. Their soft songs curl on the air. The woman comes back with her hands full of square cakes of olive oil soap. She presses it upon me, saying, "Take this to America. You need this in America." She says other things I can't understand. Then she reaches into a nest and pulls out a small bird. She makes the motion of chopping off its head and I protest, "Oh, no! Please! I am not hungry." She wants me to eat this teenaged pigeon today or tomorrow. I tell her I can't eat it tomorrow either. She looks sad. It was a big gift she was offering. "I will take the soap to America," I say. We kiss and stare at one another shyly. A line of children crouches on the next roof, watching us; they giggle behind their hands.

What is this need to give? It embarrasses me. I feel I have never learned how to be generous. In a Palestinian refugee camp in Jordan last week, I was overwhelmed by offers of coffee and Pepsi showered on me as I passed. Would I ever do that in the United States? Invite a stranger in off the street, simply because she passed my house?

Here in the village, the gifts I have brought seem foolish

when I unpack them. Pantyhose in rainbow colors, two long seersucker nightgowns for the older women, potholders, perfume. What else could I have brought that would better fit this occasion? A lawn of grass? A kitchen table, swoop of formica, so the girls might pare their potatoes sitting up at something, rather than crouched on the floor? Bicycles with sizzling thin wheels, so we might coast together down past the shepherd's field, past the trees of unripe plums? But I unpack a tube of Ben-Gay for Sitti (someone told me she needed this), a plastic bottle of Ecotrin, and give her instructions, like a doctor. I want to make it very clear she should never take more than two pills at once. She nods gravely. She tucks these prizes into her bodice, the front panel of her dress left open at one side like a giant pocket.

"Is there anything else?" she asks. And I run back to my suitcase, unfold a gauzy white scarf bordered with yellow flowers—someone gave me this in Pakistan—I carry it toward her like a child carries a weed-flower tentatively home to mother.

Now she smiles broadly, rocks back on her heels. This strange slash of cloth is a pleaser. She and my aunt unfold one another's presents, touching them and murmuring. This is the worst moment of all. I didn't bring enough, I think. I gaze nervously toward my father, who is smiling shyly. He unpacked his own presents for everyone the day before I arrived. "It's fine," he whispers to me. "We'll go buy them chocolates too. They like chocolates."

In the corner of the room sits a large old wooden trunk painted green. It wears a padlock—this is where Sitti stores her gifts, opening the lock with a key from between her breasts. She places her small pile carefully on top of whatever else is in there, and pats it all down. Janan teases her, "Can we see your treasures?" Sitti protests, locking the trunk hurriedly. "Not now," she says. "Not this minute." I think of the burglar alarms in America, the homes of old silver, furniture, shiny appliances, and remember the way I complain when somebody steals my trash can at night. And it seems very right that a Palestinian would have a trunk in the corner of the room, and lock it, and look at it often, just to make sure it is there.

In this village, which used to be famous for grapes, most of the grapes have died. A scourge came ten years ago, they say, and withered the crop. It has never recovered. Now the vines produce only leaves, if people are lucky. A few fields show traces of the old days: arbors where grapes once flourished, small rock shelters built so the people who gathered the grapes could rest in the shade. I want an agricultural expert like the ones we have in Texas to come analyze this soil. I want a farming miracle, right now, to give this village back its favorite food.

The loquats in my uncle's patio hang yellow-ripe and ready. Sitti won't leave the house alone, for fear someone will steal them. One day we almost get her to go to the Turkish baths in Nablus, but she remembers the tree. "I can't leave a ripe tree," she insists. We peel the loquats with tiny knives; their slick seeds collect in an ashtray.

We go for luncheon at the home of Abu Mahmoud, an elderly man known for his militant rhetoric. "I'm bored with him," confides my uncle. But when we arrive, Abu Mahmoud is only interested in talking about gardening. He leads me inch by inch around his property, introducing me to eggplants, peppers, apricot trees, squash. The apple tree will produce for the first time this year. He stuffs my pockets with unripe fruit—I beg him to stop. He crushes herbs between his fingers and holds them under my nose. Then he stands me on his balcony with binoculars, so I can stare at the Jewish settlement across the valley.

"No people live there," he tells me. "Just buildings. Maybe there are guns in the buildings. I'm sure there are guns."

"Are you scared?"

"I'm tired of fighting," he says. "All my life, we've been fighting. I just want to be sure of one thing—that when I wake up in the morning, my fig trees will still be *my* fig trees. That's all."

This sounds reasonable enough.

Another day I'm walking with my father and two old men to Abu Mahmoud's house, to deliver some sweets as a thank-you gift, when an Israeli tank pulls up and trains its gun on us. "Why are you doing this?" I shout in English at the tank. And a soldier rises out of the top and stares at me curiously. I wave my fist as my father tries to quiet me. "What *right* do you have?"

Several years before the official beginning of the Intifada, I know firsthand why little boys throw stones.

The wedding picture of my parents hangs high on my uncle's wall. It's slightly crooked; I keep scouting for a ladder, to straighten it. One day I realize how long it has been hanging there. "Did you put that up in 1951?" I ask my grandmother, a woman unsure even of her own age. She says, "I put it up when I got it." My father looks serious in the picture, thin, darkly intense, in a white linen jacket hanging nearly to his knees. My mother, fair and hopeful at his side, already learning about pine nuts and tabooleh. In how many houses have they lived? And suddenly I want to leave the picture crooked, because it may be the single icon of our lives that has stayed in one place.

My father and I hike to the tomb of Sheikh Omar, high

on a hill. We must overstep the lentil fields to get there. My father stoops to pluck a handful of fresh green lentils, saying, "Once you eat them raw, you never forget the taste." Sometimes I feel this way about my whole life. Who was Omar, when did he live? My father says he was a disciple of Mohammed. He lived a long time ago. The villagers know this is his tomb, so they have built a rugged mound of a mosque to honor him.

Inside, faded prayer rugs cover the floors. A ring of half-burnt candles stands in one corner. We take off our shoes and kneel. I don't really know how to pray like a Muslim, but I know there is something very affecting about people putting down shovels and brooms five times a day to do this. I like how life continues in the rooms where someone is praying. No one stops talking or stares; it is a part of life, the denominator. Everything else is a dancing away.

My father wants to show me his land. He bought it in the 1960s, before we came to Jerusalem to live for a year. Now he doesn't know what to do with it. Who can build here, knowing what shakiness sleeps in the ground? Yet people do. They do it every day. In recent years the Israelis have taken to surrounding villages with wire, calling them military zones, and ousting the villagers. The village of Latroun, near the monastery famous for wine, is flattened and gone. I remember it fifteen years ago as a bustling place. Its complete disappearance strikes me as horrendous and bizarre. This is only one erasure of many; in which camp or town do those villagers now reside?

My father's land is steep and terraced, planted with olive trees—five big ones, five small. When my aunt notices a broken branch, she stoops to stroke it, asking, "Why? Why?" She tries to tie it up again with a stalk of wheat.

"I could make a good house here," my father says wistfully. "It would make my mother very happy. It would make *your* mother very unhappy. Do you know, my mother's one great hope is that her American son will build a house and come back here to live? How could I ever do that?" I feel a sadness in my father which this land brings out, lays clean before us.

He asks why he is obsessed with property. In Dallas he scouts for condominiums, buys a block of duplexes, renovates it for resale. "Lots of people are that way these days," I tell him. "It's not just you."

"But you don't feel like that?"

My husband and I own our home and a swatch of Texas hillside. The only land that's ever really interested me is the rolling piece of blank paper on my desk. Then again, I'm not a refugee. We've been robbed five, six times, and came the closest to imagining what a refugee might feel. But we had insurance. A refugee has no insurance. A refugee feels violated in a way he might try the rest of his life to understand.

I tell my father I like his land.

We walk to a place called the Museum of Curiosity to see a woman who sells "souvenirs." She's big and ruddy, a recent widow, and welcomes us with all kinds of exclamations and flourishes. Her shop offers a jumble of Bedouin coffeepots and amber beads.

I am intrigued by the massive clay pots lining her porch. At my grandmother's house, two of these stand in the courtyard, holding water. I know they were made in this village, which was once a well-known center for pottery. Why not today? My grandmother told me, "The clay went away."

I ask the lady if she sells her graceful pots or keeps them.

She throws up her hands. "Oh, the Israelis love to buy these. Just today a man came and will return later with a truck to pick up a hundred. Maybe they use them for flowers, I don't know."

"Show me the hundred," I say.

She leads me up the hill to another small house and motions me in.

A whole congregation of giant hundred-year-old pots sits gathered, some natural pink clay color, some marked with a blurred zigzag border or iron oxide lines, propped against one another, holding one another up. Their fat-lipped mouths are all wide open. I want to fall down into their darkness, hide there until I learn some secret perpetually eluding me. I want to belong to a quieter time, when these pots stayed living with the hands that made them. I am very sad these pots are going away.

She'll get more, she tells my father. She'll go to smaller villages and buy them up. It's hard times, she says, and people will sell what they have to keep going.

We eat dinner with Abu Akram, my first cousin, age fifty-five. This trip I have tried to clarify relationships. For the first time I met a beautiful olive-skinned second cousin named *Sabah,* morning, and we teased each other like sisters.

Abu Akram is at the moment a subject of controversy. He is building a three-story house that will be the tallest one in the village. No one likes it; they claim it blocks the sky. But he wants his whole family to live under one roof, and this is the only way they can have enough room. His sons went away to the Virgin Islands to make some money, but decided to come back. One tells me how lonely he was for his village. "If my sons and daughters do not know their *own real place,* what difference does money make?"

We eat stuffed grape leaves, *hummos,* and *frikke* soup, a delicate broth thickened with wheat. We peel oranges for dessert.

Over the table hangs a hand-tinted portrait of a young man. I ask if this is another cousin.

Abu Akram says no, this is a boy who was in school while he was still the principal. The boy was shot down last year by an Israeli soldier, near the post-office, after someone threw a stone at the tires of the soldier's jeep.

Someone threw a stone? Did this boy throw the stone?

Abu Akram shrugs. "It was never clear. He used to be very good in math. I put the picture up because we all liked him."

I ask my grandmother why things happen as they do, and she says God wants them to. I think of a poem by a Vietnamese refugee girl which ends, "God cannot be mean to me forever." I ask my grandmother if God can be mean. She looks at me for a long time and her eyes seem to grow paler. I don't think she ever answers.

I ask my grandmother if I may see her hair and she shakes with laughter. "It is only as long as a finger," she says, holding up a finger.

"I don't care. I want to see it." She keeps it so well-hidden under her scarves, it is hard to imagine.

"Then get up tomorrow morning at four o'clock before prayers," she says. "My hair will be visible at four in the morning."

I set my clock.

At four she is still asleep, on top of her covers. I poke her shoulder. "Where hair?" I ask. At 4 A.M. I have no verbs.

She bounds up laughing. "Here, here, here." She unpins her white overscarf and the satiny green and yellow one underneath. She unknots a quilted maroon cap that lives under the scarves and shakes out long strands of multicolored hair, gray, white, henna-red. I touch its waves. "Nice hair," I say. It is much longer than she said it was, rolling over her shoulders. And then she goes to pray.

Small things irritate me—why the Hebrew is larger than the Arabic on road signs, even in the West Bank. My cousin Mary refuses to eat packaged yogurt because the label is in Hebrew. We go to Ramallah one afternoon to find the daughters of a Palestinian writer famous early in this century. We knock on doors to find their house. My father is carrying a message to them from someone he met on the plane.

Gentle, intelligent women, they offer us fresh lemonade and an album of old photographs to look at. Neither has ever married. They have always lived together. What irritates them? They cannot have their telephones listed. If you are an Arab in the West Bank, you don't have directory privileges. "So how many people have we missed who might have visited us? You, you took the time to look. We are occupied people, but we do not wish to be invisible as well."

My father offers to take me to the Sea of Galilee, to Nazareth. He's described Galilee's crisp little fish to me since I was a child. Surely I must want to go taste them. But I don't want to go, not now. For now I want to soak up my grandmother's gravelly voice, her inflections; it's the way I make my own tattoo.

In the mornings Hanan and Janan wash clothes in a big pan in the courtyard. Piece by piece. We hang them on the roof like flags. Our breakfast is fried white cheese, flat bread, rich yellow eggs. My grandmother wants everyone to eat cucumbers, which she peels slowly with a knife.

After lunch, I read and nap. I walk up and down the road. I follow the hillside path to the abandoned home of my Uncle Mohammed and stand on his porch, realizing how the poem I once wrote about him accurately imagined his view into the valley. It's strange to live lines you have already written. I could stay here. There are even shelves, for books. Uncle Mohammed went to Mecca on pilgrimage and was struck down, hit-and-run, by a passing car. It took a month for the news to reach this village.

In the afternoons I prepare dinner with my cousins. We stuff squash, snip mint. One evening I show them how to make mashed potatoes, which inspire my grandmother to say, "Stay here, we'll let you cook all the time."

In the evenings we sit, visit. A generator comes on for three hours and pumps the houses full of light. A television emerges from hiding. All day it had a cloth over its face. We are watching an Egyptian soap opera in which each character does nothing but cry. By the third evening, I call this a comedy. My father switches the channel; there is *Dallas*, big and clear. He says the Arabic subtitles don't fit the actual dialogue at all. When J. R. says, "What a bitch," the Arabic says, "I am displeased at this moment."

Do they like this show? They shrug. Television doesn't seem to interest them much. Maybe they liked it last year, when it was new. The point is, what does it have to do with this life?

I try sleeping upstairs for one night, so I can leave a light on late to read. This newest room of the house has its own set of steep stairs down to the outside. At 2 A.M. comes a wild knocking on the door. It takes a while for it to filter through my dreams and rouse me.

Men's voices are shouting, "Open up!" in Arabic. I think, fire? Trouble in the streets? I peek out a side window to see a group of Israeli soldiers, perhaps thirty, with machine guns. I'll be damned if I'm going to open this door.

Suddenly a story returns: my young father in Jerusalem awakened by a similar knocking and the sound of gunfire.

"What shall we do?" wailed his terrified mother.

He said, "Just cover my head."

Tonight I do exactly that, cover my head, and the knocking goes on. I am grateful for these huge iron locks.

Then I hear the soldiers jogging around to try the main entrance. My uncle is roused and steps out, groggy, in his white nightshirt. They want him to come direct them to somebody's house. Reluctantly, he pulls his suitcoat over his pajamas. As *mukhtar*, he is obliged to act as counselor, mediator, guide.

We're all nerves now, everyone awake huddling together in the downstairs big room. Janan serves tea like a sleepwalker. I wonder how many times a day she makes coffee and tea. For every guest, for every meal, between meals, before bed, upon rising, and now, in the middle of the night. I worry about my uncle. When do you know which stories to believe?

Sitti starts humming to me. My father says it's a marriage song.

"But I've been married a long time!" I tease her.

"I know. But I missed the wedding." We talk about my husband. He'll come next year. We'll walk around the whole village, do all this again.

My uncle returns after an hour. He pointed out the house, the soldiers woke the family within, searched the rooms, dumped out every drawer, and smashed the toilet, then arrested the twenty-year-old son. He's been in Syria recently. Bad luck for him.

My uncle feels very upset. He hates giving directions.

"Why the toilet?" I ask.

"They like to smash toilets. Sinks and bathtubs too. It's one of their favorite things to do."

We will not hear of this arrested boy again before we leave. He's been sucked up by silence. For the rest of our stay, I sleep downstairs.

One day my father and I catch a bus into Jerusalem. He

is going to show me the house his family lost in 1948. He saw it once from the rooftop of my school in the Old City in 1967, and he wept. I'm a little worried about trying to see it face-to-face today, especially after my father stops to uncork a nitroglycerin tablet from his pocket and pop it down without water. He says he hasn't taken a heart pill in two years, but today he's "having pain."

The Old City's hodgepodge self is a comfort, though punctuated by Israeli teenagers with artillery. An Israeli Jewish friend wrote me a letter describing the first time she ever walked through the Souk after the Six-Day War. "At first I felt victorious," she said, "but that feeling dissipated quickly, as I looked into the faces of the old Arab men in front of their shops. By the time I left through another gate, I felt like a trespasser." I buy one short broom for fifty cents from a toothless old man who sits weaving them, straw over straw. My father swears he's been there since his own childhood.

We pass a bright bouquet of T-shirts: Jewish schoolchildren with canteens and lunch pails, listening to their teacher. My father says he walked this road as a schoolboy too. We circle between massive stone walls and vendors with towers of sesame bread.

Once we cut through someone's private garden. "It didn't used to be here," he says. "This used to be a street." We pull back wires and step between.

In front of us, a flight of iron stairs ascends. "I cannot tell you," whispers my father, hand on the railing, "how many times I traveled up and down these stairs."

We seem to be standing in the middle of someone's construction. A pile of stones. A box of nails and tools.

I stare at the house where my father grew up, realizing it is not as I have pictured it. It is much larger, taller, with a view. An old-world, stone, connected-to-other-houses house.

I never pictured it connected.

A young Jew in a yarmulke approaches us.

"May I help you?" He picks up a hammer.

"We're just looking," whispers my father. "We just wanted to see something."

The man speaks cheerily. "We're renovating here. This will be one of the new dorms for rabbinical students. Ha— 'new'—but can you believe it? This building is seven hundred years old."

He talks so Brooklynish I have to ask, "Are you from New York?"

"I am. But I've decided to be an Israeli." He speaks proudly, with emphasis. "I'm what's called a New Immigrant, under the new plan; have you heard of it? I'm working for the rabbi here; do you know him? It's really fantastic being a settler—now I know how the pilgrims felt."

He's so enthusiastic, I can't help liking him. Anyone would. He's staring at my father, who's still staring at the house. "If you know the rabbi," he repeats, "he might let you see inside."

Now my father looks at him. The refugee and the settler. "I've already seen inside," he says. "I grew up on the inside. I'm an Arab. I used to live here. This used to be our house."

The man looks puzzled. "You mean, you sold it to the rabbi?"

My father shakes his head. "We didn't sell it. We never sold it."

A silence in which the settler half opens his mouth and closes it again and the Arab takes his daughter's arm and steps quietly back.

"I'm sorry," the young man blurts. He looks shaken. He puts out his hand, which my father takes. "I'm really sorry."

And I really think he is.

Back in the village, my father reports, "We saw the house," and my grandmother sits up, interested.
"What did it look like?"
"It looked—nice."

Once my father arrived from America to find my grandmother in a funeral procession, weeping and wailing for the deceased. He asked, "Who died?"
"I'm not sure," she confided, real tears on her face. "I just wanted to help them out."

No one will build a house west of the cemetery. It's bad luck, though the land appears particularly luxuriant there. My grandmother advises us that we are to give thirty pounds to the poor right before she dies and thirty pounds immediately afterwards. We tease her. "But how will we know? If you're not dead yet, how will we know you're going to die?" She is famous for her sudden revivals of health. We're to bury her with a pocket of air above her in the ground, so she'll be ready to sit up when the angels come to visit. She doesn't like to talk to people lying down. If someone reports the birth of a girl baby, she shakes her fist. I ask, "Why are you happier over boy babies?"
"It's obvious," she says. "A girl goes away with her husband and belongs to someone else. A boy sends money home and continues to belong to his own family."
"What about belonging to yourself?" I ask. "I'm married, I work, I'd give my family money if they needed it. What about belonging to the *world*?"
She tilts her head. "You're odd."

Three days before we leave, my grandmother starts

mooning around the courtyard. She plucks endless bits of invisible lint from her dress. She mumbles to the lemon tree. I ask, "What's wrong? Are you tired?"

Her face trembles and falls into tears. "I'm only going to be tired after you go. Then I'm going to be very, very tired."

When she cries, I cry.

Two days before we leave, the gifts start showering down. My aunt gives me a red velvet prayer rug from Saudi Arabia. My uncle hands over worry beads. "From *me!*" he says in English. He worked in Texas once, in a produce house where everyone spoke Spanish. The souvenir woman delivers a necklace of orange stones. Janan is stitching me a small purse the size of my passport. Her face as she sews is weighty, morose. Hanan produces a shiny-threaded scarf and takes to her bed, claiming stomach trouble. "It's a ritual," says my father. "I refuse to get caught up in this melancholy farewell ritual."

And Sitti, dear Sitti, comes to me with three trinkets from her treasure trunk in hand. A fat yellow bead, a heart-shaped locket carrying the image of the holy mosque at Mecca, and a basketball medal. Two players with out-stretched arms are pitching the ball through the hoop. The incongruity of these items makes me want to laugh. "Where did you get these?"

She swears the basketball medal came from Mecca along with the locket.

"But do you know what this is?" my father points to the players. "Do you know what these men are doing?"

She says, "Reaching for God?"

She tells us the yellow bead will guarantee a happy marriage. It's very old, she says. I notice it has a seam, as plastic things do, but I don't mention it. My aunt brings a thread and attaches the trinkets to my prayer beads. When will I ever see these people again? I wonder, stricken with how far apart our lives have planted us. I think, maybe never. I think, I will always be seeing them.

A circle of kids across the street chants at me whenever I pass them. "How are you?"—rolling the *r*, speaking the words as one word, musically. They learned it in school. They call out when they see me on the roof.

"I am fine!" I shout. "And how are you?"

Now they chirp, flutter, fly away from me. They are poor, shy kids, dressed in dust and forty colors. They have this new red Arab hair, springing out in curls, and what do they play with? Stones! Sticks! The can that peas come in! And they are happy!

My favorite, a striking girl named Hendia, wears a yellow headband and a dazzling grin.

"Hendia!" I shout. "*Shu bitsewee?* What are you doing?" She leaps like a chicken being startled from behind. Yikes! I'm being spoken to! She runs and hides.

My uncle gets mad at the racket. He steps out and waves the kids away.

On this last day I look for Hendia. I have gum for her and candies for all the kids. She is gone, says her sister, to Ramallah to have her picture taken. "Tell her to find me when she gets back."

Later I hear her piping voice. "Naimeh! Howareyou?"

I run to the upper landing and drop her surprises down. She swoops upon them, looking at me curiously.

In Arabic I tell her, "Tomorrow—good-bye."

She says it in English. "Good-bye."

She hides her face.

All the relatives file through the house to pay their respects. Sitti sits on the bed with her great-great grandson in her arms. I ask her if she knows the names of all her grand-children. "Why should I?" she says. "I say, come here, little one—and they come."

I step out into the night, pulling on my sweater, to get one last sense of what we are leaving. One village, in a ter-ribly troubled country full of cousins who should have been able to figure this out by now. What do we really know? And a shadow leaps on me, startling. It is Hendia. She has been waiting in the shadow of the loquat tree for me to emerge. No telling how long she has been here; it is the first time I've seen her enter the courtyard.

Into my hand she presses a packet of peanuts. "Good-bye!" she says again. And runs away so fast I have nothing to thank but the moon.

Local Hospitality

This is the story he told me exactly as I heard it.

He thought it would be simple going back to the village. He and his wife would visit their families, unpack the bolts of fresh velvet and cakes of sweet soap. They would sit up late into the dark, telling stories they had collected in the United States over the past four years, and everyone would be happy to see them, as if their own lives had somehow been confirmed. What could be easier?

Since their departure, their neighbor Abu Mohammed had installed a genuine white porcelain toilet in a closet off his courtyard and Zaki's father, Abu Zaki, had become the new *mukhtar,* or mayor, which really just meant he drank a little more coffee and knew a little more gossip than anyone else. Sometimes he would be called upon to settle a minor dispute, in which case he would improve upon his posture, puff up his chest, and gesture dramatically, but mostly the days in the village were as slow and roundly curved as Zaki remembered. How much can stones and chickens change?

Sitti, his grandmother, commented that Zaki was wearing paler colors. She asked in her most serious voice if he had forgotten how to pray. Zaki told her the universe he and his wife lived in now was as different from her universe as the moon from the sun. "No!" she said. "The moon and sun are not different. They float in the same sky." When he tried to tell her about the American high school next door to his apartment complex, where boys and girls kissed and held one another in the parking lot at lunchtime, she shook her head. "Ya'Allah, maybe a different sky after all," she said. She stared at him doubtfully, as if he were a new man with a name she couldn't pronounce. "Give me some bread," he said, to bring her back to earth. And she nodded, passing the bread.

His father pretended to be angry that he and his wife were only visiting and weren't going to stay. He acted as if he hadn't known this all along. Originally his sons had each gone to America to study, but later they found jobs, and now all six were in the process of becoming citizens. What sorrow must this be for the ones who stayed home? Zaki tried not to think about it. His own citizenship papers had been signed and delivered three weeks before his trip, but now he didn't feel like mentioning it. His wife Suheila would begin her citizenship soon. Once you went to America, your mind stretched out like a wide field and became too big for the village. To live back home again would be like trying to make a big thing shrink.

Zaki's father couldn't understand this. He had never left the village for more than three days, and then only to travel thirty miles to Jerusalem, to see a doctor about his closed-up ear. When he came home, he kept saying it was hard to breathe in the city, you had to share the air with too many lungs. Now he kept mumbling, "So what is this I hear? You're going back again? For what reason? You want to make more money or what? You could build a nice house here and settle down." Fidgeting and fussing when their backs were turned.

Zaki and Suheila spent a whole month telling their bundle of stories. A new cousin or old schoolmate would appear and they would tell the same story a different way. Maybe a fact would sprout wings and disappear, leaving room for something fancier. After a week, Zaki realized he'd stopped looking at his watch. He started sleeping later and arguing more. Suheila commented that people argued most where there was least to talk about. If conversation was rich and subjects many, talk kept rolling fluidly, passing over rough spots like water over rocks. But once everything had been said, you started paddling backwards, flinging water and scraping your knees. Suheila said she was seeing the village like a movie for the first time and learning who the main characters were. Suheila loved movies. She learned English at the movies. She talks a little like Omar Sharif.

As their visit neared its finish, Zaki's grandmother Sitti began making prophecies about the end of her life. "When you pack your bags," she said, "I will take my last breath. When the taxi arrives to drive you to the airport, when your plane rises into the sky. . . ." She was planning to die each time. She had said this to Zaki four years before and repeated it to every visiting brother. Zaki wondered if that were the secret to her long life—keep dying and death won't find you. She said everyone would forget her and their worlds would be filled with sorrow. She said it was impossible to leave your village and be happy anywhere else, and did they think they could bring her a better sweater on their next trip home? Zaki loved Sitti just as much as he had loved her when he was a boy. Her logic was so elegantly simple. To live as she lived would be a gift—but people didn't do that anymore. Only a few rare ones remained and the most we could do now was listen to them.

Of course there would be a huge farewell dinner the night before they left. Two lambs were to be slaughtered, the women would cook mountains of rice, and pastel egg-shaped Jordan almonds would appear in every ceramic bowl. Zaki's mother sent a verbal message through Zaki to her brother-in-law who ran a store in the next town. "Send glasses, and napkins, and some of those mints if you can give me a better price than last time. Send garlic and the largest sacks of rice. Three packages of lace for our dresses, red thread, and remember the last time you sent *hummos?* The beans were small and dried-up. Please send some better ones and I will forget the past."

Zaki carried this message half-heartedly and couldn't say he delivered it exactly as it had been sent. All the relatives would be invited, a number that might exceed one hundred dinner guests and more, if cousins of cousins decided to show. Zaki thought about the United States, remembering the pleasant dinner parties they had attended in the past few years, backyard barbecues or neat buffets where five or six couples served their own plates and sat around having relaxed conversations. In America you didn't issue invitations to a whole town—you invited someone, you knew who was coming. In the village they invited everyone and they never knew.

Three days before their departure, Zaki and Suheila decided to travel over to the next town once more to visit the home of Uncle Khaled, Abu Zaki's brother, who ran the store. He had asked them to stay longer on the day they did the shopping, but Suheila was having a headache, so they declined. Now Zaki was thinking they should at least go tour his new house more closely, since he had built it recently and was very proud. Zaki's father and mother gathered themselves up at the last minute and said they would accompany, and at the last minute three bored young cousins added on to their group, plus their father's ancient friend Tawfiq the Bird-Man. They called him the Bird-Man because he kept cages of wild birds and pigeons in his courtyard. Tawfiq never ate his birds. He talked to them. He used to say they told him how to live.

Sitti stayed home to sew on the dresses. Even with her old eyes, she was embroidering tiny golden figures, winged birds and water pitchers, along the edges of her white dress. Zaki wished everyone weren't going to so much trouble. It made him nervous. They were even embroidering a fabulous dress for Suheila at her mother's house, though she'd worn only clothes from Marshall Field's and Mervyn's since her arrival.

Uncle Khaled's place sat on the side of a hill near a grove of baby olive trees. His house was built from a new pinkish tint of stone. This seemed to irritate Zaki's father. Why couldn't he have used the same gray stone they had been using for centuries? "I heard he has a *bathtub*," Abu Zaki said in a low, disgusted voice. So what? Zaki had heard of this famous bathtub at least ten times, from ten different people, who seemed to think it an insult to tradition to have a tub inside a room. They still favored the metal tub in the courtyard, water poured out of a jug, or a shower spigot over a drain.

"Coffee or tea?" Uncle Khaled offered, obviously pleased that so many had come to see him in the middle of a Friday afternoon. The coffee was thick and sweet as ever in fine white china cups. It was the coffee Zaki had missed for four years, though they made it in the United States themselves on their sleek electric stove. Something about that coffee, lightly spiced with ground cardamom, always made Zaki feel the world was smooth and at peace. No matter that soldiers were banging the heads of citizens three miles away; the coffee offered reprieve. Zaki's mother surprised him by accepting a cigarette along with the men. He had never seen her smoke before. His father whispered, "She only does it where Sitti can't see."

They talked about the fine furniture and the artistic design of the house. Uncle Khaled's wife Nabeela, Zaki's mother's sister, was happy to see them again. In the village everyone was related at least twice. Americans say this makes the children idiots, but the village didn't seem to have more idiots than its share. Nabeela talked about their two sons, away at college in Damascus. They had to travel through Jordan to get there and back, but they were getting so smart it was worth it. This irritated Zaki's father again; on the surface, he was prouder of sons who had gone to the United States than he would have been of sons in Syria, but in his heart he wished his own were closer to home. Nabeela's sons would probably come back to the village to live when they graduated. They would marry Arab girls, as Zaki had, and settle back to have six babies and a lifetime of visiting, as he had not.

Zaki talked of prices in America and the special plate he liked to order at the cafeteria. Suheila described laundromats. They told of the brilliantly lit-up signs in the streets. At first it had seemed strange to walk or ride down a boulevard and have a hundred shining signs to look at. Here at home, the night belonged to the moon. Electricity was rationed, three hours each evening. A few people had televisions, but not refrigerators, except the generator kind, since three hours a day wouldn't be enough. Even the radios here only ran on batteries. Tawfiq began telling a bird story Zaki had heard from him before, about a bird who wanted to be a radio. It had never made sense before either. "So the bird found itself one day in a tree and began weeping the invisible tears of birds, which changed into fruits, and that is why we have all these new fig trees appearing in the village!" It sounded to Zaki as if he had two or three stories mixed up.

Nabeela leaned over to Suheila and asked her if they were planning to stay for supper. It was then around three and they'd eaten lunch after one. "Oh no," Suheila whispered. "We'll need to go back. We've promised my own parents we'll eat with them tonight."

On the table before them sat a plate of *mamool,* little domed cookies stuffed with dates or nuts and rolled in powdered sugar. Zaki's mother said Nabeela made better *mamool* than anyone else in the family, but Nabeela insisted their Aunt Mary's were much better.

"What is your job?" Uncle Khaled asked Zaki again. They all knew what his job was, but they liked to keep hearing it.

"I run a clothing store," he said. "I am manager of a clothing store that is part of a chain." They didn't understand what was a "chain." Zaki explained about businesses in America, how sometimes there were main offices in distant cities and you worked years and years for a man you never saw. Or a woman, he added, and that got them. *A woman?* Zaki had lived twenty-one years in the old country before emigrating and should have known better than to bring up a pesky subject like that. Next he made the mistake of mentioning that as soon as Suheila finished her last two counseling classes she hoped to get a job in a school for children or a home for old people.

"What do you mean, a home for old people?" demanded Tawfiq. He was nearly a hundred himself. Suheila poked Zaki. He was traveling dangerous ground with his last few comments—like walking naked in a no-man's land.

"Tawfiq, in America, some of the old people are too weak to live alone," Zaki said.

"*Haki fawthi!*" he grunted. "Empty talk!"

Abu Zaki coughed and looked around the room. A light breeze lifted the curtains. There were no screens. He rubbed his hands together in his lap and leaned forward suddenly with his serious mukhtar face, as if he were about to make a decision.

"Tell me, Khaled," he said to his brother. "Has this fancy new house changed your ways? Are you trying to bring new customs to the villages? Do you know we have sat here for an hour visiting already and you have not once mentioned any dinner to us? Don't you think the guests from America might be hungry?"

"Oh no!" Zaki almost shouted. "We're not! Nabeela already asked us and we told her we're eating later! Please, Abuki, we can take care of ourselves."

His father looked at him angrily. "Take care of yourselves? Perhaps. But who can Khaled take care of?"

"Ya'Allah, brother," said Khaled, looking sick and stuttering. "I am sorry; you know we finished lunch ourselves right before you came and I was so full I was not even thinking of food. Nabeela, what do we have to eat? Get these young people some bread and meat!"

"Please, no," Suheila was pulling Nabeela's arm. "We want nothing. We just wanted to see you."

Nabeela was making hand signals at Khaled, circles in the air, and shaking her head. "What is the meaning of this?" he shouted at her. "Speak!"

"I think we are out of bread," she whispered.

At that moment Zaki's cousin Farouki, a strange and silent man, rose and walked out of the house. "Where is *he* going?" Abu Zaki demanded. "What is wrong with that character?"

"Please Papa," begged Zaki, "don't be so angry at everyone. Let's go on with the stories; no one has the slightest appetite."

By this time Nabeela was in the kitchen, pulling out drawers. Suheila had followed her, protesting. Zaki's mother lit her fifth cigarette, while the other two cousins joined Abu Zaki's call for justice.

"We are losing the old ways," Saleem protested. "It is not important if someone is or is not hungry, but that food is offered, this is what counts."

"But it is three in the afternoon!" Zaki cried. "We are between meals now. Is anyone really hungry?"

His cousin Samih started telling of a house he had visited in the town of Ramallah where the people never fed him from sunup to sundown.

"Who were these selfish heathens?" croaked Tawfiq the Bird-Man, happy to be enraged.

Uncle Khaled looked as if he were in great pain. "I believe in the customs," he was saying, though no one but Zaki was listening. "All my life I have tried to weave together the old and new, keeping the best of the old, yet trying to move forward at the same time. In this house you will see the arches of the old architecture and yet there are plastic dishes in the kitchen. I beg your consideration for my full stomach, which forgot its manners, but soon everything will be well again."

"I'm not hungry," Zaki said loudly. He whispered to his uncle, "Listen, my father is just talking like he always does. Pay no attention to him and please, may I see your bathtub?" This seemed to make Khaled even sadder.

Farouki returned from the market with his arms full of bread, at least thirty loaves. He dropped them down on the coffee table in front of everyone. "So *eat*," he instructed them. "Eat and eat till the day is done."

Nabeela appeared with a tray of warmed meatballs and a dish of cold eggplant dip. "But we have no more bread," she was saying, till she saw the bread on the table and looked surprised. Uncle Khaled rose, saying he was going to his own store to get a better kind of bread. "But we aren't hungry!" Zaki shouted. "Are you hungry? Is anyone hungry?"

Abu Zaki, apparently not to be outdone by his brother, the poor host, or his strange nephew, stood up and said he would be back shortly with all the necessary supplies.

"Father, we're leaving!" Zaki shouted. "We're going away! We're going to fly back to America this instant without saying good-bye!"

Sometimes it works to fight logic with logic and craziness with craziness. This truth, however, cannot be depended on.

A half hour later, everyone was back. Zaki and Suheila had been muttering together in the drowsy living room, waiting for them. Two flies had mated on the arm of a chair, and Zaki's mother had gone to sleep, her ashtray full in front of her. At least sixty loaves of flat bread were now piled on the coffee tables and cabinets. Nabeela had prepared soup and a salad of cucumbers and radishes. She moved in and out of the kitchen like a sleepwalker.

Now that they had all this food in front of them, Zaki's father and uncle had stopped speaking to one another. The cousins declined. Zaki's mother woke up, tasted one meatball and some salad, but said no bread, thank you, she wasn't hungry enough for bread. Only Tawfiq the Bird-Man was eating. He picked at his food like a sparrow picks at the ground. He kept telling weird stories with wrong endings and no one asked Zaki or Nabeela anything else about the United States for the rest of the visit.

Three nights later they were all dressed and perfumed for the farewell feast when a young boy appeared from Uncle Khaled's village to say that none of the family from over there would be coming. Abu Zaki, the mukhtar, had cast a shadow over the relatives. He had insulted his own brother in front of women and his son. Neither would the family of Nabeela, Zaki's mother, be attending, since they had heard the terrible story and could not permit themselves to socialize with Zaki's family again so soon. The villages were temporarily divided—those who loved, or were related to, Khaled or Nabeela, standing firm against the mukhtar. No matter that they were related to the mukhtar just as much; for the present, they weren't claiming him. A few tender-hearted women sent consolation gifts to Zaki's mother. No one even seemed to remember Suheila and Zaki, and weren't they the ones who were leaving, the whole reason for the party?

Zaki's grandmother Sitti stood in the doorway of the house, watching the sky. "It's going to rain tomorrow," she said gloomily. "You won't be able to fly. And it's a bad sign here too, we have killed the lambs and no one is coming to eat them. That means something terrible is about to happen. If you leave us and the plane falls out of the sky, I will die."

"So will we," Zaki said, hugging her. Later they stuffed themselves with triple the usual amount of food, to make up for all the people who weren't there.

Grazing

In Aroostook County, northern Maine, I knew nothing about fiddleheads or the northern lights. I didn't even know enough not to eat the skin of a potato, my favorite part. Now farmers spray potatoes with chemicals twice, once while still in the ground, and once in the trucks. The farmers looked sad when they told me. They're absolutely certain the poison stays in the skin.

I went to see a man in the next town who knew where to find pussy willows. His wife had invited me. He was sitting on his couch eating popcorn when I arrived. "Have you seen a moose yet?" he asked. When I said no, he stayed silent for a long time. He seemed angry. Then he blurted, "I'm thinking about death today. When my parents were alive, I didn't think about it, I didn't have to. Now they are dead and nothing is standing between us. Between me and death—I'm next."

He sat there and his wife brought me a smaller bowl of popcorn. We all sat there, eating and not speaking.

A woodstove weighted the room, and a shelf of old science projects: rocks with dusty labels, mounted drawings of seeds. I could smell winter coming out of the couch—musty, smoky, so long, so cold. We went into the woods together, wearing jackets, stepping on stones between crusts of leftover snow.

"It's the ugliest time of year," their daughter said. "April always seems ugliest because it's neither green nor white." I liked the shades of brown and gray, but didn't say so. It's easy to like things you don't see very often.

Days before a boy had asked me if I really drove all the way up from Texas and I said yes, we really drove, in a car, a regular car. He wanted to know how much gas it took. "Tell me about everything between here and there," he said. I asked if he had ever been south and he hadn't even been to Bangor. His voice had the whack of a shovel in it. I wanted to stroke his potato-colored hair.

In the woods the pussy willows were growing out of a bush, where the man knew they would be. We clipped them with a pair of shears his wife carried in her back pocket. We snipped rust-colored weeds with shaggy heads and loaded our arms. We crossed a loud stream on a narrow icy bridge.

They took me to a cabin where they camp out sometimes, in summers. The door had a padlock on it and the smell of the bunk beds inside was powerful, piney. "It smells lonesome in here," their daughter said. "Let's open the windows and let the smell out." But her father said they had to wait till summer. I admitted I was still hoping for a moose, and he said, "If you walked about ten hours on that path we came in on, you'd see one for sure. Just keep walking, into the woods."

"But by then it would be dark," I said, and he said, "That's right."

Going back to their house, the daughter walked behind us. Her parents told me they'd grown up exactly across the road from one another, right down from their current drive-way. He had lived on this side of the road in a house that was now gone and she had lived on the other side, above the store. They knew each other forever, knew each other's parents, playthings, faults. It did not surprise them in the least that they were still here, together.

But suddenly he put his arm out and stopped us all, whispering, "There!" I looked hard for a moose but saw nothing. "There, across the field, the black dot moving slightly." He pulled some small field glasses from his pocket and peered through them. "A bear, stretching his arms," he whispered. He handed the glasses to me. It was a real bear, waking up. His wife placed her hand on my shoulder. "He can always spot them." Without the field glasses that bear didn't look like much, but the knowledge of what it really was astounded me. Hibernation—so long, so cold. "He'll be real hungry for the next few days," the husband said. We walked back to the house with our bounty, feeling rich.

Before I left, they took me up to the attic. Everything waited there—his father's bed, her mother's hat stand. He brought out maps and photographs. There were places nearby without any public roads. You could sneak up on a moose bathing in a lake and jump on its back and ride it till it bucked you off. He had a name for it, like a sport, but I forget what it was.

We sat on the front porch in the twilight before I left. "It's a mistake, you know," he said. "We should have been part of Canada. It's always been hard to understand." And just sitting there made me feel the way you feel when tree branches part above your head and a little light comes shin-ing through. He said, "Yeah, it's good you came. Because everybody around here knows exactly the same things, so what can you talk about?"

That night, in the other town where I was staying, a

neighbor called. My hosts weren't home, so I talked to her. "Still looking for that moose," I said, and she told me there had been two moose grazing in her front yard all morning. I shouted, "Where are they now?" and she reported, "They left, they took off. I would have called but I didn't know anyone was interested. They weren't even in a hurry."

Roses for Lubbock

They appeared to be mother and son in the boarding line at San Antonio. They were nearly the same height and leaned their light brown heads together, murmuring. When our flight was delayed, we all crowded back into the waiting room. The son carried twelve roses in careful tissue. His mother's eyes circled the room anxiously. All these traveling people with hand luggage, dressy shoes! Later on the plane, the attendant repeated "Overhead bin," but the son stroked the roses in his lap.

At Dallas, the sky sagged like a flat gray petal. They told us fog out west was making everything late. Then they gave up. See you tomorrow, they said. A student swore, a banker said he'd take the bus from now on. The roses closed their eyes and went off to a hotel for the night.

Next morning all the waiting passengers were asked to draw numbers. The roses were 67, I was 128. No one had told us we'd have to take numbers, so a lot of angry rumbling rolled around. Phone wires sizzled. A man ripped the Airlines pages out of the phone book and stuffed them into his pocket. The possibilities of chaos loomed remarkably. I took a survey; who had missed what, how many lives would be juggled because there was fog over Lubbock. The two with roses said simply, "We're really *late*." Well, so was everybody. I was reading a book called *Someday, Maybe.* The flight attendant said she'd like to tie it over her face.

When numbers were called, the roses made it on the plane. "Numbers 1 through 90." I was past being mad by now. "Wait till noon," an announcement said.

At one o'clock they said the noon flight would be delayed.

At one-thirty the roses returned. It was good to see them again. Their plane had been circling Lubbock for over an hour and still couldn't land, so it came back. "Great fun," I overheard the son saying. "A terrific morning of accomplishment."

The rest of us who had been interviewing one another since dawn felt secretly justified.

The roses looked exhausted. One was hanging its head, the outer petals slipping down like tired socks.

An announcement said there would be no more flight attempts that day, and we could all go on back where we came from.

The roses wished this were possible.

A cowboy demanded to know why, if a bird could fly in fog, couldn't a plane?

An elegant woman said she would rent a car, drive to Midland, visit a cousin she hadn't seen in ten years, and get drunk.

The roses slipped away quietly. I never saw them again. Who was it in Lubbock turning the key, pulling out of the parking lot, filing this day with the other Alones?

I'd write you if I knew. I'd say they tried hard to get there and roses mean nothing next to the way they held them, through weather and crowds, and would not put them down.

Camel Like Only Camel

We watch dubiously from the ground as the men invent saddles by balancing canvas sacks of hay atop the humps, then binding them down with strips of leather. Musty blankets, cooking pots, and stirrups are roped over the mounds, which look far too high to sit on, and preposterously unstable. But the men smile at us. "Climb up, yes, yes, this where we ride."

At first my husband, Michael, and I revolted against the thought of sharing camels with our guides. It seemed so babyish. Couldn't they ride a third beast together? They shrugged. Not sensible. We would have no idea how to click, chirrup, and whistle the secret signals a camel understands. So now we have agreed to a man planted firmly behind each of us, and holding the slack reins. My man is named Tane (*taw*-nay) and knows fragments of English. Michael's driver speaks as little as possible in any language and sings a wispy trill that pricks my skin. His name vanishes when he says it—a grace note in a minor key.

A week ago we arrived at Jaisalmer, India, the most remote city in Rajasthan, accessible by a ten-hour overnight train from Jodhpur. Freezing cold on the dusty bunk (what the Indians miraculously dub "First Class"), I reluctantly traded my last good pen to the conductor for a blanket. He wouldn't take money.

Guidebooks refer to Jaisalmer as "the most exotic city in India, straight out of the *Arabian Nights*." They do not exaggerate. A walled city high on the only hill for miles, Jaisalmer at sunrise and sunset looms fabulously, exactly matching the golden shimmer of sand and sky, as if it materialized a thousand years ago from the only color there was in the desert. Inside the walls, temples and houses of carved golden sandstone stand intricately stacked.

Banners strung across streets invited the few tourists we saw to sign up for the "Camel Safari." We saw their expeditions returning to town: dazed travelers loosely draped over camels, shirts askew. The camel drivers looked gloomily resigned. So when we were approached by a gregarious fellow in a teahouse offering "better desert trip," we listened. He touted a village called Khouri, forty kilometers from Jaisalmer, accessible by local bus. "It's the best!" he exclaimed. "Best food! Best persons! Best sand!"

We packed toilet paper and plastic bottles of mineral water in one small bag and left our satchels at the hotel. Boarding one of those buses impossibly stuffed with tie-dyed turbans, onions, and crates of corn, we became instant centerpieces. Women openly stuck their hands into my pockets and shoved me when they came up with nothing. A ragged boy squeezed up and down the aisle, passing out neon jawbreakers. Though we knew Rajasthan is called the opium capital of India, we had forgotten this till witnessing the dreamy stupor of our fellow passengers.

One man stared at us so long and hard I could feel his eyes melting in and out of focus. The seats had holes, and the shock absorbers had long gone limp, but we were teetering into the golden distances. It was amazing to see where people got off.

At Khouri village, Tane greeted us and led the way to the guesthouse. For less than three dollars each day, we would receive a private room, meals, and a pot of tea before breakfast. A plump matriarch dominated the family. She poked a finger at her ample breasts and said, "Mama." Immediately she had us sitting on straw mats on the floor, surrounded by at least sixteen little dishes of food. Some of the lunch items, like cauliflower curry, rice, yogurt, sweetened carrots, were familiar, while others, like dried desert beans sprinkled with salt, tasted odd and wonderful.

We ate on the floor alone. After lunch, Tane produced a giant scrapbook in which previous guests had written comments. Nearly all had written, "The best food I had in India." Some described their camel trips, even sketching their aching genitals. I was intrigued by the number of superlatives—for many guests, the trip had been the *most* fabulous, *most* unforgettable time of their lives—but also noted one tightly scrawled entry: "While I found my trip into the desert interesting, and am glad I did it, I would not do it again."

After lunch, Michael toured the sand dunes with his giant camera perched on his shoulder. I wandered the village of rounded earthen houses, golden and white, decorated with stark geometric designs. They had a peculiar organic quality, as if they had bubbled up from the earth and dried there. Flattened dung cakes stuck on walls to dry looked like giant polka dots.

Graceful Rajasthani women in succulent red saris and purple scarves passed between houses. They would stare at me shyly and smile, or look away. I felt awkward and bulky among them. Unexpectedly I was set upon by a chorus of

Gimme! Gimme! children shrieking wildly, jumping onto my back, pulling my hair, and trying to remove my glasses. One ripped the handkerchief out of my pocket, yelling, "Pen! Candy! *Namaste!* Thank you!" I struggled with a boy about twelve, finally gripping him by the shoulders to push him away. They thought it was funny.

Two older sisters with rings in their noses ran out of a house and tried to pull off my watch. I was kicking and slapping at all of them before wriggling away, breathless. I felt so disgusted by the episode that I spent the rest of the day in our room, gloomily reading Salman Rushdie's *Midnight's Children.* Even his most surreal images seemed possible. What was I doing here? My usual long-trip melancholia had begun to surface. I would never escape. I would feel out of place forever.

Tane had mentioned rather mysteriously that a "Swiss lady" was staying in Khouri for a while. Before dinner, I developed a sudden desire to meet her, so I asked Mama, who pointed me to a nearby courtyard.

Inside, a pale European woman in Rajasthani garments was painstakingly sorting uncooked rice in a big bowl. She nodded dully when I asked if she spoke English. "I always dress like the place that I am in," she said. This seemed rather presumptuous, but I didn't mention it. She answered my questions vaguely, as if she had no desire to speak to human beings anymore in her life. I had the feeling she was recovering from a tragedy. Did she want help cleaning the rice? She shook her head.

That night she sat by herself in a corner of the kitchen as Mama fed cakes of dung to the slow-cooking fire. A Japanese photographer guzzled quarts of *lassi,* the thin yogurt drink. He said he was photographing children at the school. "Did they jump on you?" I asked, and he looked surprised. "No, they were nice." The Swiss woman took careful bites of *chapatti*. Michael tried hard not to watch Mama as she slapped the chapattis against her own sweaty cleavage to flatten them. She had not rinsed her hands between the dung and the dough.

For after-dinner entertainment, Tane had hired some local musicians to play and sing for us. They followed us back to our room with harmonium and drums, where their music shivered off the rafters and thickened the shadows. One boy juggled a set of wooden sticks and kept losing himself as he sang, closing his eyes and falling into a rapture. Tane whispered to me that the boy's father, who had recently died, had been the village's premier musician. "The boy is being sad now," he said, during one particularly long-held note. And the room trembled. The room turned upside down.

I think we paid them thirty rupees—whatever Tane told us to—and their voices held fast in our ears long after they had walked home. I went outside and found dark mounds of camels sleeping, tied right underneath our windows. I placed my hand on the back of one, and it grunted and shifted its weight. I wondered how long it would take to make a camel your friend.

Now we are riding the camels, heading even "farther from electricity," as Tane says. Khouri had none either. We ate potato chapattis and homemade butter for breakfast. Our down jackets are tied around our waists.

Sometimes the camels strut slowly, regally. Other times they run. Are we galloping, trotting? None of the words seem right for a camel. We pass other animals as we travel: sheep, donkeys laden with clay jugs. Some villages haul water extremely long distances. A herd of oncoming cattle defers to the camels, splitting to let us pass. "Do camels like cattle?" I ask Tane. "Are there certain other animals camels prefer?"

Tane speaks gravely. "Camel like only camel."

The Thar Desert, stretching hugely in every direction, emanates profound silence. It has long been this way and will continue to be this way: vast, golden, studded with rocks and rare trees. I feel we are crossing a shrine.

When we pause at a village tinier then Khouri, three turbaned men motion us inside a courtyard. Riding camels, one quickly learns the strangest loss-of-gravity sensation is getting on and off, as the camel falls to its knees or tilts to rise.

Inside the courtyard, a baby camel stands penned in a corner, bleating desperately. Five days old, it cries for its mother, who died of impacted bowels shortly after giving birth.

Amazingly, a veterinarian is present, a handsome young man named Dr. Sharma, who walked all the way from Khouri this morning to see the anguished baby. He greets us almost with relief, speaking fluent English. There are no other nursing camels in the vicinity, and cow milk is too expensive. "I think it will die," he tells me. He's explained to the village men what they would have to do to keep it alive: prepare a thin, mixed gruel and feed it continuously. "I don't think they will do it," he says. "They have their own folk remedies. One of them caused the ailing mother to die."

I squat with the women inside a cavelike kitchen. They look me up and down sympathetically—I have so little jewelry. Touching their own dangly silver earrings, they point to my barren ears. They are heating water for the men's tea and send me out to the men's circle to drink milky tea from a single saucer, which we pass around the group. In India one must forget the memory of hygiene or be paralyzed.

As we ride off, the baby camel's cry follows us. Our own camels act edgy till we're out of hearing. I have never heard a sadder sound. Somehow Dr. Sharma's eyes echoed it when he said, "It is impossible to work here. It is all darkness. I came out from Jaipur for two years of rural service and I am going back soon. A good thing, that I am going. Otherwise I might be losing my mind."

I asked why he couldn't haul the baby back to his own house in Khouri, strapping it to a bigger camel, and mixing the gruel himself. He stared at me with his dark, dark eyes. "They would never let it go. There is pride here, even in dying."

For lunch, Tane and the Singer direct our camels into some rippling dunes. The sand feels softer, and the animals struggle not to sink. "Go take a picture," Tane tells Michael. To him, taking a picture is proof a person admires what he sees. "I bring one man here and he take two hundred picture," Tane boasts. How to explain that Michael often waits whole days and makes one exposure? Tane does not understand.

From under a rock, from flying carpets, from the stained saddlebags Mama had packed, lunch emerges. We use tin plates and sit in a soft hollow. Everything tastes fresh. We clean our plates by washing them with sand.

Duff-colored desert mice dodge past us, diving into holes. A brilliant green bird flashes out from a tree. All afternoon we traverse a golden emptiness, seeing no other person. I think of an Israeli I met in a café in Jaisalmer who asked, "Do you like it here? What have you been doing since you got here?"

I told her about the small tank of water we'd found on the edge of town. A fabulous assortment of exotic migrant birds, some from as far away as Siberia, congregated there each evening. We saw ducks that walked on water and families of wild peacocks roosting in the trees. Long trains of goats, returning from a day of grazing, would pause to drink before heading back into town. Behind everything, the rich brocade of silence wove its endless spell.

She interrupted, "Well, I think it's a *stupid* desert. I've seen deserts that have a lot more going on."

In the Thar Desert, at every moment, the sky is going on. A cloudless sky above the Thar is bigger than anything we will see again. The earth is under it. Some moments, the seam between them disappears.

Tonight we stop at Jonra village, where we will sleep. After tying our camels to a ramshackle corral filled with lambs and baby goats, Tane and the Singer unload provisions for our dinner. I realize we have been sitting on the camels' meal all day as the sacks of hay are dumped before them and Michael rubs his groin. "Next time remind me to get stainless steel underwear," he says.

I say, "Just wait, the camels ate your padding a minute ago." I try to get my camel to look me in the eye, but he grunts and stares away. Tane says his name is Winston.

Michael vanishes with his camera. Three little boys in raggedy coats surround me. One coat is made of colored strips of satin woven together. "You are a *shredded rainbow*," I tell him, and he seems to want me to say it over and over. He covers his laughing mouth. Soon the little shepherds go off to escort the goats and sheep home from whatever pocket of rare vegetation they've been grazing on. The babies have grown frantic in the pens, flinging themselves against the crossbars, hungry for their mothers.

A swollen orange moon overwhelms the sky. The Singer is peeling potatoes and won't let me help—he has only one knife. An elderly woman wrapped in black approaches and jabbers at me. Tane says, "She want to know what is your name." When I say it, she repeats and repeats and goes off holding it under her tongue. I ask for hers, but she doesn't tell. The little shepherds run back into view, followed by exuberant herds. They fling open the gate, and carry confused or motherless babies toward mothers with generous milk supplies. I wish the orphaned camel were here.

Tane has told me the wells in this village dried up years ago. Now the residents must carry their water jugs eight kilometers every day. A few use donkeys for the trek. Sheep still grazing in twilight loom like soft, moving stones.

Now a man approaches our little fire scene, speaking rapidly to me and waving his hands. I point him at Tane, who listens intently and scratches his head. "He says his father has—what you call?—the thing that make you very hot. His father is too hot."

"A fever?"

"He want to know what to do."

I have four aspirins hoarded in my little pouch and hand them over, with clear instructions that he is not to take them all at once. Two now, and two in four hours. I doubt this man has a clock. Two when the moon is at . . . that other place. I point halfway across the sky and he nods. Through Tane, I say they should keep the father warm—already the desert night feels chilly—and give him many glasses of water to drink. Tane frowns. "Remember what I tell you? No much water here."

The man looks grateful and backs away from us, holding the pills tightly in both hands.

Michael returns and we eat around the fire—potato and onion curry, cabbage, freshly patted chapattis. Delicious, but the Singer seems preoccupied, and the little boys huddle nearby, staring at our meal. I want to feed them, but Tane stops me. "They have own food."

We stare into the flames. To the west, not far away, is Pakistan. On the maps of India this area where we sit is blank, unspeckled by names. Yet each small, unmarked village feels utterly populated by daily habit, details, hope.

We're almost dozing when an extremely disheveled man runs toward us out of the dark, startling our group. He stops short of the fire, stares round the circle, and approaches me, waving a clutch of ragged rupee notes in my face before pitching them into my lap. He's jabbering breathlessly. Tane raises his hand to slow him down.

After asking a few questions, Tane translates. "This man not from Jonra. He come from village six kilometers far. He hear a doctor is staying here tonight in Jonra—you." Tane points at me. "His baby very sick. He want you to take money and—help—baby. I tell him you not a doctor, true?"

The dispensation of those recent aspirins returns to me with a jolt. How could such news travel so far so quickly? And why do they think *I* am a doctor instead of Michael, who looks far more doctorly? The man has mustered his funds to run all this way while his wife waits at home with a desperately coughing baby.

I say through Tane, "Tell me about the baby." But the father looks crestfallen as Tane explains the mistake. He looks betrayed. And I wish I were a veterinarian, at least.

It sounds like whooping cough. Tane does not know what honey and lemons are. Probably they wouldn't help whooping cough much anyway. So I say the same things about liquids and keeping warm, the magic potions we often pay our doctors thirty dollars for, and the man backs off from us, shoulders sagging.

An overwhelming disappointment lingers behind him. Our guides excuse themselves early for bed, but I sit up over the coals, depressed, imagining what it would feel like to be a doctor out here, carrying a bag of remedies to people who had been waiting and waiting so long.

Later that night, curled on a cot in the rank manger for sheep and goats, I can't sleep. Everything smells like damp wool. What if one of us were to have an appendicitis attack out here? Nine hours from Khouri by camel, only one bus to Jaisalmer daily, no telephones, radios, or relay systems. Naturally, I feel a growing pain in my side.

In cities we glorify the wilderness, but tonight I imagine the glowing lights of a city, spread out warm around us, as if they could soothe or save. I remember sleeping in a remote cave full of fleas in the Andes Mountains on our honeymoon, thinking, "What if we died tonight? How long would it take our parents to hear about it? What if just one of us died?"

Later I jolt awake as if a sheep has brushed my hand. The smell of our blankets is choking me. I stumble through the dark manger, feeling for the door, but when I find it, can't budge the heavy latch. Not a crack of light is visible from anywhere. I hear the shepherd boys giggling in their bedrolls and realize, *they're in here too.*

One rises to help me. Outside in the pen the babies take my arrival as a signal of morning and leap onto me, squealing and licking. I laugh. The moon's eye still shines its steady light. We are the only sound I can hear.

In our next days in the Thar Desert, we learn random details about desert life. If a slinky mongoose scoots across the path ahead of us, the camel must detour to avoid crossing where it crossed. This becomes quite tedious when we traverse areas thick with mongoose. It seems we are circling for hours. But Tane insists, "Mongoose very bad luck."

I ask him how common it is to spot a desert fox, which I've read about, and he says, "Very hard to see," then inhales deeply. At exactly that moment, a golden fox has materialized from behind a bush. We halt, and the fox freezes. "I cannot believe you say 'fox' and there is fox," whispers Tane. He seems nicer to me the rest of the trip, now that I am suddenly clairvoyant.

That day we also spot two great Indian bustards, among the rare birds of the world, which many expert watchers travel here to see. Bustards are tall, graceful birds with thin white necks and impressive wingspans.

Tane says we are very lucky people. He says some travelers look much harder than we do and see much less.

Visiting a rugged group of cattlemen living in a lean-to shack, we learn they are from the Indo-Pakistan border and come here for five months at a time so their bony cattle can graze. Gazing off toward handfuls of scrubby bushes, none looking soft or delicious, I think of the plump Texas cattle back home in meadows along our highways. When the men offer tea, I can barely swallow. It seems wrong to take anything from them.

Tane points out landmark stones and trees. He recognizes footprints of individuals in harder sand. "How do you know?"

"I know his shoes."

We stop at one lonely, round house where a little boy, perhaps five, is all by himself. Mama has gone to Khouri for flour. Papa is out minding the animals. Maybe they will return tonight. The boy talks to Tane, puffing up his chest. Seemingly fearless, he stands in the doorway watching us leave until we are small specks to each other.

Our skins have grown parched and browner. My lips feel bitten, Michael's hunching under his hat. Two men with that wild-looking Rajasthani handsomeness walk alongside us for a few hours the last day, bantering with Tane. Their voices keep time with the camels' tired pace. As we near our turnoff to Khouri, and I begin imagining I really recognize things, I feel drowsy, lost inside a rhythmic swoon.

Then Tane pokes me in the back. "Hello," he says. "You sleeping? My friends ask you a question. They want to know what caste you come from."

"In the United States, we don't have castes. We try not to." Actually, I thought this was a thing of the past in India too, but a few months in the country have shown me otherwise.

He repeats this answer to his friends. Now their darkened eyes glisten harder, examining me. They look puzzled, and one asks through Tane, "So how you know who you are?"

I muffle my laugh.

I used to know but I forgot.

Photo postcard with no message sent to the author's great-grandmother in Ohio, 1909.

The wedding of Miriam Allwardt and Aziz Shihab, the author's parents, Topeka, Kansas, 1951. Photographer unknown.

Naomi and Aziz Shihab digging in the garden, St. Louis, about 1956. Photo by Miriam Shihab.

The Shihab family, circa 1960. Photographer unknown.

Naomi at World Gifts, St. Louis, 1962. Photo by Aziz Shihab.

Aziz Shihab and Danny Thomas, World Gifts, St. Louis, 1962. Photographer unknown.

The author as Spring, Unity
Village, Missouri, 1965.
Photographer unknown.

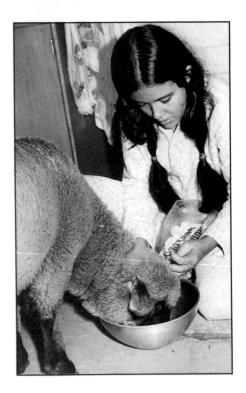

Animal husbandry at the
Shihabs', Texas, early 1970s.
Photo by Aziz Shihab.

The author at age 25. Photo by Dow Patterson.

Sitti Khadra Shihab, the author's grandmother, Sinjil
Village, West Bank, 1984. Photo by Michael Nye.

Shadows and *Anyone for Tea?*, Rajasthan, India, 1984.
Photos by Michael Nye.

The Sleep Dance from the Sleep Series, 1987. Photo by Michael Nye.

Michael and Naomi, Austin, Texas, 1989. Photo by Ave Bonar.

Sheep in the village, West Bank, 1992. Photo by Naomi Nye.

Cousins Ribhia and Janan, Aunt Fahima, and Sitti Khadra in the courtyard of the family home, Sinjil Village, West Bank, 1992. Photo by Naomi Nye.

Cousin Fowzi and his wife Adeela, Sinjil Village, West Bank, 1992. Photo by Naomi Nye.

Madison and Naomi, Oregon, 1993. Photo by Christine Eagon.

The Rattle of Wheels toward the Rooms of the New Mothers

Down the hallways came the rolling alert, at midnight, 4 A.M., with the generous humming of nurses in doorways giving instruction, promising they'd be back. From those high hospital beds with special buttons for raising, lowering, those islands on which the tailbone ached and the startled breasts grew and grew, we heard the rattling as a boat coming to save us, the answer to our unshaped cries.

I wanted to hold the nurse in my arms too, she had all the information. How to negotiate the compact swaddled bundle, to connect rosebud lips with raw and blossoming nipple, to make it hold. Something like electricity. Tapping in to the source. But who was the source? Was he? Was I? Hold him like a football, they all said, and I did not think to say how little that helped.

What if he never ate? What if his elegant eyes stayed rapturously closed in on themselves and the silent world was all he needed? An elderly nurse, Specialist in Rousing Sluggish Babies, turned him upside down, tickled his feet. She advised me to be patient. A series of swirling TV lessons—"How a Newborn Perceives"—unfolded on the screen. I attended a bath demonstration where one veteran mother just brushing up on skills offered her fleshy redhaired daughter to be dipped and patted dry. I eavesdropped on a Bengali couple in the hall anguishing over names; whatever they had produced was the opposite of what they had prepared for. I could not apply the sticker to my door, "IT'S A BOY," which declared so much less than what I was feeling. It's an Angel, a Miracle—how easy, contagious, to reduce this miracle to sex and weight.

He was . . . petite. They unwrapped him under a spotlight in the hospital nursery, to take blood counts. He was wearing tiny blinders, soaking in the glow, barely flickering an arm or leg—"like some beachcomber," my husband whispered. I stood at the nursery window watching him bask till I trembled and a nurse came to place her hands on my shoulders. She guided me toward the chamber of incubators. "Now *these*," she said, "these are worth trembling for, these are *really little,* but yours is simply yellowish. He's also slightly cold. He will be fine."

When the volunteer in striped hospital jumper came to sell me the portfolio of ugly First Day Photos, I wept. What if he never made it out from under the light and these scrunched-up eyes and closed fists were all I took home? Relics, ancient sad baby stories, poked their fingers into fitful dreams. Beyond the hospital windows, heavy rain was sheeting down, sky booming and blackening repeatedly, it was the peculiar June of endless rain, streets flooded, babies pressed to our sides.

I felt revived each time my husband appeared. It was possible to ask about our house and the world outside, to laugh together at another new father who pointed proudly through the nursery window, proclaiming to relatives, "Isn't the nose just like Cheryl's? And look at those hands, big as mine!"—then realized it wasn't his baby.

It was possible to laugh over our recent saga of birthing, how I'd sent him to the grocery store for lemons, desperate for my old favorite Arabic dish of lentils and rice with lemony salad on top, and he'd returned to find me in bed, clutching my side, "Oh, oh, something's not right," never thinking *this was it*—later, in final throes of breathing and counting at hospital, I'd puffed to the labor nurse, "Are you *sure* this isn't a false alarm?" so she hooted and told every passing nurse what I'd said.

My husband and I walked the whole wing arm in arm, watching the nurse swab the freshest babies, till a stricken cowboy, collapsed against a wall, noticed our eyes on him and blurted, "My baby didn't make it and my wife may not either"—changing the day. What could we bring this man? Coffee, juice? Why didn't the nurse take him in her arms too?

In the swaths of clean linen, the stacked towels, I wept. Buried myself in a closet, sobbing and sobbing. Why had this crossroads pumped so many tears into my eyes, abundant wellsprings, like the endless dripping of the stone cave in Syria where I'd prayed for this baby, a craggy nun directing me to drink, drink from the pool at the bottom, fill my bucket—if a hundred people filled their buckets at once, the level would not go down, she said. And I'd drunk, praying. I'd also drunk water from Lourdes, swallowed herbs, rubbed the subtle essence of rosemary and melissa oils on my belly, leaning toward this moment with senses tuned toward babies, their closed and haloed eyes, their hallowed empty hearts.

One of the four nights at the hospital they forgot to bring him to me. I awakened fifteen minutes early, preparing myself, raising the bed, straightening the covers. Far off down the halls I could hear the parade of rattling begin and

envisioned the little bundled worlds on wheels each heading toward a different door, mothers groggy and roused,
some more anxious than others, and some more ecstatic. It
was easy to notice the matter-of-factness of third- and
fourth-time mothers; I'd heard their casual chatter as they
hoisted the bundles, joking about diapers, saying, "Here
we go again." And what about the sixteen-year-old down
the hall, less than half my age, her bland face still unformed,
her rocky vocabulary a smattering of *Yeah*s and *Gee*s? It
seemed preposterous that some people fell into this experience with no apparent forethought, while others struggled
years to be here . . . maybe it was the same about everything in life.

Wheels rattling to halts at bedsides, the occasional yelp
and cry, and the one baby whose long siren of a wail stitched
all our rooms together.

I waited and waited and no wheels stopped at my door.
Why hadn't I limped down the hall to collect him myself?
Panic flashed—something had happened. He'd gone from
chilly to frozen. He'd slipped away while I was sleeping
and they hadn't told me. I pounded my call button till the
drawl flooded my speaker, "Can I help you?"

"Where is my baby?" I called out. "The wheels are heading back to the nursery already and my baby never arrived!"

"We'll check."

The gap of centuries. The aching pit of longing. The
terror of loss, now that he was finally here, and the whole
lineage of mothers, bruised and troubled, echoing behind
me . . . rosaried Mexican mothers keeping vigil at Our Sacred Heart, chanting stroking Arab mothers, the mothers
of Calcutta stoking dung fires before their tumbled cardboard shacks . . . would faith follow the fear? Would wisdom come suddenly now? And the intercom bellowed,

"They just forgot to bring him. They gave him a bottle already and he went back to sleep. Do you need the breast pump?"

How I tumbled into dreams after that, hugging the fatly anonymous hospital pillow, dreaming the lips of babies, that sucking pull, the sigh and swallow, dreaming the nights ahead when each fine-tuned whimper would pull me back to earth, unfolding fists around a finger, dreaming the earth's secret rattle as it turned in space on its ancient implacable hinge.

Nineties

For ten years after we married, my husband and I enjoyed the company of two women, his great-aunt Della and my great-great-aunt-by-marriage Leonora. We all lived in San Antonio, where none of us had grown up, which in itself seemed extraordinary.

We visited often. We talked on the telephone and went out to eat. Sometimes I'd drive them on outings together and they'd sit in the back seat together pitching wild stories and exclamations into the air.

Della loved to buy plaid blouses at discount stores and return them two days later. Devoted to soap operas and her impeccable yard—climbing yellow roses, billowing iris and the famous Esperanza Tree from Mexico—she hung up a birdhouse with a perch but no door. "So the birds could have a joke too." I didn't find it funny and she tipped her head at me. "Well, you're not a bird."

Every year on my birthday she took me to Fanick's Nursery to buy me a new rose bush, favoring ones with glamorous names like Don Juan. I like to imagine what my yard would look like now if they had all lived. She rearranged her living room furniture and pictures so often her walls were checkered with faded rectangles and nail holes. And she averted her face whenever we passed cemeteries, as if the graves were having conversations she feared might draw her in.

Leonora cracked endless sacks of pecans into giant bowls. I didn't have the patience for it—she told me to bring mine over. For her ninetieth birthday I offered to clean out her closets, having caught glimpses into their wild under-growth—Smith-Corona typewriters, milkshake makers, ancient bedpans. When I arrived at 8 A.M. she wasn't home. I peered into the dark windows, imagining her dead inside, then realized the car was gone too. For months I'd been begging her not to drive, since the day she entered a divided highway from the wrong side.

Two hours later she careened recklessly up the block, a fishing rod dangling from her back window. She climbed out puffing, lugging a bucket of two fresh fish. "I should have called you. I didn't think it would take so long. We just *had* to have something fresh for lunch." She'd risen at 5 and driven forty-five miles to Canyon Lake to fish, by herself. And I thought she needed my help.

One day it struck me that the dimension of time these two added to our lives was enormous. When they died, no one in our close circle would remember what the world was like so long ago. The farms, the fields, the wagons. Growing up without toxins in their bodies. When I was pregnant, I used to ask Leonora about the meals she ate as a child. The milk in buckets, the flamboyant silk on the corn. I'd visit Della and lie down in her sweet bed to sleep while she washed and dried her single plate in the kitchen. She set sugar cookies out on sheets of waxed paper to cool. Della and Leonora both predicted they would never see the last decade of the twentieth century. They spoke ominously of "the nineties" though they were already into their own.

When our baby was born, he favored them with grins and exuberant kicking. At two he told Della, "You are my sweetheart," stunning us all. Della, who had never married, said, "Thank God. I prayed to like just one child before I died." Leonora, who had raised ten stepchildren but had no child of her own, crawled around on the floor with him. She hiked up her dress and pitched the ball. They ate tangerines delicately, section by section. He stroked the soft fluff of her hair. He dumped Della's postcards out of their old cigar box and asked both women hundreds of questions about their hosiery and old-fashioned gas heaters.

In the same month, across town from one another, Della, nearly ninety-two, had a stroke and Leonora had a ninety-five-year-old breast removed, which seemed somehow criminal. In the same month they took to their beds to begin the slow and terrible good-byes. Della was not ready to die. She kept hoping for an alternative. She had a ramp built up to her door at home which she rolled down only once. She had us bring her Mexican food—puffed tacos and cheese enchiladas—in little cartons, though she could barely swallow.

Leonora was so ready to die she got mad at God. She said, "If God won't take me, why won't the devil?" She made deals but kept losing. She said to us, "Have a lot of fun in your lives. People just don't have enough fun." The two women asked about one another—"That poor thing." I plugged an ice chest into my car's cigarette lighter and drove little bowls of egg custard all over town.

They died within two weeks of one another, in 1989. And my tiny yellow tea roses with frilled red edges, Della's favorites among all we'd chosen, dropped their heads. The whole bush withered overnight.

I have thought of them so much and my throat still closes

up each time. What it means to have someone older than ninety who wants to know what you did today. . . . It is not the same.

My son and I planted feathers on their graves. I didn't tell him what graves were, I just said, "Let's stop here and think about how much we loved them." But he knocked on Leonora's tombstone as if it were a door, shouting, "You died on the ground, but you're in the sky now!" He seemed very sure about it.

Leonora's tombstone had been waiting for her since 1931, when her first husband, Luther, died of tuberculosis in one of the isolation huts on Zarzamora Street. They'd only been married a few years when she had to bury him. She'd always told me he was her real, true love and she kept his dapper framed portrait above her bed. Her second husband, my great-great-uncle, was a gloomy widower who needed her. She was his nurse for years and years.

In her last days, she said, "Don't think I didn't love your uncle too. He was a pretty man and I always liked pretty men. But it was a different kind of loving." I had to laugh seeing the tombstone, which must have been a shock to my great-great-uncle's children. She'd had Luther's name engraved large and the name she had carried for nearly sixty years, my mother's family name, in small parentheses.

David Crockett's Other Life

Recently the blazing purple tourist trolley, only purple one on the circuit, began idling longer then usual next to the mountain laurel tree across the street from our house. Passengers fanned themselves in slow unison—even in March, Texas heat can be oppressive—as the driver rose from the steering wheel to stride down the center aisle, speaking passionately. His shirt strained against its buttons over a generous belly and he wore a Greek fisherman's cap pulled low over his eyes. "You know wisteria? How it clusters in bunches like grapes? This tree we call mountain laurel is similar to wisteria and the fragrance of its blooming can make you reel!"

Actually, it was blooming already, and the passengers leaned forward to sniff. Fascinated by his aggressive manner, I watched—had I been one of those riders, I would have felt compelled to take notes. I would have feared being caught, like a dozing student, in a dream.

Instead I began following his slow circuit, eavesdropping. One day I intersected with him on King William Street as I pushed my little boy in his stroller, and was able to keep up with him for six whole blocks. Surely it had to be the slowest trolley ever to circle our handful of landmarks; maybe it was marketed toward the groggier tourist, who found slow-motion synonymous with relaxation. And I came gradually to understand; the driver had driven this route around downtown so long that he abandoned the standard text, inventing new narratives daily. Pressing his mouth against the hand-held microphone that blared beyond the puzzled seats out into the air, a cacophony of static: "This vine, known as Queen's Crown in south Texas, was planted eighty years ago by a magician who could make all the blossoms vanish overnight," or "This house, now inhabited by liberal nuns, boasts three gravesites in the backyard."

I could hardly blame him, even on the day I heard him pronounce a whole block boring, and it was mine. Perhaps he had told the story of the Alamo so long a harmless lunacy had overtaken him. Perhaps he had simply come to realize how our days deserve embroidery, embellishment; the long avenues between meals and sleep need more than fact to give them heart. Once I visited Oregon, amassing notes on Chief Joseph, the Columbia River, Mount Hood, and what careful detail did I carry home, discovered at random while using a local phone book? In Portland lives a man called Enzo Garbanzo. I almost phoned him. To ask what it is like traveling through the world with such a moniker, and was he ever called Chickpea as a boy?

Here, where the two-headed cat nursed a lizard. Here, where a photographer printed images of his grandmother's ghost. Here, on the battered sidewalk, a curling set of inscriptions, a whole family of names: Theodora, Leopold, Baby Emily, Raleigh the Dog!

I think of the trolley driver when caught in traffic, idling, cursing the slow light. How he must wait for chunky tourist women in horizontal stripes to board, swallowing their chatter: which side will offer the best view, do we get to see the missions on this tour? How he too must bear the clogged arteries and endless detours-in-the-name-of-progress; we live in a city that could have improved itself by doing ever so many things, but has chosen to stride forward by tearing up every street at once and laying down cobbles.

Perhaps our futures really will be improved by such aesthetic detail; I cannot balance this against the family businesses that have gone under, or the wrecking ball, or the dust.

Tell me what to tell my child. He saw the Bluebonnet Hotel, still solid as a great-aunt's shoe and frilled with concrete bows, reduced to rubble and skeletal pipe. "Mom! Mom! What did that building *do?* Did it get in trouble?"

Now he greets other buildings with a somber voice. "I saw the Bluebonnet Hotel and it was all broken. If you are not good you may get all broken too."

I will tell the man in the purple trolley what happened at a certain corner once, in the rain. It relates to nothing else but why I claim a certain corner as a landmark now and why, some days, the stories of any corners seem to swell like soaked seeds, and change.

People come to us whom we have not beckoned. The man wearing green suspenders in the next seat on the plane suddenly decides to spill forth his complicated autobiography in hushed and ominous tones. I can believe we are ultimately judged, if such reckoning there be, by how we treat them.

Once I was given a hairdresser, fragrantly cheerful, and her husband from India, who dealt in gems, to host and drive around town for a single afternoon. They came to me by way of someone else, and she needed to get to the Barber's

College for an interview. I could not send them on the tourist trolley.

We set out, the gent babbling about sapphires, in a driving rain, the kind that pushes back trees and distorts even the color of stoplights.

I tried to tell him that I had been to his country, but he broke in immediately with "The poverty was very difficult, yes, and I'm sure you found it appallingly crowded, as does everyone from the West, but don't you see, we have had many more centuries than your youthful country to develop problems and, forgive me, the collective wisdom of our country has deepened profoundly whereas the ignorance of the West . . ."

My turn to interrupt. "No, that's not what bothered me about your country at all," and he asked, "What did?"

"Arrogance."

The rain pounded hard, hard. His wife kept glancing at her scrap of address as if it might drift closer to us in the tumult. We passed Five Points, the corner where a young Mexican singer had been swept to her death in such a storm a few years back. I didn't mention it. I guided the car slowly along the curb.

Mukti gazed disapprovingly out the glass. "I always thought of Texas as being—somehow—dry."

"Yes, but when it rains here, it rains a *lot*. Don't you know how fond we are of exaggeration?"

His wife in the back seat seemed terribly nervous, fidgeting with a lipstick tube and sighing. I asked if she would be forced to give a haircut or shampoo as part of her interview.

"Well, they do it differently. What I was going to ask— do you think that you and Mukti could—maybe—leave me there—and not wait? I mean, you could go somewhere while I have the interview and come back and pick me up? I just think I'll be too nervous if I see you waiting for me."

He said, "Certainly, certainly, actually I wouldn't mind peering at some of the better gem shops and jewelry stores in town—do you think a glance at the telephone directory could guide us there, or might you know of any offhand?"

We were stopped at a light. I considered our grim possibilities as another car slammed us, hard, from behind. The floating moment after impact seemed surreal, peaceful— my first impulse, that I had been spared a horrible tour.

Pushing out from the driver's seat, I found a startled older woman in a fat Chevrolet backing away from me, looking toward the next lane as if preparing to drive off. I pounded her window, calling "Hey! What are you doing? Stop your car!"

She stared at me, her hair unmistakably permed. Already drenched, I disliked the fact that she was clean and dry.

She cut off her engine and reluctantly rolled down the window. We could both see the back of my car crumpled and shining, stripped of paint.

"I didn't mean to," she blubbered. "I couldn't see the light because of the rain and you were just, well, really stopped." Her pale hands clutched the steering wheel. She wore floral rings that might have come from an Avon catalogue, as a bonus. I said I would go call the police and she blanched, "Not the police! My husband will string me up!"

I told her mine would string me up if I let her leave and she smiled weakly.

"For insurance," I explained wearily. "You know they have to make a report."

Mukti was waving wildly through the back window of my car. I imagined him gunning the engine and driving off to the diamond caves without me.

I yelled at him, "Come out!" He looked bewildered, so

I went back to speak to him. "I need you to hold this woman here while I call the police," I hissed.

He considered his jacket sadly and slipped it off. Melinda moaned and twisted her fingers. "Are you hurt?" I asked.

"No, but I'm late."

The other driver stoutly refused to stand in the rain, so Mukti demanded that she open her back door so he could climb in. She looked less than pleased but I felt proud of him. In the meantime I had grown so cold and wet I felt a finger of hysteria beckoning at me from the clouds, the kind that makes people giggle during arguments.

"I'll be right back!" I advised Mukti to keep an eye out for a taxi and launch his wife toward her interview. I knew he would not see one but I said this to give him hope.

Where to go? I'd never even noticed this corner before, though I'd driven past it a thousand times. The doughnut shop I'd never stopped in —BEST DONUTS IN TOWN WE PROMISE—loomed somewhere nearby, but I couldn't remember in which direction. The closest business besides the local gun shop seemed to be a dilapidated drive-in a block away, striped candy-cane pink and white, in the downcast manner that said, "Once we hoped to be a big success."

Trudging through the flooded gutter, the mud, the gluey clay of the old gravel parking lots, I went singing, thinking of ruined shoes and women scared of husbands just when it felt convenient, and the song that poured unexpectedly forth from my lips tasted somehow delicious—"Oh, do you know the muffin man?"—it seemed as good a question as any. Without intending to, I had fallen into the lap of fable, on an afternoon that would better have been spent drinking hot chocolate and reading the *New Yorker*. Innocently, foolishly, I had entered the whirl.

A handwritten scrawl above the drive-in's entrance said "George's." I pushed open the greasy door. Neon video machines blinked mindlessly and a couple of teenagers dressed in black stood propped against one wall, his hand thrust inside her blouse, pumping. I called out, "George!" The lovers glanced at me, startled—no public telephone in sight.

Here, where the nipple rose with vivid delight and she pressed her tongue into the center syllable of a cry, swearing to be true to something, the pitch of desire, the hungry hand kneading her flesh. How many rooms did we pass on our daily rounds without ever imagining the passions within? And how many would we be able to stomach if we knew?

"Excuse me, is George here?"

The boy stared vacantly at me, as if such banality no longer held meaning. I pressed a stiff swinging door to what would probably be the kitchen and spotted, on a shelf cluttered with empty soda cups, a huddled phone. I reached toward it automatically, then addressed the backs before me. "Excuse please, may I use your phone?"

A grunt, a single face turned. Three men hunched over the meat table where George once slapped his fatty burgers. The face looked crooked in its own skin. "Huh."

I took that to mean Yes and rang up Emergency. "I need the police," at which point all three chefs turned toward me, wild-eyed.

"Police!"

"She's calling the police!"

"Who the hell *is* that?"

Thrust forward, a grab for the receiver. He slammed it into its socket. And there before us on the high table stood the line-up of little bags shown on the 10 o'clock news every time another drug bust makes headlines. For some reason I thought of my childhood friend Dominica, whose grandmother would, every Sunday evening, line up in little bags the cookies for her school lunches, a whole week in advance. I envied her life, and wherever she was in the world today.

"Who *are* you?" Rough hand on my arm.

"I'm a person who needs the police because some other person just wrecked my car down the block from your— establishment here. It's on the level, believe me. You can go outside and look."

But no one moved. His huge lips parted. "The hell you call the police are you outta your mind? Piss outta here bitch!"

Here, where I saw nothing, where my life flashed before me in sad snippets of wonder and the closeness of the underworld rained upon me. Where once you could say Onions or No Onions and someone would listen.

I couldn't help it. I said, "You guys are doomed" and turned on my heel. Lucky they let me leave, I guess. Out front the lovers had disappeared, perhaps into a broom closet or filthy car, and puddles spangled the lot. Rain fell softer now, like a lullaby, the swish of cars almost soothing. And off to the right on the corner, unbeckoned but miraculously arrived, idled a police car flashing its light! Mukti stood before the officer, gesturing and lecturing, probably about the traffic problems in America, probably something heroic. Both women were gone. I had only been absent a moment and everything had changed.

"Where are they?" I called, waving.

Mukti motioned excitedly, shoulders thrust back. "This lady here, the hitting one, she went to call her husband. She went walking that other way. Look, I kept her purse as hostage! And Melinda found passage to the Beauty College with another policeman who stopped and took pity, she was crying and he asked if she were hurt and she said, 'Only my future.' He said it was a matter of blocks. And now we have been having a nice discussion about opals, you know, this police here bought one for his wife . . ."

I placed my hand on the policeman's arm, tenderly. "Thank you very much for stopping." He had his clipboard poised as I fumbled for my driver's license. "I have never been gladder to see you in my whole life."

He looked up, puzzled. Why did I seem so flushed?

"When you finish with us," I whispered, "you might want to see what's cooking over at George's."

Melinda was positive she didn't get the job, though they liked her East Coast style of brushing. Mukti said our city wasn't ready for the quality of gems he had to offer. I offered to drop them at the Tandoori Kitchen but they chose El Típico Mexican Food instead. We consecrated our lips with puffed taco shells. And when I left them at the battered Park Motel I felt a sudden impulse of love, for the people we meet only once, the lives that spin out in vast rings from the moment they clicked together, stones, jumbled in a hand, then tossed.

Mukti said, "I hope your husband will not feel too distressed about the fender. I have full faith in the lady's insurance company. She looked like a lady who would pay her debts."

"But she wanted to run away!" Melinda reminded him.

"Well, yes. Maybe I'm wrong."

I think how each group of travelers riding the purple trolley shares one tilting swoop around the city, one fantastic parcel of anecdotes, and remembers—what? *David*

Crockett's fork at the Alamo, tines tarnished black. His beaded leather vest.

I could tell about the book called *My Philosophy* written by David Crockett, a rare edition, now stored in a dusty crate on the fourth floor of the Hertzberg Circus Museum. I know it's up there because I packed it away myself in 1973 after stealing it from the special collection for two days to read it first. I worked in a library, typing cards for archival books marked *Storage Only*. It broke my heart to put books into boxes and I escaped as soon as I could. And I can testify with certainty that Davy, who is usually remembered for his bravery in battle, his willingness to die for Texans though he came from Tennessee, or the raccoon tail he wore over his own ponytail, would much prefer to be remembered for his mind.

Here, the authentic engraved carriage of circus performer Tom Thumb! Imagine it, ladies and gentlemen, a human being small enough to wear this shoe! Here, the house shaped like a pig, eyelashes a recent addition! And did you know—(full stop)—why early settlers in Texas painted the ceilings of their porches blue? They had been wandering so long across the prairies they needed the sky above to make them feel at home. Also they wanted to attract songbirds to their rafters, to roost and make their nests. Do you realize what a chirping nest meant to those tired German settlers? It is proven that birds prefer to roost on porches painted blue rather than ones painted gray. The only trouble was, roaches like sunny skies too. And now we have a serious insect problem that we are working on. Here in our city. I'm so glad you could come.

Favorite Cleaners, San Antonio

Henry L. Ramirez, I am ashamed that for twelve years you knew my last name and I did not know yours.

Even "Henry" had long ago been gained offhandedly, as the presser at the hissing steam table shouted into the back of the shop. "Hen-*ry! Hen*-ry!" He wore a strip of white cloth twisted and knotted on his head, and said "Hungover" when anyone asked him how he was.

You'd come forth wiping your hands, wearing a white shirt, and smiling, that slow smile that says, "Still here, still going." Carefully you pencilled the name of each garment on a pad. Next to it you wrote a price—surprisingly low. Sometimes you cast a funny wink in the presser's direction. I cannot remember you ever being gloomy, even when temperatures soared above ninety-five and it seemed strange that people would wear clothes anyway, or need to get them cleaned.

Your business stands on Durango Street, east side, near downtown. Ten years ago the People's Variety Store (fish hooks, khaki pants, Rit Dye) was demolished, a block down. Someone put up a sleazy chicken joint that went broke within a year. Then the blocks around you were closed by construction, so an overpass could be built above the train tracks. I had to drive a huge loop to get to you. "Is this hurting your business?"

"Nearly killing it," you said, smiling.

The Chinese grocer held out, but the Texas Printing Company doesn't seem to have a door anymore. And the antique warehouse, where we once bought a British wardrobe with sweet-smelling London newspapers still folded in the drawers, has spiraled downward into caverns of junk.

After the street opened again, it took a weird jog and didn't really go by your shop anymore. You shrugged. You wrote, "Shirt, Jacket, Poncho" on the little white pad.

Sometimes a woman sat off to one side, sewing up ripped trouser seams on a treadle machine. I'd return from journeys, unpack, and drive straight toward you with a mound of crumpled clothes in the back seat, holding my breath till I saw your old car in the lot, the ornate turquoise metalwork of your front windows.

SUITS PRESSED WHILE YOU WAIT. Blocky, solid lettering. Did anyone really have a suit pressed while he waited? Did he bring it in on a hanger or did he take it off his body? I told you your old-fashioned vertical sign FAVORITE—probably neon in its youth—happened to be my favorite sign in the city. You liked that. I wanted to photograph it. "Any time." And the laugh behind your words, Henry, mild as freshly ironed jackets shimmying into their bags.

I brought you my great-uncle's giant linen tablecloth, folded up tight so you wouldn't see how big it was. Did you do tablecloths?

"Well, not really—but no one ever asked me before. I guess we could—*try*."

I drove off feeling guilty. It was the size of a tennis court. Days later when I came to get it, you raised your arms high in the air. "It just kept *going* and *going!*" you said. "It covered up all the ironing boards at once! It covered up the whole shop!" Still you didn't charge much. You treated it as an experiment.

I was worried when you went into the hospital for a month, but afterwards you looked healthy. "That's what everyone tells me—Henry, you look good. I *feel* good. Well, it's good to be back, anyway."

You put your business up for sale, even before the city condemned blocks of wooden houses on neighboring streets for construction of a controversial sports dome. "I don't think anybody will take it, but I thought I'd find out." I'd come in with blood-streaked hands after stealing roses from doomed yards. My friends and I were trying to dig up old bushes before the bulldozer buried them, but their roots went too deep. I always worried you'd say a deal had been struck. "No such luck. Who wants to run an old cleaning business, anyway?" Then the FOR SALE sign disappeared from your window and you stopped mentioning it.

Today it seems oddly intimate to imagine someone cleaning our clothes—as if the people on the edges of our lives are the ones who hold us together. I have a friend who writes poems to waitresses, casting his troubles into their cups and sturdy hands.

Today, Henry, I wish I had asked you about your childhood, your family, what you sang inside your head as you worked. I wish I had not been too shy to say, "Hey friend, what's your last name, anyway?" so I didn't have to find out from a notice taped to your locked door: *We regret to inform you that Henry L. Ramirez has passed away.* A fistful of notes on scraps of paper and cardboard crammed into the door's crack: "I need my clothes—Mary Garcia 222–3470," "Urgent—got to have my shirts—call Katie 223–4065" and not one note about you.

Doomed. No one else will ever know this corner as you knew it. No one. They'll mow this little building down and find another use for a spot of blank property in two hot seconds. It's our heritage. I'm sitting a long time in the car with my head on the wheel and my boy asking "Where's Henry?" and a pile of rotten jackets balled up in back. Then I stick my note in with the others, but this is more a love letter on an old bank receipt from the floor of the car, a crumpled cry of honor and sorrow, and nobody, no one, has an iron this size.

Enigma

He keeps the heavy doors of his old-fashioned piñata shop locked up tight since he's usually in the attic working. You have to ring a bell if you want to shop here. By then you're semicommitted, buying party favors even if you have no party in mind. Tomorrow I turn forty and today Mr. Beto, who has always seemed old, seems distinctively older. Did some wind blow through in the night? His face has grown thinner, more gently defined, his skin softly tissue-like. He's becoming his favorite substance. He's switching on lights for us, muttering, "It's here, it's all here."

Party favors loop down the walls. Plastic babies, Mexican finger traps, sparklers, poppers, whistles. Mountains of confetti for stuffing *cascarone* eggshells at Easter. Madison stares up at the crowds of piñatas dangling from the ceiling. "Does he really make all these?" he whispers to me, and Mr. Beto grumbles, "I do." He's married to tissue. He's snipped it into a million strips.

Once I climbed with him into the attic, the flamboyant topple of half-finished Batmen, turquoise sailing ships, chipmunks and brides, to ask him serious piñata questions. I used to interview men who ran feed stores and built tooth-pick dispensers. My newspaper columns appeared between ads for fertilizer and cut-rate bras. I wasn't nervous with Mr. Beto in the attic; it seemed doubtful he would wrestle me to the floor, though neighborhood legend says he has a secret room of X-rated piñatas somewhere. I've never seen it.

He told me how long it took and how much thinking it took and the sun coming in through a tiny slit of window lit up sheaves of paper along the walls. I wanted to buy just the uncut paper, plain and sheer and tropical fruit–colored, and made the mistake of saying so. It seemed to hurt him. After that I thought of him living here alone with all these faces.

Today Madison's dragging a huge pink rabbit around. Mr. Beto growls, "Put it back where you found it." How people stuff these with candy and smash them still eludes me. I can't do it. I leave them hanging till they grow dusty webs between their toes. Madison's fingering a giant birth-day cake, smiling. A fish, and a policeman. Mr. Beto could supply every party between here and Saltillo till the end of the world.

My eyes fall onto a single standing girl done in odd shades of gray and brown with the word ENIGMA planted on her chest in blocky white letters. Who's this?

I carry her by the string in her head to Mr. Beto where he sits.

Two little gray braids poke out on either side of the string. She's not smiling. She looks uncharacteristically gloomy for a piñata. Does she represent a robot? A charac-ter in a cartoon?

He's waving his graceful fingers, looking for a word with sudden urgency.

"She's like *mystery,* you know? Like something you can't answer even when it stands right next to you? Like *puzzle.*"

"Yes, yes, I know what the *word* means, but who *is* she? Is she a character from a story or did you make her up?"

He pauses. Looks as if he's deciding whether to tell the truth. "I just thought of her."

He stares at the floor. She costs eight dollars. He peers up curiously when I say I thought of her too.

It takes a long time to decide not to buy her. It seems philosophical. I could hang her over the breakfast table tomorrow when forty comes to claim me. Or I could think of her in the dark shop down the street from my house, waiting, waiting. I could visit her later when it's so hot we almost die.

My Life with Medicine

Once my mother put me on a horseradish diet for an entire week. I ate nothing but tablespoons of freshly grated horseradish, and drank gallons of water to flush out my system.

After suffering for months from a lingering bronchitis no conventional treatment seemed to cure, I was ready to try anything. Possibly my mother had learned about this treatment in one of those old-time remedy books that lived on our shelves, written by someone named Jethro or Hubert. The delicate tissues of my inner cheeks and throat blazed mightily each time I braved a dose. I squinched my eyes shut and thought about: the lips of my ex-boyfriends, the extravagant view from the South Rim at Big Bend National Park, chocolate cake—to be able to swallow. Till now I have hesitated to mention such details about my past, for fear they might make my mother seem reckless, or myself, susceptible in the extreme.

The horseradish did not make me well, but it didn't make me sicker either. I remember the lumpy horseradish-like texture of my off-white ceiling as I lay weakly in bed staring up at it, and the bones in my wrists, which seemed more prominent each morning. I was reading Jack Kerouac at the time, and had not eaten meat for years, so I could not imagine whatever meat it was that people liked to eat with horseradish to help it go down easier. My idea of a nightmare was a lamb chop sizzling in a skillet. I do think the Kerouac books I read from then on were marked by a certain tingle that would arise in my tongue upon opening one.

This treatment preceded my personal visit to one of the Filipina faith healers who had come to San Antonio to give presentations on psychic surgery. Their films showed a healer running his or her hands over the troubled region of the patient's body, babbling in some intense, electric vocabulary, and lifting what looked like a bloody kidney or tumor from the body without ever cutting it open.

A few people in the back of the tiny auditorium, where we liked to sit so as not to be called on to demonstrate anything, murmured that it was a chicken gizzard or pig liver or cow heart, and the so-called "healer" had had it up a sleeve. I listened to each possibility with equal interest. I was not devoted to believing things, but it seemed as foolish to scoff too soon. When the scratchy film showed the previously sick patient now well and smiling widely, it did not even look like the same person to me. And how were we to know? What were we supposed to do about it?

Perhaps the Filipinos hoped for contributions from the audience to allow them to continue their work. Undoubtedly we did not give much, if anything. But my mother made an appointment for me to have a "free consultation" regarding my ongoing bronchial condition, which included stabbing pains in the chest and attacks of hyperventilation so profound I would have to pull off the highway if I were driving and breathe into a brown paper bag.

She dropped me off downtown at the David Crockett

Hotel-Motel behind the Alamo. I was to visit room 17 at 2 P.M. My mother had not given our names when she called for the appointment, to insure perfect anonymity; the psychic could not check up on you in advance of your visit.

A handsome, strong-boned woman with an upswept hairdo answered the door. She motioned me to be seated on the twin bed opposite her. After staring at me for a brief moment, she looked away toward the ugly dresser with handles impersonating treasure trunks of conquistadores.

Her first words were "You breathe too much. Why you breathe so much?" I felt astonished. I was not breathing too much at that exact moment, so there was no way she could have known this by looking at me.

She closed her eyes.

"You learned exercises for breathing, is this not right? You went to a—school. They teach you make deep breathing in and out, and you were good with this, no? You show everybody how to do it, no?"

A pack of wild cards shuffled in my head and slammed on the table: the Yoga School, where I'd gone on Tuesday and Thursday evenings for many months, where we ended each session with deep breathing cycles and I was able to take in so much air and hold a breath so long, the teacher sometimes made me lie down on a platform at the front of the room to lead everybody.

"So now you need *forget* how to do it a little bit, okay? You do it—*automática*—now so your blood fill up with too much oxygen and make you dizzy. You feel dizzy when you do it, no? No good to breathe too much. Make your whole—system—lose balance." She waved her arms and threw her head around dramatically to demonstrate. "Now you need learn to do—what a dog do."

I tried to follow. "Bark?"

She shook her head. "No, that other thing," and demonstrated by hanging her tongue out of her mouth and panting. "Do it with me," she instructed.

We sat on two twin beds at the David Crockett Hotel-Motel panting hard at one another, as if we had just jogged up to the South Rim of Big Bend National Park with jugs of horseradish in our packs.

Then she stood and smiled at me. "So there you go," she said. "Train your breath the other way and you be fine. Each time you feel too big breaths coming, remember the dog." I tried to hand her five dollars but she wouldn't take it. "No, no," she said. "I do this because I like to do it." She waved me out the door. "Good luck."

What could anybody say to that?

First she diagnosed me in ten seconds, then she cured me, for free. I was remembering the dog from then on, each time my attacks started. Panting worked far better than the paper bag had, and I didn't have to carry anything with me. I just turned my head to the side.

My mother, waiting in the steamy car with all the windows rolled down, said, "Well? That was awfully quick." I could tell her and know she would believe me, but it was certainly going to be hard to tell anyone else. I have suffered no bronchitis or serious hyperventilation since that moment.

I always think people with closed minds must never have had any ineffable experiences in their lives. Otherwise how could they be that way?

Our mother birthed us in the friendly '50s without drugs, inhalants or spinal numbing. This was not considered "hip" or "intelligent" back then, but radically goofball. More importantly as regards her general character, she birthed us naturally with no moral assistance or support on the part of the nurses at St. Mary's Hospital in St. Louis, who looked askance at her request. They left her completely alone in the labor room, saying, "You probably won't be able to do it." At the last minute she rang a bell or shouted or something, and a doctor appeared. Our father was off feeling faint in a broom closet, a distant corridor. I have a picture of them leaning over the crib my first day home—mother's sensitive nose, father's thick, sensational hair.

Our mother took pesticides and toxicity seriously long before many other people did, back in the deluded years when most grown-ups still smoked. She frequented an organic farm a few blocks from our home, refused to spray our house or yard with poisons, and mulched her peelings and eggshells. She was as skeptical of chemicals as she was of antibiotics. Rather, she walked the line. We *were* vaccinated, and we visited doctors *occasionally*—chicken pox, stitches in a bloody knee—but our mother kept her radar tuned to High for Other Possibilities. Legions of vitamin bottles lined our shelves. We were safe in her interesting hands.

Our fresh, wonderfully dirty-looking yard eggs came from the organic farmer's elderly mother, who got mad at my father once and swatted him over the head with a broom. I think he'd asked her too many questions. He refused to pick up our eggs after that. Dazzling waves of heat rose from the pavement late summer afternoons when we trudged with our mother up the hill, pulling the red wagon piled high: summer squash, crisp green beans, flamboyantly fat eggplants. At our house we had little extra money, but terrific cuisine.

In Girl Scouts, the other girls brought frothy cupcakes decorated with pink sugar sprinkles for treats, but I could count on my own mother to supply us with dried apricots and nuts. No one in our chirpy circle ever groaned. They just stared at me silently: *Is this what you have to put up with?* But I knew their bones were more brittle than mine.

I never once, not once, took a white-bread sandwich to school. My friends stared at my authentic, earth-colored lunches with sidelong interest. I think they were afraid they might be contagious. My brother and I had to sit way, way back from the face of the television set, if we watched it at all. At night, our windows stayed open so cool exhalations of pine and cherry trees filtered through our screens.

With all this attention to detail, it's amazing we ever got sick. If we had a fever, we fasted a while, then ate a potato. Potatoes were supposed to soak up the heat. If we had a cold, we lay in bed with a giant stack of books and a mound of Kleenexes rising out of the sheets. The daily, domestic world felt farther away—muffled voices, vanished smells, an unfamiliar croaky voice coming from deep in the chest as if we had turned into leprechauns or aliens. There was that awful first moment when you imagine your throat getting sore, then the awful point of no turning back—sore for sure. At least a cold slowed me down, gave me Carl Sandburg, Nancy Drew and *Little Women*. It had its payoffs. Occasionally my family would visit the Unity School of Christianity, an eclectic group of positive thinkers who said people only got colds if they invited them. You could deny a cold and it would leave before it ever came. I liked lots of their upbeat beliefs, but this hogwash failed entirely for me.

As a baby, my brother once experienced convulsions and had to be whisked to the hospital in a swirl of panic. We measured all illness by that episode from then on—eyeballs rolling back in the head. Everything else was minor. Another time I unwittingly caused him to stumble into the path of an oncoming bicycle. He was rushed, bleeding and dizzy, to an emergency clinic, where they wrapped a gigantic white turban around his head like a Sikh. He wore it for nearly a month, staring soberly at me from beneath its folds. I said he was getting an accent.

Because I tended toward morning snuffliness and had already displayed dramatic allergies to penicillin and sulfa drugs, confirming my mother's reservations, I had allergy tests—the prickled poke of tiny needles up and down my back. When the specialist announced he had isolated my sensitivity—allergic to dust—it seemed ridiculous. Where could we ever go where there would be no dust?

Our mother vacuumed my walls. She pleaded with me to take the travel posters off my ceiling. I received exemption from various household chores—no shaking rugs, sweeping or vacuuming. There were certain benefits to being allergic. Years later, my brother, who had looked askance at these special considerations, did what he called "the allergy test" on me. He didn't use any needles. I had developed, after consuming six lovely bowls of fresh English strawberries on the great ship *Queen Mary*, a set of hives and announced I could never eat a strawberry again.

My brother made me a peanut-butter sandwich. After I ate it, I heard him remark, "That strawberry jam was great!" Immediately I moaned and felt the skin itching under my shirt, whereupon he leapt to the refrigerator and seized upon a jar of—raspberry. "See!" he said. "It's all in your mind! It's always been in your mind! I knew allergies were a lie."

Once I went to the doctor with my father after he lost control of our car around the corner from our house and drove into a ditch. I hit my head on the dashboard and he hit his head on the steering wheel. We felt fine, but someone thought we should go to a doctor, to make sure we didn't have any head injuries.

How did the doctor discern this? He made us walk in a straight line. He didn't stare at the wall or close his eyes.

The night before my father drove into the ditch, he dreamed it. Whenever he had a bad dream, he'd take a deep slug of his breakfast coffee and say, "I need to wash that dream right out of my mind." He liked the scene in *South Pacific* where Mitzi Gaynor washes a man out of her hair, over and over again. He was always singing it, in between "What kind of fool am I?" and "I love Paris in the spring-time."

Our mother said he drove into the ditch just to prove he was a psychic too. We knew a lot of psychics in our family. We knew swamis and gurus and theology professors and Dead Sea scroll scholars and people who were doing new translations of the Bible. This must have made our mother's parents very nervous.

Our mother's parents were God-fearing, doctor-fearing Missouri Synod Lutherans who lived in a gloomy apartment on Union Boulevard and kept their blinds drawn down all day long. I thought they liked their rooms to feel more mysterious. Our mother had shaken them up by marrying someone who not only wasn't a Lutheran, but wasn't even a Christian. How could she do this? Our mother had a mysterious smile.

"Tomorrow I'm going in for my knee again," our grand-mother would quietly announce, year after year. We never asked much about her knee. I have regretted this. Whether it got better or not after years of consultation was not discussed. The point was: she believed. She believed in going to the doctor. She would no sooner have visited a Filipino faith healer than taken a rocket ship to the moon. Appointments were sacred and paid for by a big Blue Cross or a giant Blue Shield. Years later I was shocked to hear that our German grandfather, whose parting words to us were often "Keep your belt buckled!," frequented a chiropractor on Fridays. It seemed almost—avant-garde.

Our father's family, on the other hand, were Palestinians now living in a small, stony village surrounded by almond and olive orchards, high in the hills of the West Bank. They had lived there since their 1948 ouster from their Jerusalem home. Though Muslim, their village was named for a Christian, St. Giles. They were covering all the bases. My father's family ascribed to watermelon cures ("A watermelon can heal fifty ways," our father would gently remind us, slicing the juicy pulp from the skin and placing the triangle in our open mouths) and an herb called *marimea,* of the family of sage. *Marimea* was good for stomach ailments, any variety—our father brewed it up in fragrant cups of dark tea. So it made sense that he would not object when our mother began cultivating great plots of comfrey in our yard—the furry, heavily veined leaves were said to be helpful for everything from canker sores to burns. *O we knew aloe vera before it became a household word!*

Our mother was tender but tough. She stood over me with bottles of pantothenic acid and vitamin E. "Put the pill on the back of your tongue and swallow!" she directed. "It cannot get stuck!" But of course it could if I thought so. At least vitamin Cs were suckable. Our tender-hearted father bore the burden of over-empathy. If anyone vomited in his vicinity, he would vomit too. Once, at a Christmas Eve Nativity pageant beside the Mississippi River, he and my brother made quite a spectacle of themselves.

Despite their cultural variations, our parents both placed great stock in the wet rag. Sometimes cold and draped across a throbbing forehead or wrapped around the stunned knee, sometimes smoky hot and pressed into the small of the back where the bicycle handlebar had poked, our parents and their raggedy washcloths eased, comforted, cajoled. We never doubted they could help us feel better. Sometimes our father had to comfort from the hallway, so our illnesses wouldn't grip his own psyche, but we knew he cared. We never left the house without a "Be careful" trailing us like the long fringes of a bedouin scarf. Of course we did not yet realize what a gift this was—parental concern. It was the ground everything else was built on. But we did not know that yet. We expected it.

Then our family sold everything we owned and moved to Jerusalem. We rented the upper floor of a big stone house eight miles north of the city. Gypsies camped in rocky fields nearby, playing wild gypsy drums late at night around a fire. Exotica seemed to grow more and more local in our lives.

When busloads of Turkish pilgrims passed through Jerusalem en route to Mecca, a hysterical typhoid rumor swept the city.

"It always happens," our father said mildly. "Ever since I was a little boy. The pilgrims come traveling, bearing some great disease."

But the city health officials took it seriously. At my school deep in the Old City, students were involuntarily inoculated with a community needle dipped into a small vial of alcohol between arms. I shudder now to think.

The next day a fever so great swept over me that my mother was taking my temperature every ten minutes. I was hauled to a doctor. Two more doctors appeared at the house. I saw them all raising their eyebrows. Everything they suggested felt like an experiment. No medicine helped. My whole body was draped with cool washcloths which my mother dipped into a bowl in her lap. Three or four days blended together. I blazed away. It was also my birthday and I had no interest whatever in looking at my cake.

Then my grandmother, furious because she hadn't been alerted, caught wind of my illness and bustled in from her village by taxi. I recall her high-pitched voice babbling angrily at my father in the hallway. He covered his eyes. "She says I have insulted her."

She shooed everyone out of my room and stood over me, her long white headdress and the richly embroidered bodice of her dress spinning before my eyes. She closed her eyes and began chanting prayers in Arabic, over and over and over again, like an Islamic rosary, running her hands up and down in the air over my body. She stuck a hundred straight silver pins which she pulled from her bodice into the bedsheet outlining my body, like in *Gulliver's Travels*. I think the pins must have broken the fever's current, for in less than an hour, I was sweating profusely and the fever eased. I sat straight upright, demanding *hummos* and custard and soup. Some might say the illness had simply run its course, but I had no doubt the cure was my grandmother's doing.

After that I looked at her differently.

When I sat at her side, I was secretly sitting at her feet.

I was the only family member who consumed delicious *falafel* sandwiches, replete with casual layers of lettuce and tomato, at a particular Old City lunch stand near my school, and a year later, only I entertained ascariasis, an infestation of hideous, sizeable parasites. Probably the two items went together. By the time the worms made themselves known to me ("Did you see one?"—"Yes, I saw one"—"More than one?"—"One was enough—") we had migrated to San Antonio, Texas, where botanica drugstores sold magical powders called Jinx Removers and Do As I Say. I bought some. I bought all of them. Maybe the trouble was that I kept them in their bottles with the neon labels, lined up gleaming on shelves in the bathroom. Maybe I should have sprinkled the powders across my chest.

My mother checked her herbal handbooks, but the remedies sounded excruciatingly slow. Who wants to fast in order to starve one's worms? It could take days, or weeks. I couldn't entertain them that long. Besides, I wanted to have them precisely identified. Otherwise it was like having a party for strangers.

The doctor we visited for the ascarids had never encountered them before and resorted to his medical text.

He prescribed an antidote with a skull and crossbones on the label. I did not feel good about this. With large worms inside one's body, it is hard to feel good about anything at all. He told me to go home, drink the medicine, and lie down. The worms were—ahem—supposed to be expelled some time afterward.

A few hours after I had downed the foul brew and nothing had been expelled, I could swear I felt worms slithering up my esophagus. I insisted my father call the doctor back and made the mistake of listening in on the extension phone. The doctor resorted to his text again. I thought I heard him chuckle and told my father later I wanted to kill him.

"Looks like—she could be right," he said. "Looks like—they might be expelled through vomit instead of feces. Like I told you, I never dealt with any of these before. I probably should have sent you to someone else."

He also noted, at that happy moment, that he had mistakenly given me nearly twice the dose suitable for my size, so the poison's drama might endure longer than predicted. I writhed on the floor. I called out for my distant grandmother.

No worm ever emerged from my mouth. I don't recall anything else. But when I found myself, nearly twenty years later, with ascarids again, I made sure I found a specialist who had broken bread with them on many occasions. ("Hon, you could just a' easily have picked these up on the streets o' San Antone as in the dark recesses o' Me-heeco.") Medicine had improved—now I downed two oblong pills and was done with it. "Is it true they could come out of my mouth?"

He laughed openly. "Hon, do you care? You want to get rid of them, right? Does a worm know which end is up and which is down? Your body's like a little hourglass and that sand goes any direction it can."

Doctors seem to be excessively fond of the metaphor. It disturbs me when I imagine they have used the same description to many other people. My body is one in a long line of bodies. It is also an hourglass, a vessel, an ocean, a brewing storm. Doctors repeat identical stories about other anonymous patients from one visit to another, forgetting they've told them to me before. I can never connect their stories to mine at all. The other patients seem idiotic, but their lives improved as soon as they took the doctor's advice. Even worse, I wonder if doctors are telling *my* story to them.

Our first years in Texas, my family was living from paycheck to paycheck, with me on the brink of college, when our father heard of the cheaper dental care available in Nuevo Laredo, a quick pop across the Mexican border. He took us all for a group excursion. I volunteered to be last.

As the *dentista,* exhausted by the tooth problems of the rest of my family, approached me in the chair with a set of supposedly sterilized instruments held upright in his hand (he had no assistant), he tripped on the edge of a rug and stabbed me deeply, right in the knee, with a silver pick.

Blood bubbled up through the perfect puncture wound.

I was wearing a dress I had recently finished stitching together in homemaking class. My teacher had been horrified when I refused to use matching buttons. The blot of blood grew on its hem, a symmetrical flower. I tipped my head and that room became a movie, *dentista* scrambling apologies, my father flustered, and outside the window, a man passing by with a colorful bouquet of elegantly crafted straw brooms.

Later I bought one. The brooms bore small wrapped swatches of red velvet at the place where the straw joined to the wood. I remember the elegant brooms exactly, but not the rest of the story about my teeth or my leg, which may have required a stitch or two. I like how memories have dissolved parts, neat as Alka-Seltzer in a bubbly glass.

So my father found an Anglo dentist in San Antonio who would swab our teeth with a piece of cotton and say he had cleaned them. Later this casual gentleman was indicted for trafficking cocaine.

Daren, our handsome long-haired neighbor, drove me back and forth to college for a year until he smashed my hand in the door of his van. He didn't mean to. I'd been watching him closely and he showed no particular interest in me of any kind. We were, in fact, on our way to visit a classmate at a hospital together when this happened, so I made a personal stop at the emergency room.

The doctors acted very gloomy. They wrapped my hand up tightly and had me return the following Monday to see an even gloomier group of hand specialists, who left long, doleful pauses between their words. "We will—need to—operate—and the recovery—will be—very—gradual. When—could you stand—to be without—the use of your right hand?" When? As soon as I found the world without dust in it, that was when. A tendon up the center of my hand had snapped, like a popped rubber band, and now made a hard, painful ball at the base of my middle finger.

My mother consulted her Edgar Cayce books (Association for Research and Enlightenment—we were active members in those days), which suggested numerous remedies. Castor oil compresses could be applied to the skin for injuries of tendon and bone and muscle. A small brown bottle cost $2.00 at the drugstore.

Why not? The anthem of the alternative. I attended the rest of my college semester with my hand bound tightly in flannel, a wad of cotton drenched in castor oil at the base of my middle finger. I grew used to the subtle, oily smell. And the knot dissolved. Maybe the tendon stretched out again, comfortably. Maybe it stitched itself back into place.

All I know is, when I returned to the specialists, they X-rayed my hand again and stared at me. It hadn't hurt for some time, but I thought I should see them once more since we had made a vague future date.

I am positive one of them used the word *miracle,* though he might have denied it the following moment.

The very instant I met the man I would marry, I felt I'd been struck hard over the head by a waitress's tray. We shared a lunch table. Right away I could tell he was a man to whom words like *miracle* would not appeal. This did not dissuade my interest. We get tired of ourselves very quickly.

About eight months after our wedding, we felt we were ready to have a baby.

We started "trying." Since elementary school, the phrase "try, try again" was a nemesis. What did it insinuate? You failed the first time, right? But people pretend it opens up the world.

While I was trying to have a baby, my world shrank. I kept my eyes fixed on the pregnant bellies of women at grocery stores. I envied, then hated them. I had nightmares about terrycloth bathrobes and barred slats of wooden cribs with no one inside. Having imagined conception would occur the very first time we invited it, I gradually realized my naïveté. When it didn't happen again and again for more than two years, my moods became dramatic. My steady friend never lost his faith and hope, but I lost mine on a daily basis.

I could have kept notebooks of the stupid things people say. I wrote to Ann Landers three times, but she never published my letters. A stranger asked, "So why don't you have a family yet? Too busy with your own little lives?"

Finally we visited specialists and had every test they could dream up. I had most of them. The great fear I had of anesthesia—being "put to sleep," being placed temporarily "out of mind"—far outweighed my concern over the laparoscopy I was about to undergo, so I was astonished to find myself happily swimming in rich blue water as the drug fed into my veins. The lap-lapping of waves licked the softened edges of my head as I sank into a warm sea. It was so *easy* to let go.

Perhaps insomniacs appreciate this sense of release more than others might, but one brief flirtation with anesthesia made a fan out of me. So when the next surgery rolled around—what was it they said they were going to do? Uncap my fallopian tubes, which were sealed like fountain pens? Pop the tight seed pod off the tangled stalk?—I asked hopefully, "Do I get to go to sleep?"

After the surgery, we "try, tried again," with renewed enthusiasm. But four more years passed with no results. I looked at the whole world differently by now. Frustration had become a palpable entity. The word *stress* sent me into a spin. I slammed my hand on the fertility expert's table. "Fertility drugs! Everyone else takes them, why can't I? I am not *just stressed out!* I used to be a very relaxed individual!"

His voice always sounded so intellectual, so mild. "They

won't help you. You *are* fertile. It's something else in your way and I don't know what. You remain among that small percentage of cases we can't figure out."

He charged a lot not to figure us out, and only prescribed one burst of fertility drugs to shut me up, but he was right—they did nothing. I felt chronically bereaved. I scared myself a few times in stores, imagining how easy it would be to grab a distracted mother's crying child and run. I couldn't believe how easily felonies were drifting into my mind.

Finally, far from home, I had tea with a couple whose son had been conceived naturally thirteen years after they started trying. "It's more than science, dear," the kind gentleman said, placing his hand over mine on the table. "Trust in this. There are mysterious elements at work here. I just want you to keep believing."

I can't say my belief quotient soared after that conversation, but something inside me settled down. I said to myself, "Okay, now what? If not that, what?" I went about my business.

Then a massage therapist offered a "special oil" as a gift. "What particular problem do you have? I'll give you something for that."

"Infertility." After six years I could say the unsavory word without tears welling up. She prescribed rosemary and melissa oil and told me to rub it on my belly before going to sleep.

The next week a friend who ran a natural foods restaurant appeared with a tiny bottle of herbal tincture called False Unicorn. It bore a fancy scientific name too, but the unicorn is what I remember. I've always been prejudiced against these creatures. I've told children in writing classes they could write poems about anything they like except TV or unicorns.

My friend asked, "Do you still want to have a baby? Well, put a few drops of this under your tongue every day. If you can't stand the taste, put the drops in tea. I just read about it and found some for you. Good luck!"

I can't say I felt terribly excited. I put the drops under my tongue for six days and vaguely rubbed my belly. We went off on a trip to Philadelphia and I forgot my rituals. Then strange things started happening. I ordered coffee in restaurants, but couldn't drink it when it came. I ran up a flight of stairs and swooned dizzily at the top.

After two more months of peculiarity—floods of compassion in airport lobbies, a sudden distaste for shrimp—I returned to my infertility expert, who, for the first time, grew animated. "I think you're pregnant! And I think you're almost at the end of the first trimester!"

Hadn't I noticed my loss of periods? Sort of. Did I tell him about the False Unicorn? No. Did the False Unicorn have anything to do with it? All I can say is—consider six years, then six days.

Pregnancy was terrific. I felt so inhabited and useful. I placed a pillow between my belly and the steering wheel. The world seemed gracious, filled with anticipation. Our son was delivered by an obstetrician so charismatic that if he had told us to wrap the boy in newspapers for the first forty-eight hours, I would have complied. He was the doctor I had always wanted to believe in. He was the guy who *knew his stuff.*

Later I contemplated why our process had taken so long. If we had had a baby years earlier, we would not have had *the same baby,* right? Even a month earlier, even a day. The one we ended up with, the luminous boy of well-shaped words, gleaming collector of lightbulbs and flashlights, was the one *just perfect for us.* Was his soul on hold? Did that herb simply allow the door hinge to swing open?

144

Since then, I have delivered bottles of False Unicorn to other people's doorsteps. While I have not heard of it working so thoroughly or quickly for anyone else I know, one friend swore it erased the PMS symptoms which had been plaguing her for years

San Antonio abounds with shrines, prayer *nichos,* and *milagros*—little metal charms of arms and legs and eyes and breasts and cars—pinned up by devotees at altars around town. Mother Mary is strung with expired driver's licenses. Little Saint Somebody stares out through a sea of school pictures, bent mug shots. A graffiti artist scrawls *Nothing is impossible* across the backs of bus benches all over town. I visit the Capilla de los Milagros (Chapel of Miracles) at the exact moment my mother's palm is sliced open for surgery and purchase a charm in the shape of a hand to pin up under the sober-looking Jesus. I touch his head, because I have seen everyone else doing it, and receive a potent electrical jolt. Either they have him hot-wired or it's a holy zap. At least I can have a sense that I have done something that invites the intervention of a power greater than my own.

We are very big on votive candles down here. Good thing there's an old-fashioned candle company selling seconds out of barrels right down the block. Sacks of cranberry and vanilla. I make shrines as centerpieces, with photos of friends who need good health. People stick stalks of fresh rosemary into one another's doors. We carry local oddities as gifts when we travel—little pouches, lottery candles in tall glass jars. When we spent a semester in Hawaii recently, I collected superstitions and remedies, just in case. I "never turned my back on the waves."

Immediately after Hawaii, our son and I travel to the West Bank so he can meet his Palestinian great-grandmother for what turns out to be the first and last time. Talk about startling transitions. One week we're basking on Kailua Beach in our baseball caps and the next we're wearing *keffiyahs* around our necks, skirting Israeli soldiers. "Why," my son asks in an Arab town, "do soldiers always stand with their guns in front of the drugstores? Are they going to fight the pills?" Obviously the drugstore is seen as a center of power. I don't get it.

At a hundred and six, my grandmother has grown weaker. Now we need to cure her instead of the other way around. But our powers are not as specific as hers used to be. One day I come to breakfast and someone remarks on the great red streak down my left cheek. I can feel it—as if I've been burned. It gets worse and worse. We leave her with much weeping as usual and a rare snow on the ground.

Back home I stare into mirrors. What's going on here? I visit a crazed dermatologist, the first of my life, who places me in a small rocket ship in his office and turns hot lights on me. My son, a *Star Trek* fan, is worried. "What is this?" I demand from inside. "I like to know what's being done to me!" The doctor doesn't answer questions.

The minute I step out of the cockpit, he sticks a giant needle into my left hip—without warning or explanation. "Cortisone," he mutters, when I pressure him. But he's given me such a bad shot I'll have a deep, ugly indentation in my hip for two years. I consider suing him. I forget his name.

The streak disappears for a month, then returns. I find another dermatologist who seems nervous when I say I would like to plant a fist in my last doctor's face. She says— politely—my skin looks very bad. "Could be skin lupus, need to do a biopsy." She slices into my cheek, removes a layered segment, and stitches it back together. I ask, "Could this have been caused by going from a very hot place straight to a very cold place?"

She looks mystified. A week later, her test results are inconclusive. She says a few fancy scientific words to name my streak. "I can't say what caused your problem. And I can't say it will ever be cured. But I think we should do a biopsy every year to check it." I scratch her name out of my book. The streak goes on and on. My friend in a wheelchair has said she gets sick of the question, "What happened to you?"

Then my parents give me a gift certificate to a skin clinic run by an Australian named Montserrat, who takes a quick look at my cheek and in a minute gives me the same fancy name I paid my second dermatologist hundreds of dollars to hear. "Sure, we can fix this," Montserrat says kindly. "No problem at all." I spend an hour and a half tipped back in her chair immersed in facial bliss—being cleaned, soothed, oiled, massaged, masked, etc. It's heaven. I leave with a sack of three special creams. The red streak vanishes immediately after this treatment and does not return.

Speaking Arabic

"Why, if I'm part Arab, can't I speak Arabic?" My son, age five, wanting to answer his cousin who calls him to follow her into the kitchen, where she shows him how she turns the pot of rice and eggplant over onto the silver tray. How the food slips out to stand up like a building. The sizzled pine nuts, poured over the top in a fine fragrant flourish. Then she carries it all on her head into the room where we sit, and we eat with forks from the same giant platter, which I have never gotten used to. The cousins and neighbors file in to say, "*Keef ha-lik?*"—How are you?— the door opening into a thousand rooms.

For months in America our son will be placing plates on his head. "This is how Janan would do it."

Why, if we're part anything, does it matter? I had to live in a mostly Mexican-American city to feel what it meant to be part Arab. It meant Take This Ribbon and Unwind It Slowly.

Why can't I forget the earnest eyes of the man who said to me in Jordan, "Until you speak Arabic, you will not understand pain"? Ridiculous, I thought. He went on, something to do with an Arab carrying sorrow in the back of the skull that only language cracks. A few words couldn't do it. A general passive understanding wasn't enough. At a neighborhood fair in Texas, somewhere between the German Oom-pah Sausage Stand and the Mexican Gorditas booth, I overheard a young man say to his friend, "I wish *I* had a heritage. Sometimes I feel—so lonely for one." And the tall American trees were dangling their thick branches right down over his head.

Maintenance

The only maid I ever had left messages throughout our house: *Lady as I was cleaning your room I heard a mouse and all the clothes in your closet fell down to the floor there is too many dresses in there take a few off. Your friend Marta Alejandro.* Sometimes I'd find notes stuck into the couch with straight pins. *I cannot do this room today bec. St. Jude came to me in a dream and say it is not safe.* Our darkroom was never safe because the devil liked dark places and also the enlarger had an eye that picked up light and threw it on Marta. She got sick and had to go to the doctor, who gave her green medicine that tasted like leaves.

Sometimes I'd come home to find her lounging in the bamboo chair on the back porch, eating melon, or lying on the couch with a bowl of half-melted ice cream balanced on her chest. She seemed depressed by my house. She didn't like the noise the vacuum made. Once she waxed the bathtub with floor wax. I think she was experimenting.

Each Wednesday I paid Marta ten dollars—that's what she asked for. When I raised it to eleven, then thirteen, she held the single dollars away from the ten as if they might contaminate it. She did not seem happy to get raises, and my friends (who paid her ten dollars each for the other days of the week) were clearly unhappy to hear about it. After a while I had recuperated from my surgery and could vacuum for myself again, so I found her a position with two gay men who lived in the neighborhood. She called once to say she liked them very much because mostly what they wanted her to do was shine. Shine?

"You know, silver. They have a lot of bowls. They have real beautiful spoons not like your spoons. They have a big circle tray that shines like the moon."

My friend Kathy had no maid and wanted none. She ran ten miles a day and lived an organized life. Once I brought her a gift—a blue weaving from Guatemala, diagonal patterns of thread on sticks—and she looked at it dubiously. "Give it to someone else," she said. "I really appreciate your thinking of me, but I try not to keep things around here." Then I realized how bare her mantel was. Who among us would fail to place *something* on a mantel? A few shelves in her kitchen also stood empty, and not the highest ones either.

Kathy had very definite methods of housekeeping. When we'd eat dinner with her she'd rise quickly, before dessert, to scrape each plate and place it in one side of her sink to soak. She had Tupperware containers already lined up for leftovers and a soup pan with suds ready for the silverware. If I tried to help she'd slap at my hand. "Take care of your own kitchen," she'd say, not at all harshly. After dessert she'd fold up the card table we'd just eaten on and place it against the wall. Dining rooms needed to be swept after meals, and a stationary table just made sweeping more difficult.

Kathy could listen to any conversation and ask meaningful questions. She always seemed to remember what anybody said—maybe because she'd left space for it. One day she described growing up in west Texas in a house of twelve children, the air jammed with voices, crosscurrents, floors piled with grocery bags, mountains of tossed-off clothes, toys, blankets, the clutter of her sisters' shoes. That's when she decided to have only one pair of shoes at any time, running shoes, though she later revised this to include a pair of sandals.

Somehow I understood her better then, her tank tops and wiry arms . . . she ran to shake off dust. She ran to leave it all behind.

Another friend, Barbara, lived in an apartment but wanted to live in a house. Secretly I loved her spacious domain, perched high above the city with a wide sweep of view, but I could understand the wish to plant one's feet more firmly on the ground. Barbara has the best taste of any person I've ever known—the best khaki-colored linen clothing, the best books, the name of the best masseuse. When I'm with her I feel uplifted, excited by life; there's so much to know about that I haven't heard of yet, and Barbara probably has. So I agreed to help her look.

We saw one house where walls and windows had been sheathed in various patterns of heavy brocade. We visited another where the kitchen had been removed because the owners only ate in restaurants. They had a tiny office refrigerator next to their bed which I peeked into after they'd left the room: orange juice in a carton, coffee beans. A Krups coffeemaker on the sink in their bathroom. They seemed unashamed, shrugging, "You could put a new kitchen wherever you like."

Then we entered a house that felt unusually vivid, airy, and hard to define until the realtor mentioned, "Have you noticed there's not a stick of wood anywhere in this place?

No wood furniture, not even a wooden salad bowl, I'd bet. These people—very hip, you'd like them—want wood to stay in forests. The man says wood makes him feel heavy."

Barbara and her husband bought that house—complete with pear-shaped swimming pool, terraces of pansies, plum trees, white limestone rock gardens lush with succulents—but they brought wood into it. I felt overly conscious of their wooden cutting boards. I helped them unpack, stroking the sanded ebony backs of African animals.

After about a year and a half, Barbara called to tell me they were selling the house. "You won't believe this," she said, "but we've decided. It's the maintenance—the yardmen, petty things always breaking—I'm so busy assigning chores I hardly have time for my own work anymore. A house really seems ridiculous to me now. If I want earth I can go walk in the park."

I had a new baby at the time and everything surprised me. My mouth dropped open, oh yes. I was living between a mound of fresh cloth diapers and a bucket of soiled ones, but I agreed to participate in the huge garage sale Barbara was having.

"That day," Barbara said later, "humanity sank to a new lowest level." We had made signs declaring the sale would start at 9 A.M.—but by 8 o'clock, middle-aged women and men were already ripping our boxes open, lunging into the back of my loaded pickup truck to see what I had. Two women argued in front of me over my stained dish drainer. I sold a kerosene heater which we'd never lit and a stack of my great-uncle's rumpled doilies. One woman flashed a charm with my initial on it under my nose, saying, "I'd think twice about selling this, sweetheart—don't you realize it's ten-carat?"

Afterward we counted our wads of small bills and felt drained, diluted. We had spent the whole day bartering in a driveway, releasing ourselves from the burden of things we did not need. We even felt disgusted by the thought of eating—yet another means of accumulation—and would derive no pleasure from shopping, or catalogs, for at least a month.

While their new apartment was being refurbished, Barbara and her husband lived in a grand hotel downtown. She said it felt marvelous to use all the towels and have fresh ones appear on the racks within hours. Life seemed to regain its old recklessness. Soon they moved back to the same windswept apartment building they'd left, but to a higher floor. Sometimes I stood in their living room staring out at the horizon, which always seemed flawlessly clean.

My mother liked to sing along to records while she did housework—Mahalia Jackson, the Hallelujah Chorus. Sometimes we would sing duets, "Tell Me Why" and "Nobody Knows the Trouble I've Seen." I felt lucky my mother was such a clear soprano. We also sang while preparing for the big dinners my parents often gave, while folding the napkins or decorating plates of *hummos* with olives and radishes.

I hungrily savored the tales told by the guests, the wild immigrant fables and metaphysical links. My mother's favorite friend, a rail-thin vegetarian who had once been secretary to Aldous Huxley, conversed passionately with a Syrian who was translating the Bible from Aramaic, then scolded me for leaving a mound of carrots on my plate.

"I'm not going to waste them!" I said. "I always save carrots for last because I love them best."

I thought this would please her, but she frowned. "Never save what you love, dear. You know what might happen? You may lose it while you are waiting."

It was difficult to imagine losing the carrots—what were they going to do, leap off my plate?—but she continued.

"Long ago I loved a man very much. He had gone on a far journey—our relationship had been delicate—and I waited anxiously for word from him. Finally a letter arrived and I stuffed it into my bag, trembling, thinking I would read it later on the train. Would rejoice in every word, was what I thought, but you know what happened? My purse was snatched away from me—stolen!—before I boarded the train. Things like that didn't even happen much in those days. I never saw the letter again—and I never saw my friend again either."

A pause swallowed the room. My mother rose to clear the dishes. Meaningful glances passed. I knew this woman had never married. When I asked why she hadn't written him to say she'd lost the letter, she said, "Don't you see, I also lost the only address I had for him."

I thought about this for days. Couldn't she have tracked him down? Didn't she know anyone else who might have known him and forwarded a message? I asked my mother, who replied that love was not easy.

Later my mother told me about a man who had carried a briefcase of important papers on a hike because he was afraid they might get stolen from the car. The trail wove high up the side of a mountain, between strands of majestic piñon. As he leaned over a rocky gorge to breathe the fragrant air, his fingers slipped and the briefcase dropped down into a narrow crevasse. They heard it far below, clunking into a deep underground pool. My mother said the man fell to the ground and sobbed.

The forest ranger whistled when they brought him up to the spot. "Hell of an aim!" He said there were some lost things you just had to say good-bye to, "like a wedding ring down a commode." My parents took the man to Western Union so he could telegraph about the lost papers, and the clerk said, "Don't feel bad, every woman drops an earring down a drain once in her life." The man glared. "This was not an earring—*I am not a woman.*"

I thought of the carrots, and the letter, when I heard his story. And of my American grandparents' vintage furniture, sold to indifferent buyers when I was still a child, too young even to think of antique wardrobes or bed frames. I also thought of another friend of my parents, Peace Pilgrim, who walked across the United States for years, lecturing about inner peace and world peace. A single broad pocket in her tunic contained all her worldly possessions: a toothbrush, a few postage stamps, a ballpoint pen. She had no bank account behind her and nothing in storage. Her motto was "I walk till given shelter, I fast till given food." My father used to call her a freeloader behind her back, but my mother recognized a prophet when she saw one. I grappled with the details. How would it help humanity if I slept in a cardboard box under a bridge?

Peace Pilgrim told a story about a woman who worked hard so she could afford a certain style of furniture—French provincial, I think. She struggled to pay for insurance to protect it and rooms large enough to house it. She worked so much she hardly ever got to sit on it. "Then her life was over. And what kind of life was that?"

Peace Pilgrim lived so deliberately she didn't even have colds. Shortly before her death in a car accident—for years she hadn't even ridden in cars—she sat on the foldout bed in our living room, hugging her knees. I was grown by then, but all our furniture still came from thrift stores. She invited me to play the piano and sing for her, which I did, as she stared calmly around the room. "I loved to sing as a child," she said. "It *is* nice to have a piano."

In my grandmother's Palestinian village, the family has accumulated vast mounds and heaps of woolly comforters, stacking them in great wooden cupboards along the walls. The blankets wear coverings of cheerful gingham, but no family—not even our huge one on the coldest night—could possibly use that many. My grandmother smiled when I asked her about them. She said people should have many blankets and headscarves to feel secure.

I took a photograph of her modern refrigerator, bought by one of the emigrant sons on a visit home from America, unplugged in a corner and stuffed with extra yardages of cloth and old magazines. I felt like one of those governmental watchdogs who asks, how do you feel knowing your money is being used this way? My grandmother seemed nervous whenever we sat near the refrigerator, as if a stranger who refused to say his name had entered the room.

I never felt women were more doomed to housework than men; I thought women were lucky. Men had to maintain questionably pleasurable associations with less tangible elements—mortgage payments, fan belts and alternators, the IRS. I preferred sinks, and the way people who washed dishes immediately became exempt from after-dinner conversation. I loved to plunge my hands into tubs of scalding bubbles. Once my father reached in to retrieve something and reeled back, yelling, "Do you always make it this hot?" My parents got a dishwasher as soon as they could, but luckily I was out of college by then and never had to touch it. To me it only seemed to extend the task. You rinse, you bend and arrange, you measure soap—and it hasn't even started yet. How many other gratifications were as instant as the old method of washing dishes?

But it's hard to determine how much pleasure someone else gets from addiction to a task. The neighbor woman who spends hours pinching off dead roses and browned lilies, wearing her housecoat and dragging a hose, may be as close as she comes to bliss, or she may be feeling utterly miserable. I weigh her sighs, her monosyllables about weather. Endlessly I compliment her yard. She shakes her head—"It's a lot of work." For more than a year she tries to get her husband to dig out an old stump at one corner but finally gives up and plants bougainvillea in it. The vibrant splash of pink seems to make her happier than anything else has in a long time.

Certain bylaws: If you have it, you will have to clean it. Nothing stays clean long. No one else notices your messy house as much as you do; they don't know where things are supposed to go anyway. It takes much longer to clean a house than to mess it up. Be suspicious of any cleaning agent (often designated with a single alphabetical letter, like C or M) that claims to clean everything from floors to dogs. Never install white floor tiles in the bathroom if your family members have brown hair. Cloth diapers eventually make the best rags—another reason beyond ecology. Other people's homes have charisma, because you don't have to know them inside out. If you want high ceilings you may have to give up closets. (Still, as a neighbor once insisted to me, "high ceilings make you a better person.") Be wary of vacuums with headlights; they burn out in a month. A broom, as one of my starry-eyed newlywed sisters-in-law once said, *does a lot*. So does a dustpan. Whatever you haven't touched, worn, or eaten off in a year should be passed on; something will pop up immediately to take its place.

I can't help thinking about these things—I live in the same town where Heloise lives. And down the street, in a shed behind his house, a man produces orange-scented wood moisturizer containing beeswax. You rub it on three times, let it sit, then buff it off. Your house smells like a hive in an orchard for twenty-four hours.

I'd like to say a word, just a short one, for the background hum of lesser, unexpected maintenances that can devour a day or days—or a life, if one is not careful. The scrubbing of the little ledge above the doorway belongs in this category, along with the thin lines of dust that quietly gather on bookshelves in front of the books. It took me an hour working with a bent wire to unplug the bird feeder, which had become clogged with fuzzy damp seed—no dove could get a beak in. And who would ever notice? The doves would notice. I am reminded of Buddhism whenever I undertake one of these invisible tasks: one acts, without any thought of reward or foolish notion of glory.

Perhaps all cleaning products should be labeled with additional warnings, as some natural-soap companies have taken to philosophizing right above the price tag. Bottles of guitar polish might read: "If you polish your guitar, it will not play any better. People who close their eyes to listen to your song will not see the gleaming wood. But you may feel more intimate with the instrument you are holding."

Sometimes I like the preparation for maintenance, the motions of preface, better than the developed story. I like to move all the chairs off the back porch many hours before I sweep it. I drag the mop and bucket into the house in the morning even if I don't intend to mop until dusk. This is related to addressing envelopes months before I write the letters to go inside.

Such extended prefacing drives my husband wild. He comes home and can read the house like a mystery story— small half-baked clues in every room. I get out the bowl for the birthday cake two days early. I like the sense of the house as a still life, on the road to becoming. Why rush to finish? You will only have to do it over again, sooner. I keep a proverb from Thailand above my towel rack: "*Life is so short / we must move very slowly.*" I believe what it says.

My father was furious with me when, as a teenager, I impulsively answered a newspaper ad and took a job as a maid. A woman, bedfast with a difficult pregnancy, ordered me to scrub, rearrange, and cook—for a dollar an hour. She sat propped on pillows, clicking her remote control, glaring suspiciously whenever I passed her doorway. She said her husband liked green Jell-O with fresh fruit. I was slicing peaches when the oven next to me exploded, filling the house with heavy black smoke. The meat loaf was only half baked. She shrieked and cried, blaming it on me, but how was I responsible for her oven?

It took me a long time to get over my negative feelings about pregnant women. I found a job scooping ice cream and had to wrap my swollen wrists in heavy elastic bands because they hurt so much. I had never considered what ice cream servers went through.

These days I wake up with good intentions. I pretend to be my own maid. I know the secret of travelers: each time you leave your home with a few suitcases, books, and note pads, your maintenance shrinks to a lovely tiny size. All you need to take care of is your own body and a few changes of clothes. Now and then, if you're driving, you brush the pistachio shells off the seat. I love ice chests and miniature bottles of shampoo. Note the expansive breath veteran travelers take when they feel the road spinning open beneath them again.

Somewhere close behind me the outline of Thoreau's small cabin plods along, a ghost set on haunting. It even has the same rueful eyes Henry David had in the portrait in his book. A wealthy woman with a floral breakfast nook once told me I would "get over him" but I have not—documented here, I have not.

Marta Alejandro, my former maid, now lives in a green outbuilding at the corner of Beauregard and Madison. I saw her recently, walking a skinny wisp of a dog, and wearing a bandanna around her waist. I called to her from my car. Maybe I only imagined she approached me reluctantly. Maybe she couldn't see who I was.

But then she started talking as if we had paused only a second ago. "Oh hi, I was very sick, were you? The doctor said it has to come to everybody. Don't think you can escape! Is your house still as big as it used to be?"

TROUBLED LAND

Tulips

I used to think rocks were important. When I was small, I spent whole evenings in the driveway, lining rocks into paths. Sometimes when my father drove in and out, the tires of our Buick would straddle my roadways and leave them intact. The next day I'd be out there again, placing headless acorns at revised intersections. I popped the caps off before I used them. Who can say why we did what we did?

We lived in a square white house with green shutters. My father had grown up on the other side of the earth in a house made of stones. Stones were big rocks, but related. Our next-door neighbors were a quiet family whose only son turned out to be a dwarf. In those days, we thought he was just short. He would stand on his side of the fence and I would stand on my side and we would have conversations. His mother stayed in the house doing secret motherly things. My mother played the piano. Doors and windows open, her music traveled the air. Sometimes I would be far away playing with my best friend Marcia, who later became an unwed mother, and my own mother's piano would drift down the block through the trees, a few clear notes. I thought we were lucky even when we were not lucky and I knew the future had something in store for everybody.

Tulips grew in our yard. Each spring their fat buds on incredibly slim, straight stalks lined the sidewalk. You could predict them, like cherry blossoms or redbuds; they were one of those things that came back.

Miraculously, on the same day, they would all open in radiant waves of yellow and red. I was convinced they spoke in the night, made pacts, did all the things people do to make decisions. Not like the iris, which took turns floating their silken heads, the tulips were a unanimous lot. What they did, they did together.

Quickly I forgot my rocks and concentrated on tulips. Their stalks so smooth, a pure pale green like the color I used up first in all my paint boxes. Tulips nodded gracefully when the wind blew. I loved the secret parts of them sticking up inside the petals. We never cut them or took them indoors and every year there seemed to be more crowding upward. I would weed out the soft grasses that grew too close to their leaves.

My mother was trying to teach me "perspective" and had me draw the tulips a hundred times on cheap white paper. Nothing is flat, she would say. Everything has a depth to it. Later I would stare at the house. I would think, the house is flat. Then someone would walk out the door and I would catch a glimpse of the living room, lamp and painting, and think, she is right. A house, to be a house, had to have insides. People had curves and shadows, and what about a rock? On our front porch sat a huge rock which my mother had chiseled into a woman's head. There was no end to what could be done with things.

One evening I sat in the front yard reading a book about Babar the Elephant King. Already I had made a song about him. Maybe I would not be a writer or an artist, maybe I would make up songs. A car rolled slowly past. It was plump and brown, like the cars we had in the world in those days. A mother and father sat in the front seat. Three small faces peered out of the back. They were taking a drive, like we sometimes took on Sundays. After they passed our house, the car paused and slowly backed up.

In front of our driveway, the man climbed out. He walked toward the tulips smiling, arms spread wide. "These are the most beautiful tulips in St. Louis!" he proclaimed. "The most beautiful tulips I ever saw! The most beautiful tulips there ever will be!"

He looked and waited. I should have said, "Thank you," but my mouth wouldn't open. He went back to his car and drove slowly away.

I ran into the house. I wanted to tell my mother what had happened, but instead I was crying. Something new and strange had lodged inside me, something that could never be said, even if I repeated his words exactly, something that feared the man was right.

Pablo Tamayo

Pablo Tamayo is moving today, to stay with his brother-in-law on Nueces Street till he can find another house. "Don't worry so much," he told me over the fence. "I'm a beat-up man, my wife is an old lady, I always told you the roof was gonna fall."

That's wrong. He never mentioned the roof. He used to call on the telephone and say in a gruff voice, "Who's there?" as if I'd called him. When I stuttered, he'd laugh and say, "This is me, I'm standing on your roof," but he never mentioned it falling.

I want to give him eggs, a flannel shirt. I want to tell him this neighborhood will be a vacuum without him. To go back to the beginning, making a catalog of his utterances since the day we met over the bamboo that divides our yards. I was standing on a ladder with clippers, trying to tell the bamboo who was boss. In the next yard he stooped over a frizzy dog, murmuring Spanish consolations. He looked like he might once have been a wrestler. "So," he said, looking up. "You're pretty tall, I guess." I told him I was his new neighbor and he said he was my old one. He pointed, "Look at how I put this eyeball back in my dog."

Once his dog had a fight with a German shepherd. Pablo came running to find the eyeball dangling on its string. He called a doctor, the doctor said twenty dollars at least. "So I do it myself. Good job, no?" The eye was now glassy white. It looked like it had been put in backwards. "My dog goes with me to Junior's Lounge," he said, giggling. You don't expect giggles from a man with tattoos. He told me welcome to the neighborhood, it's a nice neighborhood, I been here Forty, you know, Years. Throwing his head back when he spoke, like somebody proud and practiced, or kicking up dust, looking down like a kid, a brand-new kid.

Later I found myself wondering about him. What made this man act so happy? His house tilted, his wife had no teeth. We invited them for dinner, but they wouldn't come. "She don't like to chew without teeth in public." His car had not run in twenty weeks. Where was his history, what was his life?

"I was born in Mexico, like half the people in this town. They get born, they go north. Like birds or something." One night he showed me their wedding pictures. Such devastating changes the years make! From a shining silken couple, a future of roses, to a house of orange crates and dead newspapers, a shuffling duet of slippers and beans. "I love another girl first, her daddy was rich. He told her never marry a baker." His face goes dark for a moment. "Sometimes I still think of that. There was a rooster who rode on my shoulder but one day he changed, you know, he bit me on the leg." When Pablo speaks of the village in the mountains south of Monterrey, he stops smiling, as if those memories are a cathedral which can only be entered with a sober face.

The next day I ask him when he bought this house. "Aw, I never did. They wanted me to, in 1939. But I didn't like to pay so much money all at once, so I just keep payin' forty dollars a month till now." I want to shake him. Who is his landlord? "A bad, bad man. Once I had a good man but they change over the years. This guy, he won't fix the pipe, he won't paint the outside. I want to paint it, but he won't let me. What color do you think I could paint it?"

We stand back to examine the peeling boards.

"Beige."

Three days later he knocks at my door. "I just want to ask you. Is that the color of coffee with milk in it?"

His wife speaks no English and loves to wash. She wears a faded apron, veteran of a thousand washtubs. She sews rickrack along the edges of everything. I can imagine her getting up in the mornings and going straight to her sewing machine. In a cage outside her back door lives a featherless bird named Pobrecito. Pablo found it on Sweet Street, hobbling. She feeds it scraps of melon and bread.

Around her telephone she has pinned an arc of plastic lilies, postcards of saints, a rosary of black beads. Who is she hoping will call? If Jesus were to manifest for her in modern ways—*Buenos días!* She would say. *Mi casita, mi perrito, mi Pobrecito, mi Jesús.* I have a garage sale and she buys my battered hiking boots. Where is she planning to go?

After much prodding, Pablo tells me they have three children. Two are in their fifties, live in Houston or somewhere. "Naw, I don't see them, they don't see me." One is twenty. Pablo and his wife are more than seventy so that means she had the boy when she was fifty, at least. I ask him about this and he says he guesses it's true. Months later I hear another story from the widow down the street. The twenty-year-old is a grandson. She says, "Pablo lies."

When the boy comes home he turns on rock and roll so loud the candles quiver on our piano. His hair is longer than my hair. Pablo says, "He's had bad luck. Got married too young, seventeen, something like that, to a girl born north of the border. That means she's lazy. It's true. If a Mexican is born north of the border, her husband will walk the road of tears. So they broke up. Bad luck."

Months later, after numerous references to the road of tears, I ask Pablo for details. You mean to tell me all the smooth-faced innocent-hearted Mexican girls in local high schools are going to have husbands who walk the road of tears? C'mon Pablo, find your way out of that one. He looks at me, puzzled. And then his face cracks into its goofy grin. "I got it," he says. "They'll all get boats."

He asks what I do, why I'm always in this house chattering away on my typing machine. "I write things down," I say.

"Like what things?"

"Like little things that happen."

He looks around, shrugs. "I don't see nothin' happenin'." Then he goes indoors to make me a perfect pie. Pablo understands pie crust. For him poetry is the fluted edge of dough. And Pablo is the only one who will ever understand the delicate grammar of the engine of his car. There was no fuel pump in the city, he said dramatically, that would fit it. So he was building a contraption of wire and soup cans, like a child's telephone. He was going to communicate with his car.

One day, after nearly a month of tinkering, I heard the engine cough, choke, exhale a huge sigh. And there was Pablo passing my house, waving madly, his one-eyed dog perched in the back window. Ten minutes later he was back. There was a problem—the car could only go as far as the amount of gas the can would hold. But it *worked* now. That was the important thing, it worked. One night I dreamed that wings sprouted where the dented door handles were and Pablo went flying over the city, sending down lines of symbolic verse.

He said he would get another "Alamo seed" so I could

have a tree like the one in his yard. He said he was tired of the mud out back, he had this plan for grass. "I used to drink more beers," he said, "than any man with a mouth." That was when he worked at the hotel, when he came home with cinnamon in his cuffs. Some days now he still journeyed out to work, dressed in a square white baker's shirt, to cafeterias or hospitals to "fill in" someone's absence. "I made thirty-five dozen doughnuts today," he'd say, folding his craggy hands, shaking his head. "I don't want to be like the man who killed himself in your bathroom." This was news to me. *What man?*

Then Pablo looked worried; he'd slipped, he'd said too much. "Aw come on, I was joking, let's go hammer the fence, aye-yi-yi." He got shy sometimes, his words blurred. *What man?* And he told me his name. Howard Riley. Spoken slowly, How-ard Ri-ley, as if the name had grown longer in Pablo's head.

"He was an old man, kinda old, you know, oh what the hell, everybody's old. You're kinda old. He was old a little sooner than I was. He used to hit a golf ball in the yard, that end, this end, that end, this end. I hear this little tick, you know, like the clock, the little sound it made. But one day he went in your bathroom and shot his own head. Pow! (Finger to head.) I was at the bank. I came home with ten dollars and my wife, she said, Howard's dead. In Spanish, you know. So I went over to see him and he was gone already. They came in a car and took him. I just went to the bank! I used to think of him at night when the nuts fell on the roof. Tick, tick, tick."

"Why did he do it?"

A shrug. "I dunno. He was tired. He had nothin' else to do." Pablo stared down at his two big feet. "So let's go hammer the fence, I get the hammer, you get the nails."

Months later, on the same day I was watching him busy

at work in his yard at 7 A.M., wearing a blue-and-white checkered jockey cap, dragging a tin pail of cilantro from one mudcrease to the next, that day his faceless landlord appeared and told him they had two weeks to get gone. After forty-eight years, two weeks. Pablo came to me with the same expression my father had on the day he had to fire twelve lifetime printers from the newspaper because they were being replaced by computers.

"We gotta move."

The little dog running in circles, sniffing the ground. Another fall, pecans splitting their dull-green pods in the grass. A pumpkin pie still warm in my hands. How many pies had Pablo given us? Maybe a hundred, maybe more. Lots of times we gave them away. We don't like pie too much. But we'd keep them out on the table a while, on a small pedestal, like a shrine.

"This one's good."

He'd always say it. "This one's good." Forget any other one. Pablo in the yard with a ragged tea towel on his arm, hands outstretched.

"What do you mean, move?"

His landlord wanted to build an office. I was yelling about zoning while his wife unpinned the rosary from its wall, felt the cool black beads move again in her fingers.

"You know, he might make a parking lot here where the Alamo tree is." This year the tree had had eighteen leaves. From that seed Pablo found in a gutter. We joked so much when it came up, ugly stick. Not one leaf for months. Then he put small twigs around it like a barricade, tied them with string, little red flags, and it started doing things. His voodoo tree. Smack in the center of the yard.

I wanted to meet this goddamn landlord immediately. Where had he gone? What kind of office? With filing cabinets and dictaphones and secretaries' shiny legs? Obviously they wouldn't fit in this tilt-a-whirl house; they'd flatten it out, 'doze it under. Pablo's crooked stove. The ancient valentine heart tacked to the porch. From whom to whom? Gruff voice. "Me to the lady."

He stood there in his yard which was slipping out from under him, he stood there with hips cocked, plaid shirt half-buttoned, his hair still full on his head, and said, "I wanna tell you somethin'." That always meant, come a little closer, put down your groceries. "You know this world we got here?" He motioned with his arms. "Lemme tell you, this world don't love us. It don't think about us or pray for us or miss us, you know what I mean? That's what I learned when my father died. I was a young man. I got up the next day and went outside, feelin' sick, my face still fat from cryin'. And there was the sky. Lookin' just the same. Dead or alive, it don't matter. Still the sky. So then I started lookin' around and there was still the flowers, still the bugs, I mean *the bugs,* who cares about bugs? My father was dead and the world didn't miss him. The world didn't know his name! Ventura—Morales—Tamayo—but *I knew it.* And I say to myself, That's all we got! I know it, the barber know it, so what? This don't make me feel more bad, you know, it make me feel—better. Aw, I dunno, I gotta go find a box."

Hours later he's coming down Sheridan Street pushing a box in front of him, a giant box, like the boxes washing machines come in. He's done this before. I never knew what he did with those boxes. They went in the door and disappeared. He doesn't have a fireplace. Inside his wife is taking down the sweaters. They have the smell of sunlight in them. She's had them out on those poles and ropes so many times they're a little confused today. Now they're going someplace else. She's shufflin' around and he's shufflin' around, taking down calendars, rolling up the years. God knows where the boy is when they need him. Pablo probably rolls up his Marijuana Boogie poster without even reading it.

Once he said, "When you die, you die."

"Oh yeah? That's very interesting."

Then we were laughing ridiculously on our two sides of the fence.

Can I translate this great philosophy so it applies to now? "When you move, you move." Simple. Throw up the hands. Still we're very upset in our house. The sky doesn't know it, but we know it. The news comes on the television. I go out back. There is no other news.

The World and All Its Teeth

I'm very worried when I see the boy from my writing workshop, gloomy Chico Lopez, strolling down St. Mary's Street with Julio, who used to live next door. This looks like a bad connection. They're talking busily with their heads together, carrying sacks. I've never seen Chico look so animated before. Is it just that we don't ever expect to see people from our classes out in the world? I'm still troubled when I order a taco at El Valle and Irene from Smith Elementary School brings it to me. Wasn't she the girl who was going to go to the moon?

Then I run into Julio's grandpa Pablo Tamayo in the grocery store ten minutes later and we fall upon one another, kissing both cheeks, and his face, which smells like sweat and dogs, even smells sweet to me.

"Guess who I just saw," I say, but he answers, "Kiss her too," thumbing toward Elena, and I bump heads with Elena, who is lifting the bags of groceries into their two-wheeled cart, which they will drag home through the blazing streets. They both look thinner, as if their strands have been stretched. A big black bruise marks his left cheek and he strokes it. He says he fell down the steps by the river. He says it doesn't hurt. "But I been lookin' for you. That day I fell down, I was gonna come over to your house. I need some—help."

I tell Elena in my mixed-up Spanish that her lady friends keep knocking on our door, looking for her. They want the woman who reads the cards and I point them back toward City Street. Elena nods, but that doesn't mean anything—she always nods. We did not know she had a reputation as a *curandera* and reader of cards until they moved two blocks away and her clients in their long white cars started coming to our house looking for her. Michael used to think those cars were social workers, but I didn't believe it. A social worker would have done something for them long ago. I found a sack of faded *Lotería* cards thrown on the heap of trash left in their backyard after they moved.

La Chalupa, the woman in the rosy canoe. El Venado, the poised deer. I took them home and spread them on our front porch to air out the smell of dog.

Today I say, "Stick around five minutes in front of the store and I'll drive you." He shakes his head at me like Naw, Naw, but I know they'll be out there. I race around the store grabbing cilantro, tomatillos, a single poblano pepper. In the car he will peek into my bag and laugh. "You know what to do with all that?"

We used to close the windows on one side of our house to keep the stench of their house, the powerful doggy waves, from drifting over. Their house smelled stronger even than pork chops cooking. You wouldn't think people could stand it. Maybe living inside, they grew immune. Once Pablo left his cracked jacket lying on our couch and it took two days to get the smell out. Maybe if you loved dogs you wouldn't notice. Later our windows had nails in the corners to pin them tight against burglars and the odor seemed farther away. It was said Pablo sold dogs that were not his own. Some mornings a dog might be tied to a tree and by afternoon it would be gone. I asked him once, "Where did you get that fluffy gray dog?" and he said, "From someone who didn't need it."

"But Pablo, that's not right!" and he wagged his finger at me.

"Right, right, since when have things been right?"

I was just as curious about his customers. With all the loose dogs wandering around downtown, who needed to buy one?

We missed so many little things after they moved. We missed the way Pablo stood in his front yard pointing the hose toward his one big tree, whistling. He stood and stood, water coming out in a tiny stream. When I asked why he didn't turn the hose on harder, he stared at me. "For what?" He said trees didn't like to drink too fast. He had the patience of a porch swing, just hanging there, waiting.

I missed his lit-up face when I'd take over bowls of chili or soup. He couldn't believe our chili tasted so good without any meat in it. "I heard of chili without beans, but no meat?" He held his spoon of chili up to the light and shook his head. He said we were strange. I even missed the three red flannel shirts he wore on top of one another when the first northers blew through.

You would think, because of the criminal Julio who lived with Pablo and Elena, we could not have been such good friends. At first Julio just seemed like a bum who sat on the porch and drank beer with his shirt off and his tattoos blaring and his ponytail down to his waist. Later our lawn mower and bicycles vanished and the muddy footprints led straight from our garage to Pablo's back steps. Then our VCR and jumble of video tapes disappeared from our bedroom and we offered Julio a reward to get them back for us. He said, "I'll do what I can," without blinking. A few days later he returned to say sorry, they were too far gone already.

Another day I glanced casually into his messy bedroom to see one of my very own Portuguese coffee cups sitting on his dresser. Where did he get it?

For years I thought he was their grandson. I argued with people in the neighborhood. Alma Vasquez said, "Grandson my foot." Finally when Pablo came to us waving his census form, asking for assistance, he had to explain. If he had adopted the criminal as a baby years ago, the criminal would still be his son, yes? He wished it weren't true.

After they married, Elena wanted somebody to put little white clothes on. They hoped and hoped, but no baby came. Then Pablo met a pregnant teenager who gave them her baby. Even as he spoke so many years later, the element of invention remained distinct. You could almost feel him pulling tiny threads out of the air.

"I thought"—and here Pablo put his head in his hands and stared down at the wood of the table—"I thought it would all be different."

Sometimes he mentioned that Julio was on his back. Once he came and cried in our living room. He kept asking, "Can't you get him in jail?" He always thought that because we had been to college and read books, we might have some power.

I called the police department and spoke with a detective. "We have someone—uh—in our neighborhood who everyone including his father—uh—knows is doing bad things. He doesn't work but he always has money. He sits on his front porch drinking beer from a large bottle in a paper sack at 10 A.M. watching everybody come and go. By the time we get home our screens have been slit and our doors chiseled open. He has been seen selling VCRs at La

Paloma Lounge. The owner says she's afraid to call the police. Personally I think she's making a little off the side. The Paletta women at the end of the block say he used to peep through the windows at them when he was just a little boy. To see them in their underwear. We are talking bad news here, sir, major bad news, and no one knows what to do."

I wish I could have taken the Richter scale measurement of that detective's sigh.

He said the usual. He said, "We have to catch him doing it."

A hundred pieces of Sunday newspaper blew down the street.

We never caught him, but when he felt we were looking harder, things stopped happening. Maybe they happened in neighborhoods we couldn't see. Then Pablo came to say they all had to move out because their landlord was going to fix the house up and sell it. We were sad to lose Pablo and Elena, but glad about Julio. They'd found a little garage house behind a bigger house on the next street. It was the color of a peach. He didn't know if he liked the idea of a house the color of a peach.

"But you'll have the river right at your back window."

"What did the river ever do for me?"

They're waiting in front of the grocery store. I drive them home and Elena keeps shuffling her legs in the front seat and snorting. "You have a *lot* of friends," I say to her in Spanish. "The big car ladies." Pablo says he hates their house, it's too hot. Everywhere is hot. Ten years ago I stopped saying the word, at least during the summer. It felt redundant. Pablo says, "I'm coming over to talk to you." He asks about Michael and the baby and where is the baby anyhow? I say he's at the house with Michael because it's too—hot—to bring him out.

Then I reluctantly attend my own writing workshop at the West Side Food Bank. Somehow these people received funding to slap a poetry group in between their slices of white bread and bologna and their bean and cheese tacos. I was so shocked when they called to invite me to conduct it, I said yes. Now I'm stuck. We have six weeks to go.

So Chico arrives with his SPURS hat on backwards and Felice in a see-through blouse with a stiff lacy push-up bra underneath. I think she's fourteen. And Arturo won't ever sit at the picnic table outside with us, but has to sit way off by himself on a ledge by the trash can. Because of Arturo, thank you very much, I have to speak at a high-decibel level at all times. He doesn't want anyone to look at his paper. And Sergio without any paper or pencil ever and Ricky Gray Eagle who turned his face away when I said I liked his name and Marisela who really *loves* poetry and wrote a stark narrative about borrowing a clove of garlic from her neighbor for her mother. And Leo with his limpid dark eyes and smooth brown jaw. I would probably have dreamed of kissing him in high school. And three elementary kids who somehow got jumbled in with the rest of them.

I say to Chico, "I saw you with my ex-neighbor Julio the other day, are you friends with him?" and he says, "Aw miss, don't go messing in my private business okay?"

So I say nothing more. About that. Directly. But later when I'm talking about dignity as regards somebody's grandfather in somebody's poem, I'm looking at Chico out the corner of my eye hoping he applies it to the people he's hanging with. It's easy to see how anyone can go down the tubes.

This Tuesday they ask me to sign some schooly-looking documents vouching that I've really seen them. I say, "What are these?" It turns out my class was offered in the beginning as a trade-off for lingering detentions. I feel like mayonnaise. I feel like Little Debbie twinkie cakes.

But their hard-won sweaty sentences make up for it. I show them how to break their lines. Their hearts are already broken.

"My grandfather loved me / he really liked me too. / He gave me a ring of silver / to wrap around my dream. / He gave me a story / the size of six horses and three sheep. / He kissed me when I went to sleep. / I felt the smell of roses / circling my pillow. / He said he would always be here / but he's not. / He got shot."

Then they all want to write about someone being shot. And the worst thing is, they all know somebody.

Later I'm reading their papers on the couch at home and writing little hopeful notes in the margins when the big knocking comes at the front door, boom, boom, boom, the way Pablo always does it, and Michael answers. Pablo staggers into our front hallway and falls against the wall. This is wrong. This man used to be a boxer. He carried trays of fresh doughnuts high above his head.

"Help me move," he whispers, "into the housing where old people live."

We help him to the couch.

I bring lemonade. His sweat is dripping.

Michael says, "Someone hit you. Someone beat you up. Where did they hit you?" and Pablo points everywhere, head, shoulders, arms, stomach, legs.

"It was Julio, wasn't it?"

Pablo closes his eyes.

"You can turn him in, you know. How old is he? Thirty-five? Forty? He's been living off you forever! Kick him out! Are you waiting till he kills you or what?"

A whisper. "She won't let me. She still thinks of him—
like that baby—he was. That she took care of. I told you.
But it's worse."

"Worse?"

"Remember that time I fell down on the middle of the
floor in the night and Elena come to get you, she couldn't
remember how to call the Emergency, and you called the
ambulance and they took me to hospital and I was in hospital with that diabetes for a few weeks and then I came
home? Well in that time I was gone I think something happened to make her—think of him more like a husband than
a son."

"What?"

"She acted different when I got back. Like—the love
changed. She stood behind him different. She fold his clothes
better. She took him food in bed."

A long silence in which I am thinking of Elena in her
baggy faded aprons and what else he could possibly mean.

Michael, as usual, is brisk and businesslike. Michael
never acts shocked. "Well, I've told you for years, as long
as you let him live off you, he'll do it. As long as you buy
his food and pay his rent—what more could he need? If
you kicked him out, Pablo, he might have to work! Hardly
a tragedy! If you can't kick him out because you're afraid
of him, then you get help, like social workers or police. You
could get a restraining order if he's beating you up. Kick
him out of your house and onto his own two feet! Pablo,
he's got feet! All it would take is a little follow-through.
And come on, you want to go apply at the elderly housing
place? I'll take you."

If Pablo moved there, Julio couldn't come with him.

Pablo, as usual, isn't listening. He's staring up at the
curtain rods from which I've hung old quilt tops. He's staring at light filtering softly in through lost patterns of blue

181

boys on blue rocking horses and calico bow ties. He won't really apply for elderly housing because it would make him feel—elderly. I remember the nude kewpie doll tattooed on his forearm and lean over to make sure it's still there.

Michael touches his shoulder gently. "Pablo—we care about you. You're getting hurt."

"But if I kick him out, she'll die."

"Why?"

"Because taking care of him keeps her alive. I just know it. And if she dies, then it will be me and the dog by ourselves and the boy probably come back by then to get even." He's talking about the one worst-looking scrap of a dog that he always keeps, not the ones he sells. He's talking about a bad mess of a man as a boy. He's talking about the way problems tangle people up so hard we're ruined for years. Tied in knots. You pull the string but it knots. You open your mouth to say something new, but the world opens its mouth faster and bites you.

"Pablo," I finally speak again. "This thing you said about Elena and Julio. You didn't mean you thought—while you were gone—do you think?"

"Yeah yeah yeah I think it. I think maybe he was drunk and maybe she was already sleeping. Maybe she got confused or something. Maybe she thought it was me. I think it happened more than once too because he's acting real—close with her. God! She seems more shy, girly."

Elena, at eighty-four, is eight years older than Pablo. She's an old eighty-four too. I've seen ninety-fours that looked and acted younger. She wears those heavy knit stockings and clunky shoes like grandmothers in Bulgaria. Sometimes a scarf wrapped around her head. She never picks her feet up more than one inch when she walks.

By now the juice has sweetened him. He's stopped breathing so hard. "You need to do it," Michael says. "No one else can do it. If you don't do it, the story will just continue and you'll be in it."

Outside the street-sweeping machine rumbles by with its giant squeaky brushes. Pablo nods. "I'm—in it. How did I get in it? I was just—baking doughnuts. Sugar. I was just standing there with sugar on my hands and this soft lady come in and I have to lean way over the counter to hear her. She takes twelve doughnuts that first day and another day comes back and takes eighteen. I say to myself she must have a big family, no? But it turns out she's working for them nuns, them sisters at the church who like doughnuts, one day a week. She was cleaning. She told me later. She had nobody. I'm still married to my first wife then, but she go off with this guy named Rico pretty soon when the kids get big and boom! It's like they all went off together. I'm by myself for a while before I marry Elena and lemme tell you that time by myself was the worst thing that ever happened to me. Ever. Nobody waiting. No rice in the pot."

"But peaceful?"

He looks at me sharply. "Whadda you know? Who cares, peaceful? It's *sad*."

And I know he won't do it. He won't kick the criminal out because it might happen again. No two ragged white socks pinned up on the line by somebody else to console him. He'd have to do it himself.

I hear the strangest low-decibel dirge rise up out of the couch and the wooden floor and the fringes of the rug. It seems to come from the stack of papers I threw down. It sounds like heat hanging on for months and months. It sounds like the deep shy voice of Erica, one of the elementary girls in the workshop, who finally gave me a paper yesterday. Bent and scraped and smudged. A story about what it's like to sleep in the car. Every night her father sends her to the driveway. She says there aren't enough beds in the house. The wind presses against the car on cold nights and makes her hug her sheet, the one she keeps balled up in the back seat. But hot nights are worse because she has to leave the windows open.

"I like the car," she writes. "I can't drive it but I know it real well. I know that little hole where the ashtray used to be but it got lost. I poke my fingers in it. I have good dreams sometimes and other times scary. What if a bad person came to the car and tried to get in. One door won't lock. I sleep with my feet to that door. If you're walking down the street in the dark you can't see if someone's sleeping on the seat. My daddy told me that. I love my daddy."

Marie

On the brown stucco wall of the old hotel on South Alamo Street, a broad-lettered sign appears: MARIES APTS. Chopped-off white curtains flap screenless windows. It's one thing in Texas to have no air-conditioning and another thing entirely to have no screens. My son calls me to the bathtub in our house a few blocks from MARIES APTS. to see *A mosquito as big as an elephant.* It's filled with my blood, he says. It's been drinking me all evening. I think of Marie. Marie's apt to be a real somebody. You don't start a new business in a building like that if you're not. Let's salute women who put their own names on things: Rosie's Salsa, Lupita's Gorditas. Let's tour the mysterious ten-story "map factory" between our house and MARIES. Find out what really goes on in there, the front door locked like a cage. Lights on at two in the morning. Our neighborhood group is Arsenal Residents Mobilized for Action. This name precedes our living here and everyone would like to change it, but we are listed in all the city records this way. It sounds as if we need a map into battle. I hope Marie knows this. That she has a broom and a mop lined up under her hope.

Keys

For years I watched you, elegant raggedy man, stepping out from the sidewalk into the bus lane before the bus arrived, lining soda and beer cans where the big tires would crush them. You wore rainbow suspenders, baggy pants, a floppy carnival cap. You'd invented a wire hanger contraption that speared pop-tabs so you didn't have to bend—these were the older days, when the little tab still came loose from the can. You'd flip the tabs onto a jingling loop at your belt and slide the flattened cans into a trailing trash sack. Your cheeks burned, sun-streaked, your hair under the cap a vibrant plume of white.

I wanted to speak to you then, but it never seemed right. Say what? *Greetings, I have watched your eyes as they search the gutter for shine.* I have trailed you down Commerce Street, and Santa Rosa. You have tugged me along past hosiery displays, fresh-faced bankers, jumbles of tourists with swing-strap bags and conversations so predictable it hurts to hear.

I have praised God I was not in any of those families but I have never praised God I am not you.

Once I saw you talking to the man who demonstrates

whizzing airplanes near the *mercado* on Saturdays. Sometimes he dumps out a whole shopping cart of worn clickers
and faded red wind-up cars with missing wheels. I have
priced his goods and they are not cheap.

Standing nearby, unobtrusively examining the
CineFestival poster, I listened as you diagnosed shoppers
for him—"looking, just looking, not serious, not enough
people serious." I felt you trying to lift his spirits and sure
enough, when I turned to look, his shoulders were droop-
ing, his chin sagged. How many toys could be sold by a
man who never smiles?

After that, I loved the ring of keys that aren't keys strung
from your belt. I wondered where you slept at night, what
worn and checkered blanket held you. Through the Saturday crowds you shuffled, past the aromatic gorditas stand,
pausing to sniff, saluting the women.

You shepherd of trash, gatherer of the abandoned vessel—I thought of you after parades and Fiesta, how you
stayed out late, your dreams littered with bounty. Children
pressed against their parents' hips as the huge flower-cov-
ered floats rolled by. Your eyes roamed for rubble around
their feet.

Once near your favorite corner after the horses and trumpets went home, three girls with big ruffled skirts twirled
among bus fumes and the smallest called out to me, "Hey!
Do you remember my poem?" Of course I said "Yes" though
I had no idea. You raised your head and, for the first time,
caught my gaze. I felt shamed in my lie. Had her poem lain
there in the street between us you might have lifted it,
smoothed the wrinkles, offered it back.

One night by the lulling little river, a group of us occupied a canopied table. The first cooling autumn wind lifted
our hair. We were desperate for it. On my lap the baby

squirmed, stacking tostadas, peaked houses on a plate. At his birth one of these friends, a veteran parent, told me, "Welcome to an anxiety you have never known before and will know now for the rest of your life." Is this true? I do not find I am always anxious but everything is different, that's for sure. Spectrum of worries and joys, guitar with a thousand strings!

Under the arching bridge where mariachis strum and lovers tease, you limped, dragging your bag. I saw you stop and scan the crowd, your ruddy face marked with intent. Could you possibly have recognized me?

You approached our group. Stood beside my chair, staring hard at the small waves cast up by tourist barges. The baby reached for your belt. "Keys!" he pronounced. A friend exclaimed, "Oh! Aren't those too sharp?" My mind reeled back to India, where a waiter once chased me from a restaurant with two pop-tabs neatly folded in a napkin, calling out, "You will excuse me, but the lady is forgetting her earrings!" They didn't have pop-tabs in India; we'd smuggled in some foreign Cokes.

Then you spoke. Eyes fixed on the baby. "He knows more than we do," you spoke so loudly people at other tables turned to hear. "If we're lucky he'll grow up to tell us."

You touched his hair with a soft, light hand and he smiled. "Oh, what is in there?" You tapped his curly head. "What do you see, little one?" And addressed me seriously, as if all this time, trailing one another through the streets, you'd known I needed you. "Listen up," you said, pointing one rough finger straight into my face. "*He knows more than you do.* Got that? I tell you true."

The baby reached for your hand and you softened. "See there? He knows a lot!" You kissed his hand, his head. Eyes of our neighbors hovered on this sidewalk consecration, yellow strung lights reflecting in water, the secret glide of yellow fish.

I almost mentioned that I'd always wished to know you, but my tongue felt thick. Anyway, you were finished with us. You limped off, twisting the mouth of your garbage bag around your arm. Someone at another table hissed, "Like Santa Claus," and I looked down. Pop-tabs glittered everywhere beneath the busy feet of waitresses whose flared Mexican skirts made umbrellas for the ground.

Then the baby tugged on my shirt. He asked for more keys. I gave him real ones and he threw them down. Since he had gripped your huge collection, my garland rang thin.

Into the river, whiffs of accordion, neon. A shrouded moon spirited the sky. *If we are lucky,* you said. He'll grow up. To tell us.

Calling down the long aisle of faces, the river-flickering faces, *which way? Which way?*

Tomorrow We Smile

I used to say to my friend Juan Felipe that I like Mexico because Mexico still has a sense of the miraculous and he would slap me on the back and say, "You just like the peppers, come on, be honest," but I saw how he had *milagros*, little silver arms and legs, pinned up by his bed too. So I would tell him what happened in my neighborhood, like when José Palomo's father died, a big eagle came to light in his patio and stayed for days, just sitting there. José said it stared at him with a meaningful look and then one morning it was gone. When I tell Juan, he says we don't have eagles in the city. Maybe it was a lost bird that got thirsty from flying too long. But I see how a candle deep in his eyes is suddenly glowing and I don't mention it again.

Then there are things that happen to us personally, what about them? We first met Domingo Flores when we ran out of gas on the highway south of Uvalde, Texas. Juan, his mother, and I were headed for the border that day—to eat fragrant soup with cilantro, buy woolly ponchos and bottles of vanilla, and walk the streets of Piedras, fat with joy. We used to go to Mexico like that in those days, for soup and joy. It was before they said the vanilla had arsenic in it. Juan's mother wanted to find a set of blue tin plates and Juan just wanted to drink the air. We always came home before midnight on those trips, unless we were driving in farther, to Rosita or Múzquiz or one of those buttonlike villages that is nothing but a dusty plaza and a bar.

In the back seat Juan's mother was snoring into the Lifestyle section of the newspaper. Juan had the radio turned to *conjunto*. His eyes kept darting over the landscape like goats. Naturally no one else had checked the gas gauge. Thirty miles this side of Mexico, on the thorny stretch that somehow manages to link our lands, the engine sputtered and died.

Juan got out and poked his head under the hood. He still hadn't noticed the gas gauge. His mother sat up, startled, and touched her hair. If you've never been there, picture a drab two-lane sided by brush and cactus, no billboards, no restrooms or telephones, and very few cars. We hadn't seen another car since we left La Pryor, thirty miles back. "This could be bad," said Juan, trying to start the car again. Then he noticed the little arrow sagging below the EMPTY slash. He was embarrassed. He sat there silently, staring into the sky.

That day there weren't even any clouds to thumb a ride on. You can imagine people drowning in a sky like that.

For awhile we all sat, gazing at various items. I gazed at the dashboard and later, the pebbles in the ditch. Juan's mother stared at the *TV Guide*. Then the three of us walked in different circles, bugs trapped inside a window, hoping for a crack.

After an hour, we heard the unmistakable buzz of a car. It was strange how we couldn't tell which direction it was coming from. Gradually a 1965 Chevrolet chugged into view, from the south. It had strips of pom-pom balls pinned up around the inside and a pair of dice mingling with the

Virgin on the mirror. I like how people fix up their cars. I used to decorate mine with Arabic donkey beads and feathers, hoping some positive vehicular voodoo might occur. The pom-pom car was traveling very slowly. It stopped, engine still running, and a young man with a wide, clear face got out.

"*¿Qué está pasando?*" he asked, grinning.

He knew what was *pasando* as well as we did.

The back seat of his car was loaded with boxes, beat-up suitcases, a lamp without a head. Juan talked to him in Spanish and learned he was Domingo Flores, moving to Austin, Texas, to find his wife, who had preceded him there. He would locate work and eat white bread and buy a little TV with an antenna. Gas? Sure he would help us, *no problema.*

Juan said, "I am a man with a donkey's head."

Domingo said, "I travel slower than the donkey."

They climbed into the front seat of Domingo's portable shrine and chugged off, heading north.

His mother and I stayed with the car and fell asleep with all the windows open. She said she dreamed about when the boys were little, how they used to wear capes and underpants and jump from the dresser to the bed, shrieking. I dreamed about my mother pulling me in a wagon on the day a milk carton broke in her hands. Under a sky like that you could go backward forever.

A long time later the car of Domingo Flores chugged toward us again, a green dot getting larger.

We had wondered how Juan would return. Only one truck had roared past since his departure and the driver had a hard face.

Juan and Domingo climbed out comfortably, friends from the journey, and reported: yes, they had found gas, they had rousted the sleepy attendant from his bed, after stopping at three farms to find him, and no, there was no unleaded gas in the whole town of La Pryor, so they toted three gallons of regular and had to devise a funnel out of Prime Minister Thatcher's front-page head.

Domingo stayed around to see the job finished, his car running all the while. When Juan's mother suggested he turn it off, he said, "I can't." If he turned it off, it wouldn't start again. I'd known cars like that. Domingo smiled when our engine coughed awake and opened his palm up to heaven, as if saying, "You see?" Juan offered him money for his own gas. Back-and-forth meant he was going out of the way for us over sixty miles.

His face changed. He looked stunned and said, "No one gives me anything I don't earn."

"But he earned it!" I poked Juan. "Tell him he earned it!"

Juan went on in delicate Spanish as he counted out dollar bills from his wallet.

I thought Domingo was going to cry. He jumped back into his car and rolled the window up fast so Juan couldn't stick the money in. When he threw it into gear, the engine nearly quit. Now wouldn't that have been something? We could have driven him the other direction for a tow truck and gone on and on like that for days. But it caught, and he was off. He raised one hand, didn't look back, and swayed into the distance, like a camel.

"I think he was too sensitive," said Juan's mother, as our own car pulled forward. "A lot of those people with old *frontera* traditions still act like money and dignity can never go together."

We drove to Mexico and arrived as the shopkeepers were sweeping out the aisles at the *mercado*. "You're late," they said.

Months later, in the middle of a conversation about B. Traven and the Chiapas jungles, Juan said, "I wonder if what's-his-name made it to his wife. That car was a bomb!"

"Who's that?"

"The guy on the highway—Domingo Flores."

"I hope so." It was hard to picture Domingo in Austin among glossy governmental buildings and health-food pubs.

Juan said college towns were unnatural. "We need to live in a town where at least half the population feels like fading paint. It is important, this sensation."

The seasons slid into one another. Dallas residents were wearing short sleeves on the day a devastating ice storm struck down their trees. The Valley grapefruit growers wept on the news. One man held out his hands and said, "My orchard was all I had and now I don't have it either." At home in San Antonio pipes were bursting like fountains on every block.

Juan was off along the border somewhere, interviewing Tex-Mex accordionists for a project he said would be "the greatest tribute since *Chulas Fronteras*."

I was in Central Texas compiling an anthology of local memoirs for an arts council. Though the job paid decently, other factors kept me sobered: bank tellers asking if I were "born again" before they would cash my checks, and the general terrifying sense that all the best things—porches, grandmothers, independent cafés—were swiftly vanishing from the earth.

I called Juan's mother, who told me where he was. "S.O.S., can you come up here?" He said I sounded wistful. Two nights later I was sitting at the desk when he knocked. "Listen to this!" I yelled in greeting. "How much do you know about rounding up snakes? Today I met a man from West Texas who used to . . ."

Then I noticed he looked pale. "What's wrong?"

He sat down gingerly, holding himself forward on the chair.

He wiped his hand across his forehead.

"What's the matter?"

"There was fog on the road tonight, hanging low," he said. "About ten miles north of Austin I saw a hitchhiker and glancing over automatically—it was Domingo Flores! I slammed on the brakes and he came strolling toward me at a normal pace, not rushing like hitchhikers usually do. I yelled, "Domingo, is that you?"

He nodded and extended his hand. Casually. "You have gas tonight?" he said in Spanish, so I knew he recognized me, but the strangest part was, he didn't act surprised. Can you figure it? It's five months later, hundreds of miles from where we first met, we meet again in the fog, and he's acting nonchalant! He had a pillowcase with him that he held on his lap very closely.

I asked where he was going and he said, "Dallas." I asked where his car was and he said, "They stole it." Then he proceeded, in the most carefully measured voice, to tell me he'd arrived in Austin to find his wife living with another man. Nacho, he called him. She was living with Nacho. My heart split, he said. But he moved into an apartment near them and got a job clipping bushes or something. I asked him a stupid question, "Do you have a work visa?" and he nodded. Here he is telling me the Tale of the Splitting Heart and I'm thinking of visas.

He said he was praying she'd change her mind, leave this other guy and come back to him, her true and rightful husband in the eyes of God. But he said everything in the same flat voice. He said it like he was reading out of a book.

"I made myself a small and hopeful life." He repeated that twice. And then one night the wife, he never used her name, showed up at his door. She announced that she was coming back to him, she and Nacho had parted, she'd made a mistake. "I opened my arms," he said. That's it. "I opened my arms."

For a week they lived together, he was working, she had some job, and he "bought the television." Do you remember last summer when he mentioned the television? I guess that's the one he bought.

The next day she asked to drive him to work and said she wanted to use the car for a "surprise." It was her day off. When five o'clock came, she didn't pick him up, so he waited awhile and started walking. When he got home the apartment was stripped, television gone, everything gone, even the plates were gone.

I asked him if he'd called the police and he said no. "My shame."

"Your shame!" I yelled. "What about your anger?" Domingo acted blank. "She was my wife," he said. "I opened my arms."

I asked if he had any money, but he shook his head. "I used to," he said, "but I showed her where I was hiding it under a cactus."

For a moment I slowed the car to see if there was a place to turn around, and he almost jumped out. "I'm going that way," he pointed north. He was very stubborn about it. "I'm going to Dallas."

I asked him why Dallas and he said he had a cousin in Dallas. Did he know his address? Of course not. I said, "Domingo, go back to Mexico," and he shook his head. "My shame."

So I asked if I could put him on a bus to Dallas and he nodded. We drove into Belton to an ice-house Trailways station where they said a bus was due in ten minutes. Domingo nodded gravely. "It's luck," he said. Luck? His wife just robbed him of everything he had and he's talking about luck?

I said, "*This* time you take the money." I gave him every cent I had. He said, "You'll get it back." And when the bus came, he shook my hand and said a weird expression I never heard in Spanish before, "*Mañana sonreíremos.*"

"What does it mean?"

"Tomorrow we smile."

Now Juan sat back in his chair and covered his eyes. It was a black night, no stars. My friend had come to save me.

"Did you give him your address?"

He shook his head.

"Do you know how many highways there are in Texas?" I said.

"How many people named Flores?"

"How many people named Juan?"

That's it. That's what happened. I look for Domingo sometimes, on roads out of Dallas, on any old road.

Field Trip

Only once did I take a large group of children on a field trip. A summer creative writing class journeyed by bus to a printing shop to see how pages were bound together to make books and our cheerfully patient guide chopped her finger off with a giant paper cutter.

I had not prepared the children for anything beyond typefaces, camera-ready copy, collation. Standing toward the rear of our group like a shepherd, I felt their happy little backs stiffen at the moment of severance. A gasp rose from their throats as the startling blot of blood grew outward, a rapid pool staining all the pages. The woman pressed forward through our frozen crowd, cupping her wounded hand against her chest, not screaming, but mouthing silently, "Hospital—now—let's go."

A flurry of motion erupted among the other workers, much like the flurry of feathers when anyone steps too quickly into a chicken coop. Two people dialed phones, then asked aloud why they were dialing—couldn't they drive her to the hospital themselves? A voice at the emergency room said to place the severed finger on ice and a man who had been pasting up tedious layouts ran for ice. One boy tugged at my shirt and croaked, "The last thing she said was—you have to be very careful with this machine."

Someone dropped a ring of keys and I crawled under a desk to retrieve them. It felt good to fall to my knees. For a second the stricken woman loomed above me and I stuttered, apologizing for our visit, which had inadvertently caused this disaster, but she was distracted by something else.

"Honey, *look* at that thing!" she exclaimed, staring into the cup of ice where the index finger now rested like a rare archival specimen. "It's turning white! If that finger stays white, I don't *want* it on my body!"

We laughed hard and loudly, and the children stared at us, amazed. Had we lost our senses? That she could joke at such a moment, as the big fans whirred and the collating machines paused over vast mountains of stacked paper . . . I wanted to sing her blackness, to call out to those girls and boys, "This, my friends, is what words can do for you— make you laugh when your finger rests in a styrofoam cup!"

But she went quickly off toward the hospital and I shuffled an extremely silent group of children back onto our bus. I wanted to say something promising recovery, or praising our guide's remarkable presence of mind, but my voice seemed lost among the seats. No one would look at me.

Later I heard how they went home and went straight to their rooms. Mothers called me. Some of the children had nightmares. Molly's mother said, "What in the world happened on that field trip? Sarah came over today and she and Molly climbed up on the bed and just sobbed."

At our next meeting we made get-well cards. Come-together-again cards. May the seam hold. May the two become one. They thought up all kinds of things. I had been calling the printing shop to monitor her progress and the reports sounded good. The students had been gathering stories; someone's farmer-uncle whose leg was severed in a cornfield, but who lived to see it joined, someone's brother's toe.

I went to her home with a bundle of hopeful wishes tied in loops of pink ribbon. She was wearing a terry cloth bathrobe and sitting in a comfortable chair, her hand hugely bandaged. She sighed and shook her head. "I guess none of those cute kids will ever become printers now, will they? Gee, I hope they don't give up reading and writing too! Oh, I feel just terrible about it. They were such an interested little audience." She'd been worrying about the children while they'd been worrying about her.

Reading their messages made her chuckle. I asked what the doctors had said about the finger turning black again. She said they thought it would, but it might be slightly paler than the rest of her hand. And it would be stiff for a long time, maybe forever.

She said she was missing being at work. Vacations weren't much fun when they came this unexpectedly. But wasn't it great what medicine could do? I decided she might be one of my heroes. The pain was a lot better than it had been last week, and could I please thank those kids for their flowers and hearts?

After that I took my workshops onto the schoolyard but no farther. I made them look for buttons and feathers. I made them describe the postures of men and women waiting for a bus. Once I'd dreamed of visiting every factory in town, the mattress factory, the hot sauce factory, the assembly line for cowboy boots, but I changed my mind.

By the time our workshop ended that summer, we felt more closely bonded than other groups I'd known. We hugged each other tightly. Perhaps our sense of mortality linked us, our shared vision of the fragility of body parts. One girl went on to become one of the best young writers in the city. I'd like to think her hands were blessed by our unexpected obsession with hands.

And I continued to ruminate over field trips in general, remembering the time my high school health class visited the state mental hospital where our teacher unwittingly herded us into a room of elderly women who'd recently had lobotomies, after telling us people didn't do that to one another anymore. Or the absolutely inappropriate ventures—to the Judson Candy Factory on the day Robert Kennedy was shot. Our home economics teacher had planned this day as an end-of-school celebration.

My classmates and I stood staring numbly at vats of creamy chocolate brew. The air hung heavy around us. He was dead and an Arab had killed him. I couldn't mention the second part out loud, but it made me feel sick to my stomach. And the candy factory seemed less sensible now than ever—all that labor to make something that wasn't even good for you. A worker joked that a few of his friends had ended up in those bubbling vats and nobody smiled. How could we?

As a child I finally grew brave enough to plot a trip out into the fields years after my friends had first done it—to Camp Fiddlecreek in Missouri, for Girl Scouts. I'd postponed such an adventure due to an unreasonable fear of spiders. I felt certain a giant furry spider would crawl into my bedroll the minute I got there and entangle itself in my hair. The zipper on the sleeping bag would stick and I would die, die, die. Finally I decided a life without courage might be worse than death, so I packed my greenest duds and headed to the hills.

The first night I confided my secret fear to the girl who slept next to me. She said she'd always been more scared of snakes than spiders. I said, "Snakes, phooey!"

The next day while we were up in the hills hiking, a group of donkeys broke out of a nearby field and ran at us. One knocked me down and trampled me. My leg swelled into three large, hard lumps. I could not walk. I would have to be driven home to the city for X-rays. My friend leaned over, smoothing back my bangs and consoled me. "Donkeys! Can you believe it? Who would ever believe a donkey could be so mean?"

I had never, ever thought about a donkey with any fear. But here began a lifetime of quirks suspended on a single thread: the things we worry about are never the things that happen. And the things that happen are the things we never could have dreamed.

Neighborhood Quartet in a Minor Key

One day we go out looking for a carpet store on the old Austin Highway, zoom past it by mistake, make a U-turn in the parking lot of a Peugeot dealer, and end up buying an aged golden Peugeot instead.

The Peugeot is sitting in the sun with a price tag on its window so small we think it must indicate a down payment. I have never focused on a Peugeot before. The Peugeot salesman rides with us to the Aztec Garage so our trusty mechanic Joe can check out the car. We spend less for it than we had planned to spend for the carpet.

We keep the Peugeot for four years and it never fails us. We only drive it in town. I like the slope of the seats, the French hum of the engine. Later we go away for a few months and come home to find it dead in the driveway, as if in protest. We sell it to Ricky, who lives behind us on City Street. He knows about cars. He keeps five or six extra ones around for company.

It is strange to see our car living on the next street. I

want to stand in the backyard and call it home for dinner. Sometimes I hear it going by without us. After fixing it up, Ricky sells it to Gabriel, two houses down. Gabriel puts sheepskin covers on the seat and leaves the sunroof open a lot. It starts looking less confident, even before it gets a deep raw gash in one side. There's no telling where our car will live next. It pulls up close to every new owner.

◆ ◆ ◆

Justina's voice is still shaking. "Listen," she says, "if it's a choice between the man who takes nasty pictures or the man with the killer dogs, I guess I'll take the dogs."

She's collecting black and white feathers from the grass. Her stomach feels tipsy. Lucy, who lives next door, heard her screaming and came out in time to shoo off the dogs and help Justina gather the massacred bodies of her chickens. The dogs belonging to the new renter had burrowed under the fence into Justina's yard.

Lucy disagrees. "I liked Ray better. How do we *know* what he was doing with those boys? Maybe those boys they found naked in his bathtub were really dirty, yes? It's possible."

She omits the fact that police found pictures and camera equipment set up. She secretly misses Ray, though they never visited much. He seemed so sullen. But she liked his long strides up and down the street with his railroad cap pressed down on his shaggy blond hair. He was the only blond person in the neighborhood. And she liked that he was alone. Other single people make her feel less alien. She likes widows and elderly housing projects. Once she gave Ray part of a gingerbread cake and he seemed very shook up about it.

Now he's at the penitentiary in Huntsville. And the terrible man with *dogs* moved into his place. Lucy shakes her head at Justina. "I'll miss your extra eggs, that's for sure. I feel real sad about your girls."

Justina saved two of the hens by beating the dogs off with a broom. When the owner of the dogs gets home from work today, she plans to tell him she has the animal control number taped to her telephone. She goes inside to find a sack of dried bread heels. Maybe they won't lay again till Easter.

Lucy follows her. "The angels are off duty," she says. "I don't mean those cop angels with berets. I mean the old-fashioned sky kind. Did you hear about Isabel over on Riddle Street getting beat up by the paperboy she had for a year? He knew where she hid her money in a shoe box under the bed. I think the angels must be tired of us. We got too many problems down here on earth. They only want to be angels in paintings now. It's a good thing my mother is dead already."

"Why do you say that?"

"She believed the angels were taking care of us. It would make her too sad."

◆ ◆ ◆

Ernesto, age ninety-four, same as the century, sits on his raggedy front porch waiting for me to come outside and wave at him. He holds on to a silver walker for balance. He wears a button around his neck to press for help. He grew up speaking Spanish in South Texas, but he has never been to Mexico. Mexico is two and a half hours away. I want to take him, but he shakes his head. Too far, he says.

I feel guilty getting into my car without going over to visit. He was born on Valentine's Day. He used to have the Oldest Dog in the World but it died last year. We found it lying on its side behind a tree in the park and had to go tell him.

He gave it a fresh bowl of water every day. We covered it

with a blanket. The Oldest Dog pressed his cheek to the ground.

Now the house is so quiet, nothing ever coming up on the porch to nose around. Ernesto still says *I beg your pardon* and *I'm much obliged.* He watches the news and says he feels real bad about the Palestinians. He feels bad about the Jews too. If you watch the news it's not hard to feel bad about everything and everybody. Sometimes he tries to kiss me more than he should, a little lips instead of alongside the face, and I pull away. It must be hard to be ninety-four years old and never get touched. Doesn't someone have a service for this? A group offering Elderly Massage?

I stand with my foot poised to walk back to my house the whole time we're talking. I feel guilty about it. I take him soup and potatoes, nice soft cake. He has two lonely teeth. I say, "See you in a few days, we're going to Dallas." He shakes his head and makes the sign of the cross over me. "Oh Mamacita I will miss you too much, too much."

He says he went to Dallas once. "All those little towns between here and there, New Braunfels, San Marcos . . ." he proceeds to name every little town between here and there, in the correct order. "So many peoples!" he waves his hands when he finally gets to Dallas. "So much street-cars! I found a Mexican bakery, makin' good *pan dulce,* the best *pan dulce* I ever tasted, which surprised me, you know, I thought we had it better down here. I buy some, then later this friend-a-mine goin' to Dallas and I say, you find this bakery, you eat this *pan dulce,* you never forget it. Lemme tell you just where it is. And you know what he did? He brought me my own sack from that bakery back here on the *train.* Little dry by the time he got here, but it still tasted good. He said that train was quicker than the slow road."

"What slow road? Didn't you go on the interstate? I-35?"

◆ ◆ ◆

He looks blank. "Thirty-five? The only time I ever went to Dallas—was 1925."

Behind the mill, where hidden floury men grind wheat and bake cinnamon biscuits that sweeten the whole neighborhood, the bad boy Osvaldo is fishing. When he pitches his tangled line into the river, when he spits the butt of his bitter cigarette, you can feel his jagged edge. Tight little braid oiled to the back of his head.

Everybody's afraid of him. Nobody talks to him except to say, "Hey Osvaldo" passing on the street. That way he can think he has friends.

When stereos get pried out of cars in the middle of the night, people say, "Osvaldo did it." They curse and stamp their feet. They say his name to the police.

Someone old once told me the story of Osvaldo, which stayed stuck in my head like a splinter.

When he was just a baby his mother ran away and left him with his father and five bigger brothers all under the age of eight. I'll bet she didn't really run. I'll bet no one who runs away ever really *runs*. I'll bet they drag their heels for a thousand miles.

Well, she never came back and so he never knew any lady's lap not even just a little bit. They didn't seem to have any lady relatives either. In fact you never saw a lady of any age cross that doorstep even for a second. Can you imagine what that household was *like?* Picture it—a house full of rolled-up socks thrown like rat balls in all the stinky corners. I'll bet they didn't even *wear* socks after awhile.

I can imagine what Osvaldo grew up eating. Once I saw his father open the door of their car and a bag of groceries fell out and spilled. It was all marshmallow kind of stuff. Puffed cereal and bleached bread. Red soda. Another time, Lucy caught Osvaldo's father peeking into Lisa's bedroom window. Can you believe it? This is a father's example?

I don't know if those boys went to school or if any of them ever worked. They're all in their early twenties or late teens by now. I don't know any of his brothers' names. His brothers seem less bad, but they don't appear to do anything. Sometimes it gets so hot it feels like no one in the world's ever done anything but sit on the front steps and fan themselves and wait. Osvaldo does this a lot. The strange thing to me is that all the boys *stayed* with their father, like they're suspended in time. One even has his own kids living there with him now, but still no ladies crossing the doorstep. Baby cries and cartoons tangle together outside their windows.

So when I see Osvaldo fishing by himself, leaning over the skinny little river, I hope he catches something. I wave down at him from the bridge if he sees me. I hope it's a big fish with whiskers and I hope it looks up at him and grins.

Home Address

Yesterday we paid off the mortgage on our ninety-year-old white house on South Main Avenue. I drove from San Antonio to Austin with a cashier's check in my purse and a receipt marked HAND-DELIVERED for the mortgage company to sign. I wanted to see that stamp marked PAID IN FULL, to step back out the door into the sun and blink hard and take a full fine breath.

When I entered the marble lobby of the office building—cool and blank as any bank—beams of light were slanting through high windows onto the gleaming floor and the music playing over loudspeakers was the very same trumpet anthem I walked down the aisle to at our wedding fifteen years ago. I laughed out loud. It's been said our lives might be easier if we had appropriate background music, as characters do in movies. It felt wonderful climbing that staircase with trumpets to the second floor.

Later, back at home, I noticed all the cracks in the walls. They seemed more vivid. Now they were really entirely ours. We could fix them or not, depending.

My husband suggested we take a walk before dark. He and our son put on their baseball caps. I locked all the doors.

We passed our neighbor's yards, thirsty after fifty-seven days of no rain. We passed our ex-cat Maui, who divorced us and moved five houses down to live with the Martinos.

An elderly couple dressed in white was crossing the bridge by the river, leaning on one another for support. My husband said, "Is that us in the future?" For some reason I jumped to say, "No!"—maybe because our son just started first grade this week after getting his first short haircut and losing his first tooth and the passage of time feels tender and nearly unbearable right now—but when we got closer to the couple, I figured we'd be lucky to be them.

They looked gentle, intelligent, and still in love with one another. He helped her into a white car and closed the door. Then he looked at us. He had a fine grin and a white mustache. "Nice river you got," he said. "You live around here?" When we said yes, he pointed to the River Authority building and said, "Well, I grew up on this very spot in a lovely brick house with a full basement, all erased by now, but you can bet I do have some memories."

Naturally I wanted to embrace him on the spot and urge him to tell, tell, tell. "The house had marble pillars," he went on dreamily. "And was full of music. We kept the windows wide open, so the music floated outside into the air. My whole family is musical; in fact we run the local music company, do you know it?" He gave the name. Everybody knows it. He said, "I wonder if there's anyone around here I still remember," and pointed at a tall white house. "Mr. Stump still live there?" When we nodded, he grinned. "A little crazy, that guy."

We said yes, he was right. Mr. Stump used to stop by our driveway and tell us he was being persecuted at work for being a white man. His mother wouldn't let him get married till she died. Finally she died and he married a woman ten years his senior who beat him. I kept thinking how he was one man challenging the status quo.

The music man said this river was a lovely place to grow up. He said some days his head was still full of "the scent of pecan leaves piling up in the autumn, right here, right along these banks. Look! These are some of the same old trees." He seemed reluctant to leave us, but his wife was getting edgy in the front seat alone. I would have liked to tell him about our mortgage or invite him to dinner. Where did he live now?

But they drove off and we crossed the river to come face-to-face with Mr. Stump, who didn't remember us for a few seconds. He gave us a fabulously suspicious look. He said, "I haven't seen you in twenty years." He was carrying a plastic grocery sack full of Miller Lite Beer.

"How's your wife?" my husband asked him. And he said, "Oh! She died last November. Gave all her money away to a cousin up in Kansas just before she passed. Can you believe it? I took care of her all those years, then she gives it away. I'm still recovering. I'm putting myself back together now."

We mentioned the old neighbor we'd just met and he said, "Oh yeah, the piano man, I bought a concert grand from him once. Did I ever tell you I got persecuted at work for being a concert artist?"

"Do you still have it?" I asked, picturing a concert grand inside his ramshackle house, and he looked puzzled. "Oh yes. Hard to give *that* away." He told us his life was wrecked and all his tools kept vanishing before his very eyes, but soon things would improve.

When he was out of earshot, I said, "He seems terrible," and my husband said, "I thought he'd never seemed better."

Next we noticed a neighbor's house for sale that hadn't been for sale yesterday. This always feels disturbing and melancholy to me. We found two frogs hopping around in the monkey grass by the sidewalk. Their rough little bellies puffed in and out. Our son said the frogs were husband and wife. They seemed to live under a raised cracked place in the sidewalk.

I could feel an ache rising up from the ground, a desperate deep thirst from the roots of trees and vines. In a few yards, quiet sprinklers swished in the darkness. "How much longer till it rains, do you think?" and we all placed our bets, then came round to our own block again and the iron gate that never fit the fence, even on the first day, and has to be held shut with a shoestring.

Our porch swing was quietly hanging, waiting for us. The swing has a quilt top in its seat now, which used to be a curtain till I washed it and the oldest fabrics came out shredded. The banana palms and giant red hibiscus bush were breathing their slumbered breath, and the black mailbox on a pole stood at attention even in the dark. Its flag was down. Now and then, each detail stands out like a landmark.

We sat for a while before going in and I thought of the lady who lived in this house for fifty years before us. She raised one son in this house too. She outlived two husbands in this house. Each time we invited her back for tea, she said, "Well honey, I just don't think I can make it" though the service station attendant around the block said he saw her drive by all the time.

I thought of Norman Bodet, who lived in this house before her, whose family built it and started the travel agency I frequent downtown. Bodet Steamship and Travel still uses old-fashioned blue envelopes with little steamships floating across them. Mr. Bodet's portrait stares gravely at me each time I buy a plane ticket, which is often. He seems to say, "Can't you settle down?"

The day after we paid off the mortgage I was sweeping the back deck, moving flower pots around and humming. I don't think I'd swept it all summer. I dug my hands into the big purple plant that flourishes with no attention. I plucked off its dry leaves. I pulled out twigs and the stick of a popsicle, tucked in by some lazy someone, and startled backward when something cool slithered past my fingers. Leaves rattled and shook. I glanced fearfully behind the pot to see a long snake gliding smoothly down between the boards of the deck. Since I only saw his middle section, I can't tell anyone how long he was. I must have waked him up inside his cool jungle hideaway.

He looked—mottled. Grayish or greenish or brownish. I've never seen a snake in this yard in fifteen years and now, the minute it's all ours, surprise.

He lives here too.

Monumental

Ingrid, our neighbor, has a house of fourteen rooms, but actively uses only two of them. "Why need I more?" she proclaims in her giant German brogue. "My Dog has one and I have one. We are—ensconced." I like it when people for whom English is not a native language say unusual words. It gives me a new sense of the dictionary. Revitalizes my syllables. Her nouns are capitalized even when she speaks English.

Ingrid's hefty sausage dog lives in the kitchen and she lives in the bedroom. At night they live together. The other twelve rooms are full of her famous postcard collection alphabetized in long boxes on card tables, Texana lamps, heavily clothed mannequins, tin buckets, wrought-iron plant stands, empty flower pots, Christmas lights, girdles, garter belts, treadle sewing machines, wooden chifforobes stuffed with papers, mailing tubes, thread. If I need anything I have the feeling I could find it under her bed.

She invites us over for tea, but when we get there she never serves it. We look at her postcards. We look and look and look. The cards feel thick and tangible. Some bear the haunting soft tint of antique coloring. The black-and-whites feel crisp and particular. How could such a solid world have been lost so quickly?

Carriages and top hats. Black coupés with running boards. A twist of the parasol and we're off!

Sally's looking through the box of "Famous Ladies" and I'm looking through "Monuments." The Eiffel Tower, the Leaning Tower of Pisa, the Sphinx at Giza, a marble George Washington in the capitol building at Richmond, Virginia. Late afternoon light drifts across Ingrid's white chenille bedspread through cracks on the sides of her window blinds, scrawling the same sentence I read on my grandfather's bed in 1957.

Ingrid's voice grows suddenly sad. "Have you noticed they are making no extravagant Monuments in the World today? Have you seen any new Statues of Liberty lately? Or Towers of Babylon? Presidents' Faces scripted on a Cliff! Now people build for Quickness. They put them up and fall them down. Boom. Few Years and the Walls are cracking. The Life is not—indelible anymore."

We stack the cards neatly back into place, arranging their fine straight edges. Swooning, I cannot remember what month it is. I mention the Arch in St. Louis. She says, "That's thirty years ago, dearie." At our feet the sausage dog scratches his nails on the floor. She invited him in. He clicks and spins. He smells like sweat and summer and old hair and bald spots and no mail but advertisements and bad news on the television set. He smells like somebody else's leftover dinner set out on the stove.

I'm breathing the sweet lost dust of monuments as I lift my eyes to Ingrid's smooth white arms emerging from her sleeveless summer blouse. It's sheer yellow, goldenrod color. Her arms look sleek, marbleized, perfectly curved. At 2 A.M. in bed with the stinky dog they lie on top of her covers in the pool of light from the street lamp outside. No one sees how they glow.

Bread

My grandmother kept rocking on her haunches, moaning, "*Laysh? Laysh?*" Why, why? We were leaving her again. The cousins shuffled in to kiss on both cheeks and gaze at our bags till I had to step outside.

Neighbor children drifted home in the dark with their little sticks and songs. In the mounded oven's doorway, I found my aunt Fahima stooping, fanning the coals. She was baking giant discs of bread for her sons in America, crying, "This big is my love, this rounded and perfectly pocked," slapping the dough.

Next morning a mountain of huge soft loaves lay stacked beside my pillow. I would carry the bread in a tea towel, loose in my lap. I would place my nose in the bread to breathe.

Toward Ramallah we drove, past embroidered bodices, fields of sumac, the blaze of weeping strung out behind us. Each stone marked a minute we would live apart. At a roadside vegetable stand, someone was sweeping, swinging an old broom. I wished for such an average day.

In the airport at Tel Aviv, we begged my uncle to leave

us, go on back. But he had to stride ahead, turning faces with his red and white *keffiyah,* repeatedly comparing his watch and the clock on the wall. When they put us in the slow line, the line for trouble that we earned without even trying, he shook his massive head. He could see he wasn't helping. Said his favorite little English, "Okay," and turned away.

I heaved my suitcase onto the table. A young Israeli flipped the pages of my passport, exaggerating names. "Syria, E-gypt, Jor-dan, *Saudi Arabia*—why you want to go there? For what reason you go there and then come here?"

Each time I was asked to explain to an official how a human being might love a grandmother, a village, my tongue knotted up. Blood swelling inside my veins.

"Did you talk to Arabs? Did any Arab enter the room where your suitcase lay?"

Their wild fluttering when I answered, "Every hour. Every day."

So they X-rayed my socks. They X-rayed my white nightgown, my toothbrush, my extra shoes. Each item lifted onto a cart, separately, and wheeled away to another place. The shame of what we had become, marks against one another, though the olive tinted his skin as it tinted mine. I could feel the awkwardness: "You understand—we have to check the lining." Yet the man seemed so familiar, as if we had shared a textbook in Algebra Two. I knew his hair, the line of his nose. Even when fury roared and reddened my cheeks, the equation for hating did not come clear.

He seemed embarrassed, his breezy manner peppered with pain. Planes were leaving for Frankfurt, London, Paris. I'd forgotten what I held until he placed his head down on the bundle in my arms to inhale its fragrant yeast and a mother's love for her sons rose up around us. He bowed to the bread, reaching out for it.

"Who made this?"

"Fahima made it. My aunt Fahima, in the old *taboon*."

His hands softening, the slope of his jaw. "It's very fresh, yes. You could leave it here with me. I would take good— care—of it. I think there is no better—food." He smiled. For one moment his eyes returned my steady gaze. Did I believe him? He did not X-ray the bread, but handed it back, gently.

Behind us a couple from Bethlehem shifted uneasily, muttering. My uncle would be curving up the long road home by now, resting his eyes on blank spots where villages used to be. My uncle, who had only a few years to live, who would not be allowed entry into Jerusalem to a hospital after his heart attack because he didn't have a permit. "Next time I'll plan better," they say he mumbled before he died. Now my grandmother had someone else to call out to in her sleep, "Come home, come home."

On the other side of the ocean, my cousins would open their arms to take the bread. They would blink hard and break it into wedges, filling their throats, stomachs, picturing their mother's rough hands dusted with flour, the way she tore warm loaves into strips when they were children, and brought the food to their mouths.

Broken Clock

What does time look like from your chair? Once you cowered in a ditch as Turkish soldiers on horseback roared past. Your family remembers this when they try to calculate your age. You don't throw anything away. You've saved bits of a smashed blue plate, a broken clock. Recently my father heard of a blind woman in the next village with a documented age of a hundred and six who had known you all her life. Take me there, he said. He stood in the outer room while the woman's son addressed her loudly. "You remember your friend Khadra Shihab's youngest son Aziz?" The woman shouted back immediately. "You mean that awful boy who broke his mother's heart by going to America? Of course I remember him! How could I forget?"

My father, in the next room, shrinking to the size of a button. Ushered into the woman's presence with a stuck jaw. A peep. "How old is my mother?" She said without hesitating, "A hundred and four." They had always had two years between them. You know if someone else is a little younger than you are, but not much. You know. She remembered, in fact, when Khadra was born, in those other houses, that other world. When they were very young, even then, two years. "And what will you do now?" she asked him. "After so much being away, how does it feel to return? Does anything know you now? Do the trees know you? Does the prayer know you? And where do you go when you leave here? Does this place really let you leave?"

STILL THE SKY

Poetry

The library shelves opened their arms. In the library everyone was rich. I stacked my bounty, counting books, arranging their spines. Bindings of fresh new books smelled delicious.

On television Carl Sandburg strummed his guitar, his voice a honey-sweet dream of rolling, rollicking words. His white hair looked lit up from inside, like a bulb. I read every morning, every night: if you knew how to read, you could never be lonely.

If you know how to read, it made sense that you might, one night in a Chicago hotel, ask for a large piece of pale construction paper—not the easiest thing to come by in a hotel—and write down something you felt that day when you saw the streets that were also bridges lifting up for boats to pass under. When you tipped your head back to gaze at the giant towers in which a thousand people worked who had never even *thought* of your name. It was worth saying.

You could take it to school and give it to your first-grade teacher, who didn't like you. Pretend it was a present.

She would hang it on the bulletin board in the hall and weeks later, far from that trip, a girl in school who was bigger than you would pause to say, "Did you write that poem?"

"Ho! Yes. I almost forgot."

She smiled. "I read it—and I know what you *mean*,"— skipping off to join her friends at the monkey bars.

She knew what I *meant*. That was something. That was a wing to fly on all the way home, or for the rest of a life.

Banned Poem

(East Jerusalem, 1992)

The Palestinian journalists have gathered in a small, modestly elegant theater that could have dropped out of any neighborhood in Paris or New York. We're shivering, having just whirled through a gust of bone-chilling wind on the street outside. Our friend tells us it's always cold and windy on this one street.

Mulling together with their notebooks, the journalists—mostly men in dark jackets, a few using *keffiyahs* for scarves—speak quietly. Some sit at tables, smoking over small cups of coffee and plates of sweets.

I feel overcome by a speaker's worst horror—nothing to say. Too much, and nothing. What could I possibly say that these people might want to hear? Why would a group of beleaguered journalists wish to listen to a Palestinian-American poet who lives in Texas?

We shake hands, greet, get introduced. The niceties of human encounter weigh heavily upon the room. Moments later, as if detecting my sudden reluctance, they speak of canceling today's meeting, or gathering tomorrow instead, once they have better spread the word. Apparently not enough people have arrived to make them feel the crowd is a respectable size. I tell them the smaller the better. I would be happiest to speak to a mouse just now.

Because it is not hard to have some idea of their situation, and because their faces house such strong dignity nonetheless, I keep asking questions. How do you stand this life here? How do you sustain hope?

And the answers come slowly, cloaked in the mystery that says: We keep on going. See? We wake up and we keep on going.

Amidst daily curfews, closures, and beatings, my friend the bookseller arranges her lovely series of British Ladybird books for children. "I never know, on any given day, if I will be able to come to work, since I live in the next town."

At a famous east Jerusalem restaurant, Walid stuffs succulent carrots and baby eggplants, stirring a pot of lentil soup for my five-year-old son. I think of Walid's gracious greeting to everyone who enters. "You may sit where you feel best." We've chosen the table next to the heater every time.

My new friend the English professor teaches contemporary American and British literature behind a university door riddled with at least fifty ungrammatical bullet holes. Israeli soldiers approached the campus recently while the students held a small party, a rare occurrence in Intifada times, to celebrate the end of semester. "The party had nothing to do with politics," he tells me. "You know that relief which comes after exams, before break, that sense of lightened load and sweeter days? A very momentary sense, I can assure you, particularly here in the occupied territories. My students were eating cake when the soldiers started shouting outside. The students called down to them, 'This is a private gathering,' and they started shooting. Believe me, there was no more provocation than that. We are leaving the door with the bullet holes to remind us of the terrible times we live in."

The times. They are hard to forget. And the journalists carry notebooks and pens, though every paragraph they write must first be submitted to the Israeli censors. In my mind a censor is a huge hulking man at a wide desk with a cigar and a massive ink pad for stamping NO NO NO. The journalists file into their seats. I say how often journalism has frustrated me, and maybe that is why the world needs poetry too.

After the start of the Intifada, our local newspaper in Texas ticked off the Palestinian dead in tiny token back-page notes: 76th Palestinian dead, 425th Palestinian dead—as if keeping score in a sporting event. Only when the number fattened to a ripe round 500 did the victim receive a story. Ibtisam Bozieh, age thirteen. She'd dreamed of becoming a doctor but was shot in the face by an Israeli soldier when she peered curiously through the window of her village home, perhaps to see what was going on out there.

After reading that slim story, I could not stop thinking about Ibtisam Bozieh. She followed me, in waking, in troubled sleep. A small poem was born, written to her, which includes the lines "When do we become doctors for one another, Arab, Jew, instead of guarding tumors of pain as if they hold us upright?"

The journalists ask for a copy of the poem. I read a few others. I try to tell them, in a way they may believe, how many Americans I know, both writers and otherwise, who have their interests at heart. But quite obviously we do not run the government. They grow energetic. They tell me we will meet tomorrow too, same theater, same hour. Tomorrow my father, the retired Palestinian-American journalist, will speak, and I will sit in the audience. This sounds better to me.

Next day a small hubbub greets us in the theater, a brimming excitement. The journalists arrange a microphone for my father. Today a few women with strong, careful faces filter in with the men. The way they look at me, I can tell what they think of the United States. Tear gas canisters scattered in the fields by Israeli soldiers say, "Made in Pennsylvania." My grandmother's village home was gassed yesterday as we sat in it, for no reason, as if to give us a small taste of what people experience here on a daily basis. My female cousins stayed shockingly calm. "Don't worry," they said to me, unscrewing the cap on a little bottle of perfume. "It goes away in twenty minutes."

My friend Lena arrived late for a meeting this morning because her shaken neighbor told her this story: yesterday soldiers dragged off the neighbor's husband while he took care of his little boys, ages four and two. The soldiers left the boys locked in the house by themselves, after smashing the toilet and bathtub and sink. "This is a new tactic," says Lena. "Israeli soldiers like to smash Palestinian bathrooms. Don't ask me why." Water poured into the rest of the house; the little boys stood on chairs, screaming, till their mother came home from work and found them.

I keep thinking of those signs in the United States at construction sites: YOUR TAX DOLLARS AT WORK HERE. I keep feeling dizzy, as if the stories create an altitude unsuitable for living. Yet journalists and date-cake vendors and taxi drivers and schoolgirls in blue pleated skirts keep on living, if they are lucky. A boy in a stationery store arranges a display of children's vivid stickers shaped like chipmunks and ducks and bears, as he would at a happy sales counter anywhere. What happens to people to make them worse than chipmunks and ducks and bears?

Yesterday after our meeting the journalists translated my poem about Ibtisam into Arabic the minute we headed down the street to Walid's restaurant. I can picture them— smoking, arguing over words. They submitted it to the censors with the rest of their stories last night. It came back today slashed with red Xs, stamped at the bottom of the page REJECTED ENTIRELY in Arabic and Hebrew. The journalists have encircled it with barbed wire and placed it on red velvet under a frame, presenting it to me at the microphone in front of the crowd, a gift to take home. So I may remember them and the shape of their days. "Now you are one of us," they say. It's a strangely honorable linkage, to be rejected by their own censors.

Think of it: two peoples, so closely related it's hard to tell them apart in the streets sometimes, claiming the same land. The end of the twentieth century.

I keep shuddering. I keep feeling gripped, as if someone has placed an icy hand on my shoulder. None of this does any good for Ibtisam, of course. She's probably buried in her high-up village between the craggy, endlessly patient olive trees. It seems wrong to me that soldiers wear olive-colored fatigues.

Women of the West

In those vagabond months we followed roads early and late, often yawning widely, in our little silver station wagon with the Texas license plates. This day we had left Walla Walla, home of the famous fat onions, before dawn. I'd heard that in Walla Walla a rich onion fragrance sweetens the air like those towns in California where broccoli scent clings to your clothes, but it must have been the wrong season because all I could smell was furrowed ground.

We had stopped in a town along the Columbia River where a few early fishermen in rowboats leaned into the mist. We ordered homemade cinnamon rolls just like the two craggy gents at the counter were eating. They looked like they had been fishing and not catching much for a long, long time. Our little boy ran in circles around our table singing, "I can't say Columbia, I can only say River!"—a weird little chant he'd made up. He could say anything he wanted to.

I read the placemat titled Women of the West and learned about the numerous curves of Miss Jane Barnes, first white woman to set foot in the fur-trapping settlements of north-west Oregon. I had heard of her often and imagined her courage, but never her curves. I had not known that, after inciting "envy, admiration, and passion" among the settlers for years, she'd returned to England to regale bar patrons with tales of "uncivilized Oregon," nor had I ever heard that Sacajawea had saved the journals of Lewis and Clark from sinking into raging rapids at the same time she saved her own baby. Nor had I ever heard, when I could have used it, about occupying a baby by tying a chunk of fat meat to his toe on a long string, so if he happened to choke, the toe's reflex would rip the treat from his throat. Exhausted pioneer mothers must have thought that one up. Suddenly our predawn drive back to Portland seemed substantially easier.

The waitress refreshed our coffee cups, pouring slowly. She seemed groggy and pleasant, and she liked our dancing child. I complimented her placemats and she said they had a whole collection of Women of the West stories at the front desk; this mat, simply an excerpt. Also they carried a cassette of someone reading the same stories, which you could listen to in your car.

We had driven up and down the Columbia River many times by now, in and out of towns like Astoria and Corbett, towns where history feels palpable in the streets—in Clatskanie, white settlers carried in a disease that completely erased the Clatskanie tribe—and I swear you can still feel a hum of regret, a wailing and keening, in the piney air. We felt ripe with questions—Why, Who lived here, What did this used to be? The first moment we'd actually seen a salmon pushing upstream in a shallow creek had been a stunning epiphany. So I felt tempted—books and tapes. This duty we feel, growing older, to learn as much about the past as we can . . . but our car was stuffed. We'd already pitched a few clothes and toys. But we also kept adding things—miniature blackberry conserve, stones with mossy sides. How to balance the two impulses? So I decided against the tape and went to the restroom to wash up.

On a wall near the sink loomed an old metal case with a strangely primitive handlettered sign—PERFUME DISPENSER—and a slot for 25¢. The amount had been erased and changed over the years. Three fragrances were lettered above the knobs—MUSK, CHARLIE, JOVAN—and a recommendation, PRESS PLUNGER FIRMLY AND STAND CLOSE. I was immediately attracted by those last two words.

Excited, I fumbled for a quarter and pressed it into the slot. A resounding plunk. The gust of perfume that shot out came strong as artillery into my ear, so I felt momentarily dazed. I staggered back to our table, awakened and reeking. *Do you notice anything different about me?* Exhilarated by this discovery of something new—old, perhaps, but new to me—and unashamed as if I had just discovered a pass through the mountains or secret stream. What a thrill it must have been, for women or men either one, astonishing even to imagine. Now we follow the ranger signs that tell exactly how many paces to the Fairy Waterfall and feel grateful.

In such a buoyant manner, then, I listened with my new musk-tinted hearing to the waitress count our change, and emerged into the river-rich air, back onto the road. In this way I too became a Woman of the West.

Used Cars on Oahu

A hum of anticipation overtook fellow passengers as our jumbo jet landed at Honolulu. We had our noses pressed to the windows for the green hump of island coming into view. Fragrant orchid leis awaited us, as did lumbering buses, warm beaches, and that vision of relentless relaxation that people seem to embrace in a big way.

My husband had been very solemn since our departure from San Antonio. He was dubiously contemplating his immediate future on an island not very wide. This man who grew up on the gulf coast of Texas, who likes neither to swim, nor fish, nor sail, had been a reluctant convert to the news that I'd accepted a semester-long invitation to be visiting writer for the English department at the University of Hawaii.

Our first concerns were to meet the one-room dwelling we'd been offered, gain our bearings, and buy a car. This last sounded easy—how hard could it be to find a car in a city utterly jammed with them? The streets of Honolulu run bumper to bumper even in early afternoon. I felt thunderstruck by how all these vehicles had made it to the middle of the Pacific Ocean.

We bought the local *Advertiser,* picked up the free *Penny Pincher,* and settled in at a neighborhood coffee shop where the specialty seemed to be hot dogs wrapped in small waffles. Someone had told us we'd find a used car for $500-$700 since cars in Hawaii often resell over and over. People sometimes bought their own cars back again after sabbaticals on the mainland or seasons in Tahiti.

The cars under $1,000 sounded dangerous, but we identified a crowd of possibilities in the $1,500 range. Racing up to my campus telephone, unrolling the heavy louvered windows, we learned our first island truth—hang on, or everything blows away. Tradewinds roared down the valley, crashing through trees and windows—we were specks in the path. Auto ads swirled up out of our hands.

As we were phoning, a second truth came clear—no one stays home much in Honolulu. One evening we called sixteen numbers at a reasonably homey hour—8:30 P.M.— and found one real voice to talk to. Where was everybody? *Kamaainas* (natives, or long-time residents, as opposed to tourists) are quick to say they rarely visit the places tourists go. They don't even eat in the same restaurants. It seemed unlikely they'd all be at a beach in the dark, anyway. Were they still working? Contrary to their leisurely image, island residents frequently keep more than one job, to pay soaring rents and mortgages. ("I moved here because I love diving," a young woman at Midas Muffler would tell me days later. "And I haven't been to the beach since I came, because I'm always at work.")

Slowly we gathered a few appointments. The first car we visited lived in an elegant neighborhood halfway up a steep mountain. Since we were living halfway up another mountain, test drives on vertical slopes seemed critical. We liked the ten-year-old car but, with its 125,000 miles, thought it overpriced. A gracious Japanese man named

Jimmy explained he was showing it "for a friend" who had moved to the North Shore, so he couldn't barter. He kept proclaiming its good points. Wasn't it immaculately kept? Wasn't the clock attractive? We ended up trading Buddhist quotations.

The next car we visited lived down at the docks because its owners resided on a houseboat. A voice named Don would meet us at a palm tree near a dumpster. His ad contained a misprint, he explained on the phone. It said $1,800 but should have read $800 due to a minor problem—the front passenger door hinges had rusted away. When you opened the door, it dropped down to the ground. Everything would be fine if you never opened that door. Don and his wife found the door a real "bummer," but we might not mind it. This price slash perked our interest considerably.

We found Don, deeply suntanned and smooth, amidst a sea of bobbing hulls. He rode with us on a test drive around Diamond Head. He showed us where he went surfing every morning. He used our first names easily, pointing out the aquarium and the zoo. The car made a deep grating sound every time we paused for a light. What was it? Don said it wasn't anything. The car had always made that noise.

Look, a terrific sushi bar! Don couldn't tell us enough. We kept reining in the conversation. The only thing Don's car *didn't* like was sitting. If you let it sit for a few days without turning it on, it would rebel and refuse to start for awhile. Then, as you were driving later, it would just turn off. But if you let it rest about ten minutes, it started up again. No problem. When was the last time it had rebelled? Three days ago. But see, here it was, driving again! The world was a good and reasonable place.

Don stood back while my husband and I discussed his car. "I don't mind the door," I whispered to my husband. "It's this stopping thing that bothers me. What if it turns off on the highway?" Don was whistling, gazing out to sea. He'd come to Hawaii, a "high cardiac risk," ten years ago. He and his wife had planned to sail around the world, but once they found such a lovely spot, decided to stay. "Just wait," he said. "It will happen to you too."

In a flurry of good will, we called out to Don, "We'll take it!"

He ebulliently offered us a future sail on his boat.

Did he want money down? No need. We could bring him the cash right here at this dock after the banks opened on Monday. We walked away with his keys in our pocket by mistake and he had to chase us.

It was Saturday then. We spent the day feeling good about things, visiting the famous Japanese department store, eating Thai noodles and writing letters. It was, as a writer friend describes, the high slope of the loopity-loop ride that becomes one's life. But Sunday morning my husband and I each awakened in a state of extreme agitation, knowing we'd made a mistake.

"We can't take that car," my husband said. "Obviously it has something terribly wrong with it. Don's just been lucky. We were infected by his enthusiasm. The car's going to fall apart any moment! A rusted door, sure—and what else is rusted after sitting down at the docks all those years? Did you *hear* that *sound?*"

I agreed. God, we were reckless. We might have purchased a cigar factory if happy Don had offered it to us.

We began trying to call him back. His phone rang and rang. I walked away each time my husband dialed; I couldn't bear to be present when he gave Don the bad news. But Don didn't answer—surf was high, sun bright, no telling what wave Don floated on just then. The trunk of his car had been stuffed with boogie boards and snorkel tubes.

All Sunday, between phoning Don, we looked at other

used cars, feeling like impostors. We were driving a Toyota borrowed from our landlords which boasted quirks of its own, such as a headliner which had ripped out over the driver's seat and flapped madly around the driver's head. We hadn't anticipated needing air-conditioning in a breezy place like Hawaii, but driving the Toyota in heavy traffic changed our minds. Now we were getting pickier.

A vastly bosomed Australian in a tight red tank top met us at an intersection with her fading little Sprint. Ten years ago Loretta had come to Hawaii for two weeks—suddenly everybody's story. I took an instant dislike to her car, despite its air-conditioning, despite her need to return to Australia to be with her dying father.

A SURF NAKED slogan was slapped across its back window. I could feel years of grit ground into the carpet as I climbed into the cramped back seat. My husband startled me by asking her lowest price and agreeing to have the car checked out by a mechanic. They would reconvene next week. I had no good feelings about this car at all and continued to say so to my husband, as we stopped at pay phones to dial Don's number.

We drove to the town of Kailua, to a car lot speckled with balloons and a swivel-hipped salesman named Dave. The car we'd seen advertised was gone by the time we arrived. But I shocked my husband by showing interest in a giant gas-guzzler. Dave assured us the guzzler would have no trouble at all climbing high slopes and swooping down to sea level again. My husband whispered, "Are you *nuts?* Have you seen the price of *gas out here?*"

Dave promised to call us if anything better rolled in.

I was growing obsessed by a man named Buddy, whom I'd spoken to before we met Don, and whose Nissan we hadn't seen yet. It wasn't his exactly—it belonged to his son, who had joined the marines. Buddy had a haunting low-key manner on the phone, which now, in retrospect, seemed very attractive. I'd dial Buddy again every time my husband called Don.

"In the islands," someone had written me, "the first thing you do is buy a cooler. Then you fill it with drinks. You put it in the back of the car and take it everywhere with you. It's a must!" I kept picturing Buddy and Don off with their coolers while we struggled to find a car we could put one in.

We drove up to the settlement of Waipahu, dissolute with chain restaurants and tacky apartments. A monosyllabic salesman took us out in an Escort that buzzed a high pitch and wouldn't shift. "Humph," he said. "Rough. Humph." At the next lot a salesman named Mick blew up when I inquired why a station wagon was so cheap. "Don't ask questions like that! See for yourself!" The car had no battery, for one thing. Mick slammed the hood shut, his round belly straining his Aloha shirt.

A snazzily dressed young woman at the next lot looked downcast when we identified our price range, which was soaring higher by the moment. "You could only get an old junker for that." She took us out back to see two cars with flat tires.

"That's it," my husband said gloomily, driving back toward Honolulu. "We have to rent a car for a few days while we search. We can't borrow this Toyota any longer." Our son, who had just asked if we were going to be looking at cars for the rest of our lives, pointed out the fifth rainbow of the day drooped between two mountains. "Daddy didn't see the first one," he clarified, "so it's *our* fifth and *his* fourth." The balloon from Dave was losing its zip.

Somehow we bypassed the airport exit, where we imagined all rent-a-cars to be, and had to take at least a ten-mile turnaround to get back there. Then the agency we wanted—

the cheapest, of course—turned out to be located elsewhere, under a freeway. Driving toward it silently, we spotted a totemic Texas name lettered on a warehouse—Lone Star Auto Repossessions. It looked sweet, but closed. I wrote down the address.

Giddy travelers with duffle bags were hopping out of buses in front of the rental agency, wearing candy-colored shorts. They'd already rented all the cheaper cars. We took a hefty Cavalier and I startled myself by gunning the engine as I drove out of the lot. My husband followed in the steamy Toyota. Flipping the air conditioner to high and finding a radio station that played old-time Hawaiian music made me feel a little better. Driving back into town, I realized the exits were starting to look familiar.

We stopped at one more pay phone and Don answered, shouting a warm "Michael!" to my husband, which made it harder to tell him we didn't want his car. My husband winced, but said Don remained congenial throughout the conversation. He agreed we shouldn't take it if we had any second thoughts. We didn't mention third or fourth thoughts. I figured this nixed our sailing trip. Little did Don know he would become a part of our daily vernacular— Don this, Don that, wonder what Don would think, hope we don't run into Don over there.

Buddy was still at the beach.

The next morning Buddy answered. No, his son's car wasn't sold yet. He offered low-key directions to his house. "Take the Likelike Highway, you know which one? It looks like Like-Like. But they say Leeky-Leeky. Well, come through the Wilson Tunnel. Take a right, then a left, then a curly curve, then a sort of straight, then a jog." Every street he mentioned started with a *K*. My notations had a rhythmic, esoteric quality.

He didn't say we'd go completely under the high green

spine of mountains that composes the magical center of this island, or through clouds, or past temples. He didn't say we'd end up at Kaneohe on the other side of the island, blinking in the brightness, and have to stop at a dive shop to get our directions deciphered. He didn't say one street changed its name in the middle either. I had to call him back two more times.

At last we found him up a crowded driveway, surrounded by cars in various states of decline. He startled us by not even having the keys to the battered red one we wanted to see. We couldn't get inside it or start the engine or do a test-drive. My husband seemed dumbfounded. I asked, "But when will you *have* the keys?" and Buddy said, "Oh you know, maybe couple a days maybe couple a hours. That boy a mine's in town just now but when he come, he take off, go see friends, beach, you know the story."

"Does *he* have the keys?"

Buddy said, "Well you know, now that you mention it, I'm not sure." A lanky black man in his sixties, Buddy grew more animated when we asked about the instrument in the back of his own station wagon. A bass, yeah. He'd played with the Inkspots. Heard of the Inkspots? Now he sat in with other bands on weekends—the Neuro-Leptics, a group of doctors. Come any time! Also he distributed Fountain of Youth Shampoos and Creams. We waited while he went inside for samples, creamy pink conditioners, a succulent green gel to use after too much sun.

"Nice guy, your Buddy," my husband said as we drove back to our side of the island. "Can't say much for his rust heaps, but a hell of a guy."

We drove straight to Lone Star Auto Repossessions, encouraged that we could even find it again, and met a cool Texan in exile on crutches who seemed more interested in the tostada chips he was munching than in business. We examined the pictures pinned to his wall—himself in a hospital bed, tubes taped to his body. "I'm a stuntman," he said. "That's my real life. I just do this on the side." I liked his voice. "Go take yourselves a look."

Outside we zoomed in immediately on a Nissan Sentra exactly like the car we own back home. Simple and clean, it boasted fifty thousand miles and one cigarette burn on a door handle. A young Hawaiian named Manny in a shirt printed with bright hibiscus poured two quarts of transmission fluid into the engine and suggested we drive around the block. He climbed into the back seat.

I could barely urge the car onto the access road—it refused to click into gear. Manny noted calmly that we were leaving large pools of transmission fluid behind us. At the first light, dark smoke poured forth from the engine. Manny said, "It got a problem, yeah? I thought it had a problem." I jumped out of the front seat and asked him to drive. By traveling five miles per hour he was able to coax the heaving beast back home.

It seemed unlikely we'd continue to be interested in this loser, but my husband felt suddenly inspired. Hawaii was starting to grow on him. What if a new transmission could be installed before we made our bid to the bank? The bank or Lone Star, their broker, would foot the repairs.

The stuntman seemed dubious, but open-minded. "Usually you take the car as is, know what I mean, but I realize if you can't even drive it away from here . . . well hey man, who knows?" He called the bank. The banker was all tied up. I could picture him with a bunch of other bankers in floral shirts, their heads bent over a table. In Hawaii, if somebody wears a necktie, you ask him, "What's wrong?"

I asked Manny if Hawaiians really went to the beach in the dark and he said night surfing had always been his favorite sport.

For two days the banker remained tied up. We kept phoning Lone Star to ask if they'd gotten through. We said Howdy. We called them more times than we had called Don. Once the phone rang and it was Dave from Kailua informing us about another clunker. We could barely remember who he was.

I was beginning to think we might spend five months on the telephone. Finally the busy banker responded positively. We drove to Lone Star to pay $50 down. They said they'd never done anything like this before. I overheard the mechanic's name—Fernando. Our car was being taken to Fernando. All day I made mental votive offerings in his name.

We turned in our rented car and said a firm No to Loretta the Australian, who asked my husband, "Would you be more interested if I told you I found out my car is an '85 instead of an '84?" We began riding TheBus (epitome of generic designations, with both words run together on the side). TheBus cost 60¢ to anywhere, exact change only, and seemed to stop every half-block. We didn't care. Finally we had focused our hopes. That our bid would be more than three times what we initially intended to pay didn't even bother us. We weren't phoning the circled boxes in the newspaper anymore.

When we returned to Lone Star, the entire staff was guzzling pizza. They offhandedly pitched us the keys and we pulled out of the lot by ourselves nervously. Would the car shift? Would we make it around the block five times? I kept wanting to back up. Just to be sure. Manny said, "Congratulations." We'd stood in line at the bank behind Robert McFarland, Reagan's ex-advisor, to withdraw $3,400 in cash. (Five months later on Christmas Eve we would sell it for exactly the same price to a Hawaiian sovereignty activist who would withdraw her own money from the very same bank. We would refer only briefly to the car's mysterious tendency to get five miles to the gallon. We suggested she have a tune-up.)

At the wheel of our own vehicle, we felt uplifted, self-propelled at last. Our confidence increased once the car had conquered the steep hill to our little studio apartment, which grew homier quickly now that we could drive around buying tablecloths, a coffee pot, and old cereal bowls from the local Goodwill.

And our new car came with its own sticker in the back window, which seemed to describe our situation entirely—"Lone Star ** Hawaii." We had fallen into one another's arms.

Thinking of the millions in this world for whom a car remains a wish, I felt slightly shy about the luck of a shiny white Sentra when just a few days before a fussy Filipino bus driver had shouted us to the back of his bus. He didn't like the baggage we were lugging. I noted, in a list of "Do's and Don'ts in Hawaii," that people didn't honk their horns much—in fact, we hadn't heard a horn since we arrived.

And I realized how quickly the eye falls into habits—we couldn't stop noticing cars for sale everywhere, in the parking lot at Longs Drugs, or the Foodland supermarket, or displayed in people's yards. We evaluated them unconsciously. Driving past Makaha, on the dry, less friendly part of the island, up to a sign that says END OF THE ROAD, we saw an old Chevrolet parked on the sand.

RUNS GREAT!!! $75.00!!! exclaimed exuberant white lettering across the front window. But there was no phone number, no further information—just a car announcing itself against the brilliant, wild expanse of waves.

Mint Snowball

My great-grandfather on my mother's side ran a drugstore in a small town in central Illinois. He sold pills and rubbing alcohol from behind the big cash register and creamy ice cream from the soda fountain. My mother remembers the counter's long polished sweep, its shining face. She twirled on the stools. Dreamy fans. Wide summer afternoons and clinking nickels. He sold milkshakes, cherry cokes, old-fashioned sandwiches. (What did an old-fashioned sandwich look like?) Dark wooden shelves. Silver spigots on chocolate dispensers.

My great-grandfather had one specialty: a Mint Snowball, which he invented. Some people drove all the way in from Decatur just to taste it. First he stirred fresh mint leaves with sugar and secret ingredients in a small pot on the stove for a very long time, concocting a fragrant elixir of mint. Its scent clung to his fingers even after he washed his hands. Then he shaved ice into tiny particles and served it mounded in a glass dish, permeated with mint syrup. Scoops of rich vanilla ice cream to each side.

My mother took a bite of minty ice and ice cream mixed

together. The Mint Snowball tasted like winter. She closed her eyes to see the Swiss village my great-grandfather's parents came from. Snow frosting the roofs. Glistening, dangling spokes of ice.

Before my great-grandfather died, he sold the recipe for the mint syrup to someone in town for one hundred dollars. This hurt my grandfather's feelings. My grandfather thought he should have inherited it to carry on the tradition. As far as the family knew, the person who bought the recipe never used it. At least not in public. My mother had watched my grandfather make the syrup so often she thought she could replicate it. But what did he have in those little unmarked bottles? She experimented. Once she came close. She wrote down what she did. Now she has lost the paper.

Perhaps the clue to my entire personality connects to the lost Mint Snowball. I have always felt out of step with my environment, disjointed in the modern world. The crisp flush of cities depresses me. Strip centers. Poodle grooming and take-out Thai. I am angry over lost department stores, wistful for something I have never tasted or seen.

Although I know how to do everything one needs to know—change airplanes, find my exit off the interstate, charge gas, send a fax—there is something missing. Perhaps the stoop of my great-grandfather over the pan, the slow patient swish of his spoon. The spin of my mother on the high stool with her whole life in front of her, something fine and fragrant still to happen. When I breathe a handful of mint, even pathetic sprigs from my sunbaked Texas earth, I close my eyes. Little chips of ice on the tongue, their cool slide down. Can we follow the long river of the word *refreshment* back to its spring? Is there another land for me? Can I find any lasting solace in the color green?

White Coals

Scarcely anything bigger than the questions I didn't ask. What happened to my mouth? I traveled all the way across the ocean with my mouth and couldn't get the questions out. A stiff-haired cat perched on the high stone wall between leafless brambles staring down at me. The cat with his elegant command of two silences. It was *cold*. My grandmother had *bare feet*. She held her feet by a crooked brazier of whitened coals. She turned her hands over and over. In the six years since our last meeting a tiredness had gathered itself, stonelike, in the corners of her eyes. She could say anything she wanted but she didn't want much. Holding her gaze to the floor, she wouldn't look up for pictures. I wanted to describe the silent women on Maunakea Street in Honolulu who sit all day poking needles through the hearts of flowers. The tight purple orchid, its silken lips. I wanted to ask advice: What should we tell our child about his living? But my mouth went heavy, my mouth wouldn't say. It said, Would you like these socks? My grandmother who will never wear a lei, I string you with questions, from a great distance each one flies to your shoulders, pulsing, a bird turned into a flower, folding its wings.

Talk, Talk, Talk

It seems ironic that after my vocal cord diagnosis, when the doctor recommended I desist from talking for seven to ten days to let my throat rest, the first thing I wanted to do was tell everyone about it.

How first he pressed tiny pads of cocaine up my nose—an extremely minimal dosage, he assured, though I must say that one moment I cared quite a bit about the ominous-sounding procedure I was about to undergo and the next minute it all sounded just fine to me.

Then he sprayed anesthesia down my throat. "It tastes like rotten bananas," the nurse assured me in advance, with clear warning not to let it travel back up into my mouth and mix with saliva or my whole tongue would go numb. This was one of those instructions that sounds very easy until you actually have to do it.

Once I was properly deadened, the very tall and for-mally gracious doctor pressed the thin arm of a lit telescope up my nose and down my throat, and my son, who had been watching from the corner with mild interest as he sucked the straw of a chocolate milk, perked to attention.

Actually the telescope was rather like a straw. But less pleasant. The doctor peered into a little window to see what he could see.

My tonsils had *atrophied,* a word I disliked hearing applied to anything on my person, even something as useless as tonsils. And my vocal cords had little calluses where they pressed together. He checked through the other nostril, then whipped that telescope out, confident. "This won't take a day off your life, but you need to be much quieter for a while so your cords can heal, and then you need to go to a speech pathologist to be retrained. You need to learn how to talk and sing so you don't do whatever it is you're doing. There's nothing I can give you, no antibiotic, no surgery, they're actually only the size of pinheads. You know how you can get a callous if you garden? So what do you do to get rid of it? Stop holding the little shovel that way." I was feeling dreamy all of a sudden, lost in the gardens of metaphor.

He went on. "You know how easy it is to regain a callous once you've lost it? Very easy. So that's why you need retraining." I kept nodding, flushed with the sense of enormous humility I feel in the presence of doctors. They tell me obvious things and I feel deeply grateful. Maybe this has something to do with being a closet dunce.

I left his office silently, after paying the $205 fee though $55 had been quoted on the phone. It was that telescope test that puffed up the sum. An era of my life had ended unexpectedly and I couldn't imagine life on the other side. The door of fast and frivolous gab had just slammed shut. Maybe this would be good advice for a writer—save all that talk, honey, and get to work. I felt relieved not to have throat cancer. I didn't quite know how I'd answer my friend whose letter said, "I really miss you and that little husk in your voice."

Back home my husband tells me he's been suggesting I speak more quietly (and less, though he's too polite to say it) for years, for free. "And you feel like you've had a revelation or something?" He shakes his head, this man who does not share my humility in the presence of the medical profession, this man who fainted when he got a gamma globulin shot.

I'm stirring honey in a cup of hot lemon juice. I'm wrapping my neck in a pink bandanna. I, who always felt secretly attracted to understated moderates and bare minimums, have found talk the one venue in which it is very easy to go the extra mile.

I have answered ten questions when only one was asked. To me, gossip has never been a dirty word. It's the interesting part. Why pretend?

So what will I do? I'll give up giving advice, for one. That should cut things back considerably. I'll shake my head more. I'll leave the answering machine on even when I'm sitting right next to it—the only problem is, you have to return calls *someday*. I find it harder to call later than to answer in the first place. I'll say, "Thank you!" with less enthusiasm to checkout clerks. My son and husband know I talk to everybody—strangers, friends, friends of friends, even ex-friends, with similar gusto. I'll give it up. I'll become the margin on the page.

This summer we placed stones on the site of Thoreau's reclusive hut. We walked completely around Walden Pond, jabbering about solitude all the way.

I'll stop singing along with Annie Lennox and Lyle Lovett. I'll stop telling stories out loud to myself in the car— a major sacrifice since this shameless private dialogue has always been the one conversation that helped me figure everything out. Temporarily, anyhow. I'll have to do it in my head.

Meanwhile, I'll light candles to Talullah Bankhead and Tom Waits, those saints of the gravelly ranges. I'll hope the

Israeli woman who called me the minute I got home from the voice doctor and talked for twenty-four minutes doesn't call back. She wanted to establish "an ongoing conversation" with me to be printed in her Jewish-Arab dialogues book. "Can't it be written down?" I croaked. I didn't want to go into the telescope details.

"No, no," she said, " that's a completely different experience. There's nothing like the spoken word." It took her twenty-four minutes just to figure out the logistics of when we *might* talk. When we hung up, she said *Shalom* and I said *Salaam* and I thought how loud the air conditioner in the kitchen sounds, now that I'm not supposed to drown it out.

One Moment on Top of the Earth

For
Palestine
and
for Israel

In February she was dying again, so he flew across the sea to be with her. Doctors came to the village. They listened and tapped and shook their heads. She's a hundred and five, they said. What can we do? She's leaving now. This is how some act when they're leaving. She would take no food or drink in her mouth. The family swabbed her dry lips with water night and day, and the time between. Nothing else. And the rooster next-door still marked each morning though everything else was changing. Her son wrote three letters saying, Surely she will die tonight. She is so weak. Sometimes she knows who I am and sometimes she calls me by the name of her dead sister. She dreams of the dead ones and shakes her head. Fahima said, Don't you want to go be with them? and she said, I don't want to have anything to do with them. You go be with them if you like.

Be my guest. We don't know what is best. We sit by her side all the time because she cries if we walk away. She feels it, even with her eyes shut. Her sight is gone. Surely she will die tonight.

Then someone else who loved her got on an airplane and flew across the sea. When she heard he was landing, she said, Bring me soup. The kind that is broth with nothing in it. They lit the flame. He came and sat behind her on the bed, where she wanted him to sit, so she could lean on him and soak him up. It was cold and they huddled together, everyone in one room, telling any story five times and stretching it. Laughing in places besides ones which had seemed funny before. Laughing more because they were in that time of sadness that is fluid and soft. She who had almost been gone after no eating and drinking for twenty days was even laughing. And then she took the bread that was torn into small triangles, and the pressed oil, and the soft egg. She took the tiny glass of tea between her lips. She took the match and held it, pressing its tiny sulfuric head between her fingers so she could feel the roughness. Something shifted inside her eyes, so the shapes of people's faces came alive again. Who's that? she said about a woman from another village who had entered her room very quietly with someone else. She's lovely, but who is she? I never saw her before. And they were hiding inside themselves a tenderness about someone being so close to gone and then returning.

She wanted her hair to be washed and combed. She wanted no one arguing in her room or the courtyard outside. She wanted a piece of lamb meat grilled with fat dripping crispily out of it. She wanted a blue velvet dress and a black sweater. And they could see how part of being alive was wanting things again. And they sent someone to the store in the next town, which was a difficult thing since you had to pass by many soldiers. And in all these years not one had ever smiled at them yet.

Then the two men from across the sea had to decide what to do next, which was fly away again, as usual. They wished they could take her with them but she, who had not even entered the Holy City for so long though it was less than an hour away, said yes and no so much about going, they knew she meant no. After a hundred and five years. You could not blame her. Even though she wasn't walking anymore, this was definitely her floor. This voice calling from the tower of the little village mosque. This rich damp smell of the stones in the walls.

So they left and I came, on the very next day. We were keeping her busy. She said to me, *Marhabtein*—Hello twice—which is what she always says instead of just Hello and our hands locked tightly together. Her back was still covered with sores, so she did not want to lie down. She wanted to eat whatever I had with me. Pralines studded with pecans, and chocolate cake. They said, Don't give her too much of that. If it's sweet, she'll just keep eating. She wanted cola, water and tea. She wanted the juice of an orange. She said to me, So how is everybody? Tell me about all of them. And I was stumbling in the tongue again, but somehow she has always understood me. They were laughing at how badly I stumbled and they were helping me. It was the day which has no seams in it at the end of a long chain of days, the golden charm. They were coming in to welcome me, Abu Ahmad with his black cloak and his cane and his son still in Australia, and my oldest cousin Fowzi the king of smiling, and Ribhia with her flock of children, and the children's children carrying sacks of chips now, it was the first year I ever saw them carrying chips, and my cousin's husband the teller of jokes who was put in prison for nothing like everybody else, and the ones who always came whose names I pretended to know. We were eating and drinking and telling the stories. My grandmother told of a woman who was so delicate you could see the water trickling down her throat as she drank. I had brought her two new headscarves, but of course she only wanted the one that was around my neck. And I wouldn't give it to her. There was energy in teasing. I still smelled like an airplane and we held hands the whole time except when she was picking up crumbs from her blanket or holding something else to eat.

And then it was late and time for sleep. We would sleep in a room together, my grandmother, my aunt Fahima, my cousin Janan of the rosy cheeks, a strange woman, and I. It reminded me of a slumber party. They were putting on their long nightgowns and rewrapping their heads. I asked about the strange woman and they said she came to sleep here every night. Because sometimes in such an upsetting country when you have no man to sleep in the room with you, it feels safer to have an extra woman. She had a bad cold and was sleeping on the bed next to me. I covered my head against her hundred sneezes. I covered my head as my father covered his head when he was a young man and the bombs were blowing up the houses of his friends. I thought about my father and my husband here in this same room just a few days ago and could still feel them warming the corners. I listened to the women's bedtime talking and laughing from far away, as if it were rushing water, the two sleeping on the floor, my grandmother still sitting up in her bed—Lie down, they said to her, and she said, I'm not ready—and then I remembered how at ten o'clock the evening news comes on in English from Jordan and I asked if we could uncover the television set which had stood all day in the corner like a patient animal no one noticed. It stood there on its four thin legs, waiting.

Janan fiddled with dials, voices crisscrossing borders more easily than people cross in this part of the world, and I heard English rolling by like a raft with its rich *r*'s and I jumped on to it. *Today,* the newscaster said, *in the ravaged West Bank* . . . and my ear stopped. I didn't even hear what had happened in this place where I was. Because I was thinking, Today, in this room full of women. In this village on the lip of a beautiful mountain. Today, between blossoming trees and white sheets. The news couldn't see into this room of glowing coals or the ones drinking tea and fluffing pillows who are invisible. And I, who had felt the violence inside myself many times more than once, though I was brought up not to be violent, though no one was ever violent with me in any way, I could not say what it was we all still had to learn, or how we would do it together. But I could tell of a woman who almost died who by summer would be climbing the steep stairs to her roof to look out over the fields once more. Who said one moment on top of the earth is better than a thousand moments under the earth. Who kept on living, again and again. And maybe an old country with many names could be that lucky too, someday, since at least it should have as much hope as invisible women and men.

Heterick Memorial Library
Ohio Northern University

DUE	RETURNED	DUE	RETURNED
1.		13.	
2.		14.	
3.		15.	
4.		16.	
5.		17.	
6.		18.	
7.		19.	
8.		20.	
9.		21.	
10.		22.	
11.		23.	
12.		24.	

Heterick Memorial Library
Ohio Northern University
Ada, Ohio 45810